CW00944920

FALSE WITNESS

By

Harry Giller

Copyright © Harry Giller 2022
This book is sold subject to the condition that it shall not, by way of trade or
otherwise, be lent, resold, hired out, or otherwise circulated without the publisher's
prior consent in any form of binding or cover other than that in which it is
published and without a similar condition including this condition being imposed
on the subsequent publisher.
The moral right of Harry Giller has been asserted.
ISBN-13: 9798830451017

To my wife Linda, without whose love and support this work would never have come to fruition.

This is a work of fiction. Names, characters, businesses, organizations, places, events and incidents either are the product of the author's imagination or are used fictitiously. Any resemblance to actual persons, living or dead, events, or locales is entirely coincidental.

CONTENTS

CHAPTER 1

The duct tape across her mouth was making it very hard for the young girl to breathe. The small, dark place was very hot, and she had no idea where she was or why she was there. She cried uncontrollably, but there was no one to hear her. Desperate to see her mum and dad, she was scared that she never would. She was afraid about what was going to happen next, but more than anything she was terrified that the man would come back.

Karl Smithson was well aware that being stuck alongside a police car in a traffic jam was not a good place to be if you were driving a stolen car. Although still a young man, a long career in crime had led him to believe that he was a man to be reckoned with, a somewhat misguided view considering his three previous jail sentences. Nevertheless, he did possess a certain level of cunning backed up by his own feelings of entitlement and his undoubted ruthlessness.

As Smithson edged his car slowly forward in the outside lane, he saw that the police officer in the front passenger seat kept his head down as he looked intently at something on his lap. Once he was directly alongside the police car, both held up by traffic lights and the number of other vehicles on the road, Smithson just looked straight ahead. Having studiously avoided looking at the police officers as much as he possibly could, Smithson risked one quick glance to see if they were paying any attention to him. He looked over just in time to see the thoughtful look directed his way from Steve Brown in the driving seat, but the passenger still paid him no attention whatsoever. The look from that copper told him he that he could be in trouble. If they followed him, he would know for sure.

When the lights changed to green Smithson's car inched forward and he indicated to turn right at the junction ahead. Instinctively Brown pulled into the outside lane directly behind the other car, intending to follow it. Something was not right, he didn't know what, but he intended to find out.

Having watched the police follow him in his rear-view mirror, Smithson began to plan his next move if, as he expected, they pulled him over.

Initially Inspector Richard Wade was so engrossed studying the presentation to senior officers on his laptop that he didn't even notice they had turned off onto a dual carriageway at the traffic lights. He soon did though and slammed the computer closed as he sat up and looked around.

Brown had a quick look out of the corner of his eye as he heard Wade close his computer, waiting for the expected angry questions. He was not disappointed as the Inspector demanded in a loud voice to know what was going on and why they had turned off. Without pause he told Brown that they had to be at Force Headquarters by 3 p.m. and that if they were not, it would be the worse for him.

Steve Brown had gone too far to stop now and attempted to explain why he was following the car and his intention to stop it. He knew it was the right thing to do and was certain he had good reasons to do so. He tried to explain to Wade that there was something not right about the car and the driver, even though he couldn't say exactly what it was. He reassured Wade that it would only take a few minutes to check the car out and then they could be on their way, getting to Headquarters in plenty of time. Typically, Wade would not be mollified and demanded they turn round.

Realising he was getting nowhere trying to reason with the idiot next to him, Brown pressed on with his plan to stop the other car as soon as possible, thinking ruefully, 'I might as well be hung for a sheep as a lamb'. He undoubtedly made things worse by pointing out that, as it was a dual carriageway, it would be difficult to turn round on this particular road anyway.

Through gritted teeth and as calmly as he could, Wade demanded to know what made Brown so sure there was something wrong with the other car that necessitated it being stopped, particularly against his instructions.

Steve Brown replied in about the worst way he possibly could, explaining that whilst it was difficult to say why exactly, other than he just had a feeling that that there was something wrong with the driver. He thought to himself, although he didn't say so, that it was instinct developed over many years in the police.

Brown quickly went through his reasons for thinking the saloon car should be checked out. The car was a grey-coloured family saloon, not new, but very well cared for. The driver was quite youngish and scruffy looking so the car didn't really seem to fit him. Whilst alongside each other he avoided looking in their direction as much as he could, unlike most people who couldn't seem to resist looking into a marked police car. They usually have a surreptitious nervous look as if they have this urge to see what the police are doing, and what it's like in a police car. Sometimes it's just them making sure they haven't done anything wrong. If anything, it was like the driver was trying to turn his face away, without making it too obvious. On top of that, the whole Force had been looking for a grey saloon for the last two days.

Unimpressed with Steve's explanation, Wade wanted to know more about the grey car everyone was supposed to be looking for and any suspects involved. When Brown told him there were no suspects, nor did he know why they were looking for such a car, Wade became even more angry.

By this time Brown was turning left into a road marked Grimston

Lane, following directly behind the grey saloon car. He told Wade he would stop the car and quickly check out the driver if Wade would call it in to the control room so their whereabouts would be known in the event of a problem. Wade never moved or attempted to use the radio, just staring fixedly ahead as if he was washing his hands of the whole business.

Steve Brown switched on the blue lights, indicating that the car ahead should pull over. It immediately began to slow and started to pull into a lay-by. He made one final attempt to get Wade to call in their location and what they were doing, even going so far as to explain that it was for their safety. All he got for his trouble was a scornful look.

Brown gave up. The idiot was more concerned about how things looked than basic officer safety. With that thought he suddenly became aware that Wade wasn't wearing his stab vest, in direct breach of standing orders. He realised he couldn't see a utility belt either so that meant he didn't have his baton and handcuffs with him or his CS gas for that matter. He decided it would be wise not to say anything else, thinking that it was up to Wade if he wanted to disregard the orders he was so fond of enforcing, whilst putting both of them at risk.

Steve supposed he could have called it in, but not wanting any more conflict with Wade, decided that for once he would leave it, going against all his training and experience. 'Let's just get this done and get the prick dropped off at HQ as quickly as possible', he thought. He already knew that Inspector Wade would not let this go and that there could be repercussions.

The grey car stopped.

Brown stopped his car about twenty feet behind it. He knew he should ask control to check the vehicle on the Police National Computer, or get Inspector Wade to do it, but thought better of asking him. He supposed he could soon do it once he'd spoken to the driver.

He got out of the patrol car, slamming the door behind him in his annoyance at Wade, and started walking towards the other vehicle. As he did so he realised how warm it was, though he couldn't understand why he should be surprised considering it was early August. It was a lovely day indeed and was hopefully going to get better. He was due to finish his shift at 4 p.m., and then he was meeting that new blonde admin clerk for a drink tonight and, if he was lucky, a lot more.

Brown realised that his mind was wandering and told himself he needed to pay attention to what he was doing. Still, it was a nice thought and it spurred him on to get this sorted out as quickly as possible so he could get on his way. He was well aware that instinct was far from infallible, and that the vast majority of vehicle checks such as this came to nothing, even though every now and again you could strike gold.

As he got nearer, he could see the car was a grey Ford Mondeo and just what excellent nick it was in, though it could do with a good clean. He also realised the engine was still running. The thought came into his mind that police officers tried to approach vehicles from behind in these circumstances to prevent being run over. It would not be the first time that had happened to a police officer whilst checking a vehicle.

A further random thought entered his head. The driver could always reverse over him, so, without really thinking about it, he stepped to his right so that he wasn't approaching the car from directly behind.

Why was he being so cautious? Steve Brown couldn't understand it, this was the sort of thing he did a dozen times a week. Something was making him apprehensive. He couldn't pin it down, but he had an odd sixth sense that something was not right. However, his logical mind told him it was more likely down to the behaviour of his Inspector who hadn't even bothered to get out of the car. He felt as if he was on his own, which maybe wasn't such a bad thing.

A white delivery van drove by, the first vehicle Brown had seen since turning into Grimston Lane. It had obviously come from the dual carriageway as well, but where it was going was anybody's guess. The road was very quiet and there was not a building in sight.

The driver got out of the car just as Steve Brown reached the rear of it. He stopped and they stood facing each other. He still hadn't switched the engine off and had left the door open. There was no sign of anyone else inside.

The man, whose name Brown would never know, was in his mid to late twenties, about five-feet-nine inches tall and slimly built. He had longish fair hair that looked as if it needed a good wash, very much in keeping with his generally scruffy appearance. He had a thin face, was unshaven, and Steve could see that his eyes were very dark and expressionless. Brown saw his eyes flick towards the police car and quickly back again.

The car driver spoke first. "Can I help you, officer?" He had a local accent and was quite well spoken.

Steve Brown said, "Just a routine vehicle check, sir. Are you the owner of this car?"

"Yes I am. Is there a problem?"

Brown replied, "Not at all, as I said, just routine. Would you mind telling me your name please?"

"Why do you need to know that? I haven't done anything wrong."

"It will allow me to confirm you are the lawful owner of this vehicle, then we can all be on our way. Have you got any documentation to prove who you are and that you own the car?"

Karl Smithson shrugged and said, "I think I've got something in the car, I'll get it."

He sat on the edge of the driver's seat with his legs hanging outside and reached over to the passenger-side glove box, hoping it contained some useful documents. As he reached inside, his mind was whirring as he realised just how precarious his position was. If he couldn't talk his way out of this then he was in a lot of trouble, and for a lot more than a poxy stolen car. How much did they know? Could he persuade them to let him go? Had they called this in? Could he manage two of them if necessary?

He stood up again, holding some paperwork in his left hand, more as a distraction and delaying tactic than a serious attempt to establish the car was his. Then he had a huge stroke of luck as Richard Wade got out of the police car and hurried over to join Brown. Smithson hoped that this officer, who he realised was an Inspector, didn't have new information, but his fears were soon allayed when he told Brown that he was in a hurry and to get a move on. Steve Brown ignored Wade. There was something about the scruffy car driver that unsettled him, his instincts were on full alert mode. He still had no idea why.

Smithson made his decision. He knew Brown was the real danger and that he had to be the first one he took out, but they needed to be close together for him to manage both of them. He would have to be quick, so very quick. As always, he became very calm before it started. He would decide when he did it, he already knew how.

Inspector Wade was completely oblivious to everything but his need to get to Headquarters as quick as possible. Nothing else mattered, certainly not a stupid vehicle check.

Displaying his lack of experience and in defiance of all his training and common-sense, Wade positioned himself between Brown and the car driver, facing Brown, as he shouted at him to hurry up.

Smithson had a clear view of Wade's back, but could hardly see Brown at all, so it followed that Brown was unable to see much of him either or, more importantly, what he was doing. He couldn't believe that the idiot Inspector had given him the edge he so badly needed.

Smithson took the opportunity to quickly take his knife from his inside jacket pocket and hold it down at his right side. It was a fearsome weapon, about eight inches long, honed to razor sharpness with a point like a stiletto. It took only seconds, the result of much practice and familiarity. Neither officer saw anything.

Steve Brown was shocked at Wade's complete lack of awareness and reacted quickly, grabbing hold of Wade's right shoulder with his right hand, he pulled him to one side, away from the grey car. At the same time Brown stepped forward towards the driver so that he could see him again, all his instincts screaming danger, but he still had not the faintest idea why.

Smithson took a step forward at the same time and Brown only had time to see a savage grin on his face and that his right arm was coming up towards him. It doesn't happen in slow motion like they say in books and films, it happens in split seconds. Steve Brown felt the blow to his lower stomach just below the area protected by his stab vest and believed he had been punched. He tried to move forward but couldn't, and then, for some reason he didn't understand, fell to his knees. Then the pain started, the agonising pain like his stomach was on fire. He put his hands to his midriff and felt the wetness before looking down to see blood running onto the dirty road. His blood.

He felt weak and fell forward onto all fours, desperately trying to locate the maniac before he attacked him again.

Brown looked to his right and found him. He was stood holding a blood-stained knife towards Inspector Wade who was knelt on the ground, with his arms outstretched, pleading for mercy. Steve Brown wanted to shout to Wade, but he couldn't, he wanted to tell him to get up and fight or he would be killed.

Smithson only had seconds. He needed to finish it and get on his way before somebody came along the road. He couldn't believe the crying, snivelling officer in front of him, still on his knees from the push by his colleague. He sobbed, "Please don't hurt me, I won't tell anyone. Just let me go. Please!"

Enough was enough, quick as a striking snake he slashed at the policeman's throat. God knows how but Wade saw it coming and tried to throw his body backwards. He couldn't evade the knife completely and was slashed across the chest, his white shirt turning instantly red. He screamed in agony and terror although, if truth be told, the wound was not particularly serious, though undoubtedly painful. He tried to stand, but his legs were like rubber, and he fell to his knees once more.

Brown, still conscious, could only think, 'Why didn't you put your vest on, you fucking idiot?'

Realising Wade was not finished, the man went towards him with the knife raised, intent on completing the job. He jabbed out with the knife towards Wade who, unbelievably, threw himself to one side, and so was stabbed in the upper chest near to his left shoulder rather than through the heart as intended. He screamed in agony and fell to the floor, pouring blood. The wound was once again painful beyond belief but miraculously the knife had missed anything vital. He could survive the injury if blood loss didn't get him.

Smithson was getting angry, seconds were being wasted, and he became careless. He turned his back to Steve Brown whilst he pursued Wade.

Somehow Steve Brown, who had always been a fit, strong man, found an inner strength, allowing him to ignore the pain, if not forget it, and manage to get to his feet by holding onto the side of the grey car. He would never be able to explain it, but he had an overwhelming desire to help Wade, a man he disliked intensely, even more so since he had witnessed his craven cowardice when faced with danger. A lifetime of training and experience kicked in, he could never leave a colleague, no matter what the personal cost. It was ingrained, you always, always backed each other up.

Still trailing blood and weak as a kitten, Brown shuffled towards Smithson, the sound of his approach covered by Wade's continued screaming and pleading. At the last instant he must have heard or sensed something and started to turn around just as Steve Brown threw himself forward and grabbed hold of him. They fell to the ground with Brown on top, his weight pinning Smithson to the floor. Once again he raised the knife and lashed out towards Brown, stabbing him in the top of his shoulder, near to his neck, just above his stab vest. For a second time, but this time more by good luck than good judgement, he had managed to avoid Brown's stab vest, causing another serious injury to the officer.

Again, the wound was excruciatingly painful, but Brown kept his grip on his attacker, knowing that if he let go, he and Wade would both die. He screamed to Wade to help him, but he just stared at Brown and never moved. Brown's weight made it difficult for Smithson to free his arm for another strike. Summoning the last of his strength and ignoring the pain, Brown threw his head forward, butting his enemy as hard as he could on the bridge of his nose, stunning him and causing his eyes to stream with tears, whilst blood gushed from his nostrils. Brown then locked his hands in his attacker's long hair and began to bang his head repeatedly on the road surface until he lost consciousness, the knife falling from his grip.

Brown could see Wade looking at him, but he appeared deep in shock and was not moving.

He shouted at him, "Wade! Get my 'cuffs. Come on! Move, man, move." He knew he couldn't last much longer and was frightened his attacker would soon regain consciousness.

Wade looked dumbly towards the two men on the floor.

"Get my fucking 'cuffs before he comes round. Hurry!"

Slowly Wade seemed to shake himself and, covered in blood, started to crawl towards Brown. He reached into the pouch on the back of Brown's utility belt and freed the handcuffs, before fastening one end to the man's right wrist. He was clumsy and unused to the task, so it took two attempts to manage it.

Steve Brown knew Smithson was still a danger, especially as they were both injured and he was still relatively unscathed. They needed to fasten him to something solid, and quickly. He looked around anxiously, near to panic, finally realising the car was the obvious solution.

"Richard, come on. Help me drag him to the car, we'll fasten him to it."

Wade looked shocked to be called by his first name, but it got his attention. Brown rolled off the injured man and with the last of his strength grabbed his jacket and crawled towards the car, pulling him along the ground with Wade's help. Thank God he wasn't very heavy. Between the two of them they slowly covered five agonising feet to the rear of the grey Ford Mondeo, where Wade fastened the other end of the handcuffs to the rear towing eye. Their attacker was now shackled securely to the car, preventing him from doing further harm.

Not a moment too soon as he came round and went berserk, screaming, swearing, and lashing out with his feet at Steve Brown who managed to roll and crawl out of range, before he lost consciousness. His last thought was, 'What was that about? Who the hell is he? What the fuck has he done?'

Wade managed somehow to get to his feet and stumbled back to the police car where he fell to the ground with his back resting against the front wheel. He was dazed and disorientated. He didn't know what to do.

The whole incident, from stopping the car to its conclusion, took just over two minutes.

Richard Wade felt very tired and thought it would be good to sleep, but then he remembered what to do and pressed the red button on the top of his radio to summon urgent assistance. He knew he needed help, and soon, but characteristically it never entered his head that Steve Brown, the man who had just saved his life, was in much greater need than him.

CHAPTER 2

The harsh beeping of the alarm reverberated around the room, causing all those present to look up, concerned to see where it was coming from. A red flashing light was clearly visible on the C Division console, even after the operator silenced the audible alarm.

The Police Force Control Room, even on a Wednesday afternoon, was a hive of activity with several operators sat at individual consoles, each with its own bank of computers. They were responsible for maintaining radio contact with patrol officers, allocating work, and managing the police response to incidents.

The alarm activation alerted Civilian Operator Joan Armitage that one or more officers was in trouble and needed urgent assistance, something she had dealt with many times before. The activation cut across all other radio transmissions and allowed the operator to hear what was happening via the officer's radio, and to send help. Having immediately shut down the annoying beeping noise, but left the light flashing, Joan tried to identify the officer on her computer screen and to listen for messages. All she got was silence.

Sergeant John Wilkinson, Joan's immediate supervisor, went straight over to her console. He was a careful and considered man who didn't hurry unnecessarily, being a great believer in the maxim 'more haste less speed', particularly as he was all too well aware that most of these activations were accidental, but you always had to be careful and follow procedure.

Wilkinson was ready to step in if needed but thought it unlikely. Joan was one of his best and most reliable operators requiring the minimum amount of supervision. In fact, she was often used to train new staff members. She was in her mid fifties with a wealth of experience, telling anyone who would listen that she had been doing the job before they had computers. It had not been especially busy in C Division today, but even though she was feeling tired, and soon to finish her shift, she responded in her usual competent and professional manner.

The first problem was the silence. Usually with an accidental activation you heard officers talking about mundane matters, often to their acute embarrassment. The second problem was that the computer usually identified the officer concerned immediately, but today it didn't. All it did was to give a radio serial number, but not who it was issued to. Finally, all the radios could be tracked by GPS, but for some reason this one did not give a location for the radio and its user.

Joan tried a radio message, asking the person activating their alarm to identify themselves and the nature of their emergency. No response. A second message requesting all personnel to check their radios for an accidental alarm activation was also met with silence. John Wilkinson was becoming more concerned and decided he needed to step in.

He instructed Joan to keep trying to contact the officer concerned, and told the nearby C Division call handler, who worked with Joan, to ring the Communications Branch to find out who the radio was issued to and if there was any way it could be tracked. A quick look at the system showed GPS locations for the other staff on duty. The system was working.

Wilkinson next asked Joan how many staff were booked on the radio in C Division at that time. When she replied twenty-three, he instructed her to call them all one by one in an attempt to identify whoever had pressed the alarm. This was by no means a foolproof method for two reasons. Firstly, it was clear that whoever had the radio had not booked onto the system, and secondly, as they were multi-channel sets, an officer from another division could have come into C Division and tuned in to their channel without telling anyone.

Before Joan Armitage could begin the roll call of C division officers, everyone in the Control Room heard the muffled groan and the unintelligible whispered word over the radio, so could every officer with a radio in C Division. Then a last gasped word, a weak but clear "Help." Now they knew it was for real.

Because it was so unusual for incidents such as this to go on so long without being resolved, everyone in the Control Room was paying more and more attention, none more so than the Force Duty Officer Inspector Sharon Parker. She was in overall command, her role being to ensure the efficient operation of the Control Room, but more importantly to take initial control of any serious incidents until senior officers could take over on the ground. So important was her role that she was able to authorise the emergency deployment of firearms officers and, if necessary, use of their weapons. Clearly an important and stressful role with the need for quick and decisive decision making, with the potential to get it horribly wrong.

Sharon Parker had heard the initial alarm but felt no need to intervene. However, she did use her systems to monitor C Division radio transmissions. She was watching closely but couldn't see anything she could add to Sergeant Wilkinson's actions. However, she was starting to think she may have to activate a full force roll call to locate the caller if they could not be identified as a C Division officer. That would be extremely difficult, if not impossible, and she was not sure it had ever been tried before. Time was passing and someone could be in real trouble.

On hearing the call for help, Inspector Parker stepped in immediately, her first orders being of a practical nature. All external calls were to be diverted to another call handler, thus freeing up the C Division call handler to assist Joan. She then instructed Joan to tell all the C Division officers to cease whatever they were doing and to return to their vehicles and standby for further orders. Furthermore, they were to stay off the radio until they received further instructions.

Next, she asked John Wilkinson to prepare a plan to carry out a grid search of the division to find whoever needed such urgent help. This was followed by asking the operators in the Control Room to tell all staff in other divisions that, as it was near to shift change-over time, everyone was to remain on duty in case staff were needed for a major search. She knew there would be no grumbles this day from those having to stay at work for an extended tour of duty. Finally, she checked if the Force helicopter was airborne, and when discovered it was not, she gave the order that it should lift immediately and head to C Division airspace.

Whilst all this was going on, information came in from the Communications Branch. It was not good. The personal radio in question was a spare set issued to C Division and whoever was using it had not input their personal details. As the radio was brand new, the GPS system had probably not been activated. They had no other way of tracking it.

There was still no response to Joan's increasingly frantic messages.

Inspector Parker considered activating the Force mutual aid plan. Put simply it was a system whereby all divisions would send officers to another division to support them when any major incident was happening. She decided to wait but realised it was time for the C Division Commander to be made aware of what was happening.

She contacted Chief Superintendent David Moss on his mobile phone and quickly updated him on events and what she had done so far. He immediately wanted to know how long since the alarm activation and, when told it was over five minutes, he decided the Force mutual aid plan should be activated at once. His thinking being that it looked like a search was going to be needed and the more staff he had the better.

Sharon Parker was becoming more concerned by the minute and wondering if there was anything else she could do. She then remembered the roll-call of C Division staff and, in view of the fact that no further calls had been received, told Joan to do it now.

All the while Steve Brown's GPS signal flashed, showing him in Grimston Lane.

CHAPTER 3

Frank Hodgson was lost, and he was late. He was sure he was following the directions he'd been given, turn left onto Grimston Road and half a mile down the road he would come to the farm for the delivery. Even from the elevated position of his van's driving seat he couldn't see any farm. It would later be discovered that he'd mistakenly entered Grimston Lane into his Satnav and so had no chance of finding the correct address.

Frank remembered passing a police car a few minutes ago so decided to turn round and ask them for directions if it was still there.

As he drove back down the road, Frank decided he was fed up with delivering parcels and should give it up, but he did that most days and never quite managed to leave. Ah good, the police car was still in the lay-by, and he could see that the grey car was still there as well. Nothing could ever have prepared him for what he was about to see as he drove closer.

He had nearly drawn level with the car when he realised something was wrong. The police car passenger door was open, as was the driver's door of the other car, which also had its engine running. Then he saw the people and slammed on the brakes, coming to a skidding halt.

He saw one man laid face down not far from the grey car and then another leant against the police car. He wondered why the second man was wearing a red shirt, and then to his horror realised it was soaked in blood. As if he wasn't spooked enough already, he could see someone else at the rear of the grey car, his face blood streaked and with an expression of uncontrolled anger and pure hate.

Hodgson slammed the van into reverse and got to the end of the lay-by before he realised that the man wasn't following him. He stopped and made sure the doors and windows were locked. Frank was in a state of near hysteria and grabbed for his phone on the dashboard, knocking it into the passenger footwell. He got it back and dialled 999.

A calm voice answered immediately and said, "Emergency, which service do you require?"

He managed to croak out, "Police, quick."

Another voice came on. "Police, what is the nature of your emergency please?"

By now Frank was almost back under control and managed to gasp, "There's two policemen. I think they're dead."

The operator was typing the information into her computer as she spoke to Frank Hodgson and needed all her composure as she heard those horrific words.

"Ok caller what's your name and location?"

"It's Frank Hodgson. I'm in my van in Grimston Road."

"Alright, Frank, are you safe?"

"I think so, I'm locked in my van. The other man's just looking at me."

The operator continued to update her computer with the information from Frank, which had flashed to Joan Armitage's computer screen as Grimston Road was in C Division, but at least a mile away from Grimston Lane. Joan was busily dispatching staff to the location given by Frank Hodgson, watched by Sergeant Wilkinson and Inspector Parker.

The 999-operator continued to speak to Frank, "Help is on the way, sit tight. Frank, I'm going to stay on the phone with you till the police get there. Ok?"

"Thank you."

"Frank, what is the other man doing?"

"He's just looking at me. It looks like he can't move."

"Ok, Frank, they'll be there soon."

Sergeant John Wilkinson, watching carefully, could see all the C Division officers displayed by their call-signs on the GPS computer display racing to Grimston Road. They were all moving except one.

"What's that call sign?" he asked Joan Armitage.

She quickly checked and replied, "That's odd. It's Steve Brown, he's normally first there if there's any trouble."

"Look where he is, Grimston Lane. Are we going to the right place? Send one patrol there at once, we could have got this wrong. When you've done that, try raising Brown."

Of course Joan Armitage's calls were unanswered. She continued to talk calmly into her radio, trying to reassure the officer, whoever it was, that help was on the way and to hold on.

Wilkinson turned to Inspector Parker, saying "Boss, I think we're going to the wrong place, and we may know who the officer is now."

She replied calmly, "We'll know soon enough."

A deathly hush overtook the Control Room as everyone waited for news. The silence was broken when Chief Superintendent Moss entered the room having come from his office two floors below. Sharon Parker took him to one side and quietly updated him. At his suggestion she directed someone to contact Ambulance Control, requesting paramedics to attend Grimston Lane as well as those already racing to Grimston Road, just in case. He also suggested a request for the Air Ambulance, it looked as if it would be needed.

Still they waited. It seemed like hours but was only minutes.

The first message came through. Grimston Road was negative. All patrols were now diverted to Grimston Lane as a matter of considerable urgency.

CHAPTER 4

There was blood everywhere, and Richard Wade knew most of it was his. He couldn't tell where it was coming from, but the pain seemed to be all over his body and was almost unbearable.

He knew that he was sitting on the ground leaning against a car wheel, uncomfortable, wanting to move, but couldn't. Somebody else was laid on the ground, not moving apart from his dark hair blowing in the slight breeze.

He wasn't sure what had happened. How had he got here? Had he been unconscious? Everything was confused. Why was that man shouting at him? Who was he? Why didn't he help him?

The pain was getting worse. He could hear sirens now. They were getting closer, and now it sounded like there was a helicopter. He knew help was coming, but what was happening?

There was another car, it was grey, and he could hear banging above the sound of its engine. It seemed like he was being assaulted by non-stop noise. Sirens, helicopters, car engines, banging, and that man, who wouldn't help him, kept shouting "fucking bastards" over and over again. The man looked very odd, knelt down at the back of the grey car like he was holding onto it for some reason. He'd read somewhere that in near-death experiences some senses became heightened, and he guessed hearing was included.

He knew he was going to die; it wasn't fair. In a brief moment of clarity, he realised it probably never was.

There were other voices, but there was no one else there. At least he couldn't see anyone. Then he realised the voices were coming from a radio. Someone was talking, a woman pleading with him to answer, and telling him to hold on, help was coming.

He knew it would be too late. Maybe that was for the best, because suddenly he could remember everything.

Then he saw a patrol car pull into the lay-by in a squeal of brakes. An officer got out and raised his radio to his mouth.

"Charlie Tango One Two to control, urgent message."

"Go ahead, Charlie Tango One Two."

"In attendance Grimston Lane. I've got two officers severely injured. I need help, lots of help. My God! It's a blood bath. Send ambulances please and tell them to hurry."

"All received. It's on the way. What is their condition?"

PC Paul Thomas approached the man leant against the police car. He was covered in blood and barely conscious, but he was alive. The officer recognised Inspector Wade and tried his best to reassure him. As he went towards the other injured man, who was lying face down on the ground and was clearly a police officer, he noticed for the first time another man handcuffed to the rear of a car who was almost hysterical, shouting abuse and kicking out at Thomas in frustration.

Realising he presented no imminent danger, Thomas ignored him and went to the officer on the ground. He saw immediately that it was Steve Brown and that he was in a bad way. He felt his neck and could only feel a very weak pulse.

"Charlie Tango One Two update."

"Go ahead."

"It's Inspector Wade and Steve Brown. They both have knife wounds and Steve's really bad. They've got somebody cuffed to a car as well."

"Okay the ambulance will be there in a minute."

Other patrols started to arrive, including supervisors, bringing order to the chaos. The Force helicopter hovered above, filming the whole scene. Ambulances arrived, followed soon after by the press who constantly monitored police radio channels and were quick to pick up on any ongoing incidents.

It was a crime scene and was quickly taped off. The unknown man shackled to the grey car was arrested on suspicion of attempted murder and driven away under heavy escort. The man's knife was left on the ground to be recovered later by Scenes of Crime Officers and, when later examined, it would be established that his fingerprints were on the hilt.

Richard Wade's injuries had been assessed as non-life threatening and he had been transported to hospital by ambulance, accompanied by another officer. He kept mumbling "banging noise", but it was just assumed that he was delirious.

Steve Brown had not yet been moved. A trauma doctor and paramedics from the air ambulance were working frantically to revive him. After ten minutes the doctor stood up, peeled off his gloves, and shook his head. PC Steve Brown was declared dead at the scene at exactly 1438 hours, never knowing why he had died. It was now a murder enquiry.

At least one officer could be seen crying. Others stood in numbed silence, staring at the body of their fallen comrade. Unusually, there was none of the normal meaningless chat that police officers and other emergency services staff often engaged in where death was involved. They would talk about anything but the body on the ground, always careful not to be disrespectful to either the victim or their families. They tried to have normal conversations in an effort to distract them from the horror they had to deal with. It was simply a way of keeping things at a distance, not letting it touch them more than it had to. A coping mechanism if you like. It didn't mean they didn't care, but they couldn't let it hamper the work they had to do at the scene. Today was different. It was one of their own, a colleague, a friend, someone they had been on boozy nights out with. There was nothing they could do to distance themselves. It did much more than touch them. It hit them like a punch in the stomach.

Brian Donovan was the duty patrol inspector. He had arrived at the scene shortly after Paul Thomas and started to get things organised, including allocating an officer to take care of Frank Hodgson. He was taken to the police station and arrangements made to take a statement from him.

"Charlie Sierra Five to control."

Joan Armitage was still operating the radio and told the Inspector to go ahead.

"I can confirm Inspector Wade has been taken to hospital and that Constable Steve Brown was declared dead at the scene at 1438 hours. Please relay this information to the Custody Suite where the arrested man has been taken and to the senior investigating officer."

Brown's body would remain at the scene until the pathologist attended and he, along with SOCO and CID Officers, had finished their work.

The news was met with stunned silence in the control room. Joan Armitage began to shake uncontrollably, and tears could be seen running down her face. Sharon Parker had her relieved immediately and then settled down to complete the many tasks awaiting her, not least informing chief officers. She also needed to get onto the Press Office, even nowadays the murder of a police officer was still front-page news. Chief Superintendent Moss had already left to go to the scene, and to make arrangements to inform the relatives of both officers.

CHAPTER 5

Inspector Brian Donovan became aware of something annoying him, eventually realising that it was the engine of the grey car that was still running. He shouted to no one in particular, "Switch that bloody engine off, now!"

Paul Thomas headed towards the car and was quickly reminded by Inspector Donovan that it was part of the crime scene and may contain vital evidence. As he reached inside the car, he did wonder why officers always thought they had to state the bloody obvious, as if he didn't know it might contain evidence. He switched the engine off, leaving the keys in the ignition. It seemed very quiet now, as both the police and air ambulance helicopters had left, and there was no passing traffic because the road had been closed by police.

About to return to his post guarding the scene, PC Thomas heard noises from the rear of the car, his first thought being that it was just the engine cooling. A further distinct bang convinced him that couldn't be the case, especially as it was coming from the rear of the car. He walked round to stand near the car boot. Nothing. He was about to leave when he heard a barely audible tap which he was convinced came from the boot.

Thomas went over to Inspector Donovan and said, "Sir, I think I can hear noises from the car boot."

"What is it?"

"I really don't know, Sir. It sounded like banging."

"Come on, let's have a look then."

Donovan was still the senior officer at the scene and, whilst very sceptical, supposed it should be checked out. What else could possibly happen on this shit day?

Standing next to the car with Thomas he couldn't hear anything. He said to the Constable, "Are you certain you heard banging from the boot?"

"Definitely, Sir."

Donovan had a difficult decision to make, did he open the boot and risk damaging a crime scene or did he just leave well alone? One option was to contact Control and let someone else decide, but it wasn't in his nature to dodge the difficult issues.

"Okay, Paul, we'll open it. Get the keys from the ignition. I don't want to use the boot release and risk disturbing things inside the car."

Whilst capable of making difficult decisions, Donovan was also a careful and methodical man who liked to think things through. He decided that as they had no idea what was in the boot, if anything, he needed reinforcements and so called over another couple of Constables. Satisfied they could deal with any threat that may emerge from the boot, he next beckoned over the Scenes of Crime Officer who had just arrived. After establishing that the man had a video camera, he instructed him to film their actions and anything that may be revealed in the boot. Finally, he summoned the officer who was recording events at the scene to make a note of the time and what they were doing.

Satisfied that he had covered all eventualities, Donovan nodded to PC Thomas.

Thomas took a deep breath, put the key in the boot lock and turned it. He threw the lid up and gasped in surprise. Brian Donovan was the first to recover, shouting, "Get her out, for God's sake just get her out!"

Paul Thomas reached into the boot and lifted the girl out. She was about 10 years old he guessed, but very slight with short, fair hair and a pale complexion. She was wearing a dirty blue dress and laid on a grubby bedspread of some sort. However, they were not the first things he noticed, all his attention focussing on the fact that the girl had her hands tied behind her back and grey tape across her mouth.

He sat her gently on the floor, supporting her with his hand on her back. None of the officers present at that moment would ever forget the look of absolute terror in the young girl's eyes. Paul Thomas, who had children of his own, did his best to reassure her. "We're police officers, you're safe now. I'm going to take the tape off now, I'll try not to hurt you."

With that he took hold of the corner of the tape and slowly pulled it from the girl's mouth, touching it as little as possible and putting it into an evidence bag held out by a Scenes of Crime Officer. The other SOCO continued to film the scene. The girl gave a huge gasp, as if trying to suck in all the oxygen around them, and began to cry.

Thomas then said, "Hold still, I'm going to untie your hands." However, the second SOCO stepped forward and used a penknife to cut the rope binding the girl's hands, doing his best to preserve the knots. He then placed the rope into another evidence bag.

Paul Thomas clasped the girl tightly to his chest, repeatedly telling her she was safe now and no one would hurt her. She continued to cry but seemed reassured by his words. He had to ask the girl's name twice before she was able to reply, in a barely audible whisper, "Linda." He didn't ask her any more questions, but continued to soothe her, stroking her hair, and holding her close. She seemed to settle. He couldn't care less if he was destroying forensic evidence that may be on her clothes, all that mattered was looking after her. He tried to turn so that he was between her and Steve Brown's body which was still at the scene. It would be there for some time yet, and they were still awaiting screens to put round it.

Inspector Donovan used his radio to call the Control Room using his personal call sign. "Charlie Sierra Five, urgent message."

Joan Armitage's replacement, who had been fully updated, replied at once, "Go ahead, Charlie Sierra Five."

"Ambulance required to scene, urgent."

"Charlie Sierra Five, ambulance en route, what is the nature of the emergency?"

For some reason Donovan did not want to pass the information over the radio, aware that any number of people would be listening. Other officers, press, and lots of nosy civilians.

"Charlie Sierra Five, please ask the force duty officer to ring me as soon as possible on my mobile phone and I will update."

Sharon Parker was still monitoring, at least with half an ear. She had had some difficult conversations with a number of people, including the chief constable, the deputy chief constable, the detective chief superintendent, and her own boss. She was well aware that her actions, along with those of her staff, would be scrutinised later with any errors magnified and criticised. In all honesty she thought they had done well and had nothing to worry about, but you never knew when senior officers got an attack of the nine o'clock 'shuddas'. That was when they arrived in their offices at nine o'clock each morning and reviewed previous events with the complete clarity of vision provided by hindsight. They could always be relied on to be critical, identifying real or imagined shortcomings with a bad habit of saying 'you shudda done this' and 'you shudda done that'.

Wondering what on earth could be next, she found Inspector Donovan's number on her system and called him. She knew Brian only a little, but well enough to know that he was steady and reliable, not given to drama.

"Brian, Sharon Parker, what's going on there now?"

"Hi Sharon. You won't believe this; we've just found a young girl tied up in the boot of the car at the scene. She seems ok, but she needs checking out at hospital."

As force duty officer, Sharon Parker had access to information not available to others, usually for very good reasons, which prompted her next question.

"Have you got a name from her yet, Brian?"

"All she has said so far is 'Linda'."

Sharon could not help a sharp intake of breath and wondered how much more could happen today. She knew that this enquiry was about to move to whole new levels, if that was possible.

"Brian, what I am about to tell you is highly confidential. Two days ago, a girl by the name of Linda Ross was kidnapped and ransom demands were made. As you appreciate, these things are kept confidential and there is a news blackout. Are there any press there now?"

"Yes, loads of news reporters and TV, they're well back, but they must have seen what's going on."

Inspector Parker then said, "Ok, the ambulance will be there shortly. Make sure an officer goes with her. It might be a good idea to use a car to follow, if you've got one spare, to keep the press back. I don't need to tell you it's 'no comment' all the way. I'll get officers from the incident room to meet her at the hospital."

Then, in a rare show of emotion, said, "Thank the Lord something good has come out of this bloody awful day,"

Brian Donovan couldn't help being a little put out on being told how to deal with the press, but realised Sharon Parker had had a very harrowing day, as had he. He'd lost one of his men, and that would sink in sometime later when he let it.

"Alright, Sharon, she seems to have taken to Paul Thomas, I'll send him. No one else knows what's happening, and they won't hear it from me. Speak to you later."

Some of the Control Room staff thought it a little odd to see her smiling, but Sharon didn't care. She was going to make some more phone calls, many to people she had already spoken to but, at least this time, there would be some good news to pass on.

CHAPTER 6

Inspector Parker checked the number and then rang the Ross kidnap incident room, a closely guarded operation. She asked to speak to the senior investigating officer, who she knew was Detective Superintendent John Munro, only to be told that he was in a meeting.

"This is the Force Duty Officer, get him to the phone immediately please."

The detective who answered the phone still hesitated, reluctant to interrupt Munro and risk his sometimes-volcanic temper. However, he recognised the urgency in Sharon's voice and, realising it was an order anyway, decided he better get the boss. After all, he'd been bollocked by senior officers many times in his career and one more wouldn't matter much. He knocked and entered Munro's office to be greeted with scowls from Munro and the two detective inspectors in the room.

He quickly informed Munro that the force duty officer needed to speak to him urgently, and when told to put them through hurriedly left the office.

Seconds later the phone on Munro's desk rang. Picking it up he gruffly said, "This better be good, Inspector, we're a little busy here." Normally the most punctilious of men, it clearly displayed his tension and the pressure he was under.

Sharon Parker replied a little testily, "We have not had the best of days ourselves, Sir. Are you aware of today's events?"

It must be understood that Munro and his team were working away from the main police buildings and not monitoring the Force radio so would have no idea of the afternoon's tragedy. In actual fact, an old police station had been re-opened to house their incident room, allowing them to run the enquiry away from prying eyes and as secretly as possible. This attempt to conceal their involvement was because, as is usual in kidnap cases, the perpetrators had stipulated that police should not be informed. The press had agreed to a total news blackout of the story to assist the police in maintaining the secrecy, but it would have only needed one gossiping officer to let the cat out of the bag.

Munro replied, "What events?"

"Less than half an hour ago one of our officers was stabbed to death and another seriously wounded."

Before she could continue Munro interrupted her, "My God, I'm sorry to hear that, but I don't see what I can do."

"Sir, if you will please listen. The officers were checking a grey car when they were attacked. Other officers have since recovered a bound and gagged girl from the boot of the car. She gave her name as Linda."

Munro had a torrent of questions, some of which he started to ask at once. "How is she? Where is she? Where did this happen? Has the scene been preserved?"

"Sir, she seems fine, but is on her way to the General Hospital. The incident took place in Grimston Lane and the scene has been preserved. You should also know that one man is in custody and is currently on his way to George Street station, also that the press are at the scene. They can't fail to have seen what happened."

Munro, his thoughts whirling, said, "Thank you, Inspector. I'll take over and get some of my people to the scene, the hospital, and to George Street. Thank you again."

He put the phone down and quickly updated his team, allocating officers to the different tasks he had mentioned to Sharon Parker. He decided that it was his job to take the good news to the parents but stressed to the officers attending the hospital that he needed a positive identification of the girl as soon as possible. He knew it was highly improbable that there could be two girls of the same age in the same situation, but he needed to be certain.

As he drove to the parents' home, he couldn't help but feel satisfaction that, as the result of his decision to release information about the grey car, the girl had been found. The sighting of the car by a witness was about the only solid information they had, even though they could not be certain it was involved. He had agonised long and hard before deciding it was a chance worth taking so long as officers didn't know why they were looking for it. Secrecy was everything in kidnap cases.

It appeared to have paid off handsomely with the girl having seemingly been found alive and well.

However, he would not be human if it didn't occur to him that the officer may still be alive if he had known exactly what he was getting into. Munro had done his best by instructing that control should be informed for guidance prior to checking any suspect vehicles. He suddenly realised, with considerable anguish, that he hadn't even asked the names of the two officers involved.

The ripples of the incident in Grimston Lane continued to spread outwards.

Inspector Parker's next call was to the chief constable's office. She knew he would be visiting the scene shortly and, no doubt, would be required to answer questions from the press. How could he not when one of his officers was dead and another injured? He needed to be made aware of the latest developments before some smart reporter tried to trap him into an indiscretion by asking questions about the girl.

On ringing the chief's office, she was told he was already on his way to the scene and from there would be going to see Steve Brown's family. She quickly rang his car phone and spoke to the staff officer before being put on to the chief constable.

Charles Newman was an extremely calm individual with a habit of careful consideration before he did or said anything, not a bad trait to have in his position.

"Hello Sharon, what have you got for me now?"

"Sir, you need to know before you get to the scene that we believe Linda Ross has been recovered safe and well from the back of the car stopped by Inspector Wade and PC Brown. We think the press witnessed her recovery, so you should speak to Inspector Donovan at the scene for a full update before speaking to any journalists."

"Thank you, Sharon, I will. You sound tired, when do you finish your shift?"

She replied, "Very soon, Sir."

"Thank you for your efforts today. You and your staff have done well, very well. Please pass on my thanks."

"Thank you, Sir." She hung up.

'What next?' she thought. Oh yes, the custody suite at George Street. She rang the custody officer to inform her that PC Brown had died and so the soon-to-arrive prisoner was now a suspected murderer. Inspector Parker then told her about the kidnapped girl and explained that officers from the Ross Incident Room were on their way. She did suggest that no mention of the girl should be made to the prisoner, and that perhaps it would be best left to the other officers when they arrived. It was hard to see what advantage could be gained as Smithson would surely be aware the police would find the girl.

All across the Force, different branches and departments were dealing with the fall-out from the assault on the two officers and the Linda Ross kidnap. Decisions had to be made how to proceed and who was to do what as the number of tasks increased minute by minute.

Meanwhile, burglaries were committed, road accidents occurred, shoplifters went about their business, and married couples fought. In other words, along with the extra demands placed on the Force by the two incidents, normal business continued, and police officers had to be deployed to deal with a myriad of tasks.

Whilst travelling to the scene, Charles Newman pondered how best to deal with the two major enquiries facing his Force. One possibility was to have two teams dealing with the incidents, the existing one on the kidnap and a second one to deal with the murder of Steve Brown. After consulting the detective chief superintendent, he decided that the two enquiries were inextricably linked and should be dealt with as one enquiry, headed by Detective Superintendent Munro.

Munro was informed and readily agreed.

CHAPTER 7

It was still not quite 4 p.m., little more than an hour since Wade and Brown had set off on their fateful journey.

The arrested man was just entering the custody suite under heavy escort. Linda Ross was arriving at the hospital with her new best friend Paul Thomas, shortly to be joined by her overjoyed parents and a relieved Superintendent Munro. Richard Wade was already in casualty having his wounds assessed by the best the hospital could provide. As the story of the day spread, he was already being accorded hero status, before people even knew about Linda Ross.

The prisoner was brought into the custody suite handcuffed to one officer and accompanied by a further three. A number of people found urgent reasons to be there, to see the police killer, before the custody officer ejected those who were there without legitimate reasons.

Police Sergeant Mary Jackson was the custody officer having only come on duty in the last hour. She immediately instructed the officers to release the man from his restraints and then to bring him to the counter where she asked him various questions, none of which he answered. She was not unduly bothered, having dealt with many prisoners who had adopted the same tactics, and, in any event, she was sure fingerprints would identify him.

She noted on the custody record that his nose had been bleeding recently, and that his clothing was covered in blood. She could not help but think that there was no way he had got that much blood on him from a bloody nose. Everything was videotaped in the custody suite, and it was vital that he be treated properly, with no suggestion of 'special treatment' by any of the officers in retribution for his crimes. He was taken to a separate room where his clothing was seized and placed into paper bags for forensic examination before he was given a boiler suit to wear. His injuries were photographed for evidential purposes and to establish that he had received those injuries prior to his arrival in the custody suite.

He was then put in a cell to await examination by a police surgeon. A police officer was stationed at the door to ensure he didn't harm himself, as he was considered a suicide risk, but also to record any comments he might make.

Sergeant Jackson understood the man was under arrest for attempted murder. As a result of the phone call from Inspector Parker she knew he would shortly be further arrested for the murder of Steve Brown and no doubt the suspected kidnap of Linda Ross.

By the time the killer had reached his cell, Richard Wade was in a private room being assessed by a hospital consultant. The slash across his chest was deep and about two feet long from shoulder almost to his waist, whilst the stab wound to his shoulder was also deep it had not hit anything vital. Nevertheless, because of the number of stitches required, he would be given a general anaesthetic whilst his wounds were treated, preventing the investigating officers, who were desperate for a full account of what had happened, from speaking to him that night.

Chief Constable Newman attended the scene to satisfy himself that matters were being dealt with properly, although in reality he had little doubt that they would be. He thanked Inspector Donovan and his staff for their work, particularly in releasing Linda Ross, for it had now been confirmed that was who she was. For a few minutes he watched the specialists examining the scene, including the pathologist who was examining the body of Steve Brown.

Charles Newman knew he was a distraction, maybe even a

hindrance, to the people doing their job, but also knew they would be disappointed if he did not show up. He was enough of a politician to know that he had to be seen and photographed by the press, with his image as the concerned and caring leader shown on the television news. None of which meant he wasn't in actual fact concerned and caring.

His main contribution was to ensure that arrangements had been made for refreshments to be brought to the scene, knowing it would be a long and tiring night for all concerned.

His final task was to talk to the press. He explained that he would not be able to answer any questions as he was not in possession of all the facts, and announced that there would be a press conference at police headquarters later that day at 7 p.m. He steadfastly refused to answer any questions relating to the recovery of Linda Ross from the boot of the grey Mondeo. His only other comment was to pay tribute to two brave officers, one of whom had lost his life and the other who had been seriously injured doing their job, protecting the public.

The chief went immediately to the hospital where he was met by Chief Superintendent Moss in whose division all the activity was taking place. Both men were feeling the strain of recent events, especially losing one of their officers, which the good news about Linda Ross could not quite overcome. They saw Richard Wade shortly before his surgery, when he was clearly groggy and still in shock. Making sure he had everything he needed, they thanked him and made clumsy attempts to reassure him, though in truth there was little they could say.

Whilst the two senior officers were visiting their injured officer, Detective Superintendent Munro entered the same hospital by a rear entrance, well away from the press. He was accompanied by John and Mary Ross who, two minutes after arriving, were tearfully re-united with their daughter.

The parents, grey-faced with worry and tiredness, couldn't let go of their only daughter and cried unrestrained tears of joy and relief, thanking anyone and everyone in sight. Linda was guarded by police officers, including Paul Thomas, and cared for by a small number of staff who had been informed of the circumstances, then sworn to secrecy.

John and Mary had just about composed themselves when they were informed by the doctor that their daughter had not suffered any injuries and had not been the victim of any sexual assault. This time their tears of relief took longer to subside.

John Ross was a local man made good. His engineering business had prospered to such an extent that he was a millionaire many times over and had almost made the Sunday Times Rich List. However, he had not forgotten where he came from and still lived in the area, where his business was based. His daughter, who had arrived after seventeen years of marriage, was his most precious possession. When she was taken, the pain was almost unbearable, and he would willingly have given his entire fortune to get her back.

Having been told of the manner of her release, he insisted on seeing Richard Wade and was taken to his hospital room. Wade was still awaiting his surgery and, having already had his pre-op medication, was not fully aware of his visitor or what he had to say. On leaving the room Ross said to Superintendent Munro, "Whatever he needs he gets. I'll foot any bills. I want him to have the best." Munro thanked him and left it at that, knowing that, at the moment, Wade was in good hands and already getting the best treatment available.

Back at the custody suite things were also moving. The man had had his fingerprints taken and they were being urgently checked in efforts to identify him. He still refused to speak and had not responded when offered the opportunity to speak to a solicitor. At the moment that probably didn't matter too much as there were many enquiries yet to be done before officers from Munro's team would have sufficient information to question him.

Meanwhile, the police surgeon arrived and examined the prisoner in the surgery attached to the custody suite. He had an injury to his nose, which was sore and painful as the doctor found out when he touched it. The man maintained his silence, refusing to say how he had received the injury. He had some grazing and bruising to the back of his head which led the doctor to conclude that he needed X-rays of the injuries.

Finally, before he went to hospital, the doctor obtained various samples from the prisoner for forensic analysis. These included scrapings from his fingernails, swabs of the blood on his hands, and samples of the man's own blood and hair.

Later that night it would be established that the nose was broken, but not displaced, and that the back of his head was merely bruised and grazed with slight bleeding, but no fracture. Therefore, he was returned to custody with no further treatment, other than instructions that he should be closely monitored as was already happening anyway. Head injuries can be funny after all.

At 7 p.m. a press conference was convened at the Force Headquarters, where Chief Constable Charles Newman read a prepared statement to a packed room. Dozens of national and local reporters were in attendance along with TV cameras and crews from all the major TV news networks. The reporters were expecting much more than the story of the dead and injured police officers, important as it was. They knew a local girl had been kidnapped but had observed the total news blackout requested by the police to protect the victim as was usual in such cases. They also knew that their colleagues at the Grimston Lane scene had witnessed police release a girl from the boot of a car and take her to hospital. It didn't take a genius to make the connection, two and two usually did add up to four and they now expected their reward for co-operating with the police.

Much care had gone into the preparation of the statement, ensuring that no information was released which could harm the ongoing investigation or prejudice any future court proceedings.

He began:

"Ladies and gentlemen, thank you for attending on what is a very sad day for this Force and the police service as a whole. Today one of our valued colleagues lost his life serving and protecting the public and another received serious knife wounds. At this stage I am not prepared to release the names of the officers involved, I expect to do so tomorrow. The injured officer's injuries, whilst serious, are not believed to be life-threatening and he is expected to make a full recovery. As you know, this incident took place in Grimston Lane shortly before 3 p.m. today when the officers were engaged in the routine check of a motor vehicle. A man is in custody and assisting with our enquiries. Following the suspect's arrest, officers discovered a young girl secured in the boot of the vehicle. She was the subject of ongoing enquiries into her kidnap, and I am pleased to tell you she is unharmed and has now been reunited with her parents. She was liberated and safely returned to her family as a direct result of the actions and extreme bravery of my two officers. I will not be giving any further details regarding the kidnap or the assault on the officers as enquiries are ongoing. It will not be possible at this stage to identify the girl or her family, but on their behalf and my own I would like to thank the press for their discretion in not reporting this matter up to the present time. I would also like to thank the public for the many messages of condolence and support we have received in this difficult time. Thank you for your attention."

Mr Newman refused to answer any further questions, telling the assembled press that there would be a further press conference at 2 p.m. the following day, when he hoped more information could be given. He left the room ignoring the barrage of questions and requests for personal interviews, leaving his press officer to placate the irate journalists.

About 8 p.m. that night, Police Constable Steve Brown was finally removed from the dusty lay-by in Grimston Lane and taken under police escort to the city mortuary, where a post mortem would be carried out as soon as possible.

Around the same time a blonde clerk, who had spent several hours getting ready, waited in a city centre bar for her date. She had been so engrossed in her preparations she had neither seen the television nor listened to the radio and so was ignorant of the day's events. When Steve Brown hadn't arrived or contacted her after three quarters of an hour, she was near to tears and left the bar. Her only thought being 'All coppers really are bastards!'

CHAPTER 8

The following day the enquiry headed by Superintendent Munro started to gather pace as more and more information came into the incident room. Additional officers could now be brought in to assist in the investigation and to concentrate on the numerous lines of enquiry. Because an arrest had been made and the kidnapped girl located, they were now able to operate in the open without the risk of publicity jeopardising the safety of Linda Ross. However, they had to progress rapidly so that they were in a position to charge the detained man before custody time limits expired. In fairness, they had a lot of evidence already, but would need to tidy up lots of loose ends.

The first and most important news was that they now knew who their prisoner was. Fingerprints had identified him as a local man by the name of Karl Smithson, 28 years old, with an extensive criminal record. He had previous convictions for theft, burglary, drugs offences, and violent assaults, often with weapons. He had already served several periods in prison and for some reason, yet to be discovered, he had made the move into the big leagues when he decided to kidnap Linda Ross.

His home address, a flat, was quickly located and visited by detectives and scenes of crime officers, who discovered an evidential gold mine. They found photographs of Linda Ross and her parents along with notes recording their home address and daily habits, such as the time she left the house to go to school and the route she took.

It would later be established that Smithson had worked for about two months at the Ross factory before being sacked for poor time-keeping and attendance. By all accounts he had not been at all happy about his dismissal.

Handwritten copies of the ransom note were also found, which were believed to be the kidnapper practising. However, in true television fashion the eventual note delivered to the family was made up of letters cut from magazines and glued onto a sheet of paper. Smithson had stupidly left the magazines from which the letters had been cut in his flat, as well as the glue and similar paper.

Officers recovered the receipt for a caravan booking at a nearby holiday camp which, when visited, was quickly identified as the place where Smithson had held the girl during her kidnap ordeal. Food, children's clothes, and videos were among the items found and it was clear both beds had been slept in. A single bed was found to have a length of chain fastened to the bed leg and, poignantly, a teddy bear in it. Forensic tests would later identify fingerprints, hair samples, clothes fibres, and DNA belonging to both Smithson and Linda Ross.

As well as the forensic examination of the caravan, detectives conducted enquiries with the owners of the site and other caravan dwellers, most of whom were on short holidays. As it was August, practically every caravan was occupied providing a large number of potential witnesses.

The owners were quickly able to identify Smithson as the occupant of the caravan and to confirm that it was only rented for a three-day period. Furthermore, it had only been booked the previous week, once again showing a lack of advanced planning. He had paid cash and given a false name.

Some of the holidaymakers had seen Smithson, but none had actually spoken to him. They thought he had deliberately avoided them, but most were happy about that as they didn't much like the look of him.

Two people had seen him take a girl into the caravan, thinking she looked a little subdued. They had thought it odd that they hadn't seen either of the pair outside, particularly as the weather was so warm and sunny. At the time they wondered if the girl had been ill.

A gardener on the site had noticed the occupant of the caravan, who he was able to identify as Smithson, load some rolled-up bedding into his car boot on the day of Steve Brown's murder. He said it looked a bit bulky and not very clean but couldn't describe it any further. Detectives had wondered how the kidnapper had managed to get Linda Ross into the car boot without being seen and were now sure she had been wrapped in the bedding. Certainly no other method had been identified.

Previously, some more charitable officers had speculated that Smithson may have put the bedding into the car boot to make the girl more comfortable. Now they were certain of the bedding's significance it quickly dispelled any notion of human kindness they had wrongly believed Smithson may be capable of.

As for the grey Ford Mondeo, that was found to have been stolen and fitted with false registration plates. Smithson had broken into a house, stolen the car keys, and then the vehicle itself from the driveway. It contained similar forensic evidence to that found in the caravan, establishing beyond any doubt that Linda and her kidnapper had been in the vehicle.

The duct tape taken from the girl's mouth had Smithson's fingerprints on it and the rest of the roll was found in his flat, along with similar rope to that used to secure her. All things considered, there was plenty of evidence to convict Smithson for the kidnapping. It was quickly established to the full satisfaction of the investigating team that Smithson was working alone.

It all provided further proof, if it was needed, that Smithson was incapable of the detailed planning needed to carry out such a serious offence. Having left a plethora of evidence, there seemed little chance that he could ever have got away with his crime, even if Brown and

Wade had not intervened. Added to that it would surely not have been long before investigating officers had got to him from the list of ex-employees that they were already going through, especially with his criminal record.

Considering the enquiry had been running for two days it was perhaps surprising that they had not identified him before now. If they had, Steve Brown might still be alive. It was only a small team investigating the kidnap, mainly to ensure that security was maintained, but recognising how often these kinds of cases went wrong, Munro had requested additional admin staff, which had been refused on the grounds of cost. The admin staff would have been tasked with conducting criminal records checks on all John Ross's current and ex-employees. Who knows how different things might have been had it been done quicker.

Shortly, specially trained officers would interview Linda Ross on video tape, which would later be played in court, if required, to spare her the ordeal of giving evidence in person. No doubt the story she could tell would be the final nail in the accused man's coffin.

Other detectives concentrated on investigating the murder of Steve Brown and the attempted murder of Richard Wade. Once again there would be forensic evidence to link Smithson to both crimes, but by far their most effective and compelling evidence would come from Richard Wade's eyewitness account.

CHAPTER 9

At 11 o'clock on the morning following the murder, Detective Superintendent Munro accompanied by Detective Inspector Amy Clark went to see Richard Wade in hospital with a view to getting an initial account from him. On arrival at the hospital, they were informed by medical staff that Wade's surgery had gone well, without problems, and that over a hundred stitches had been needed to close his wounds. They confirmed he was fit to be interviewed.

On entering his room, they could see that Wade was awake and a nurse was helping him to sit up, making sure he was comfortable. Already the room was full of flowers and 'get well' cards from well-wishers, who were mostly members of the public with no connection to the injured officer. It was a slightly odd phenomenon that people felt compelled to send such things to someone they didn't know, but not an unwelcome one. Perhaps it showed there was still a bond between the police and public, and this was their way of showing their appreciation and support.

Wade was very pale and managed a wan smile when they introduced themselves and explained why they were there.

His voice was little more than a whisper when he said, "I've been expecting you."

Munro said, "The plan is for us to get an initial account of what happened yesterday on tape if that is alright with you. Then we'll prepare a statement from the recording which you can read and sign if it's ok. It saves making lots of notes."

"That's fine if it makes things easier. First off though, please tell me how Steve Brown is."

The two detectives looked at each other before Munro said, "Has no one spoken to you?"

Wade looked intently at them and said, "No they haven't, and they won't put the TV on for me. What's going on?"

Munro said, "I'm sorry to have to tell you that Steve didn't recover consciousness and died at the scene."

"So, he didn't manage to tell anyone what happened?"

Munro looked thoughtfully at Wade but did not reply. DI Clark stepped in and said, "He never spoke, but I can tell you that the man you handcuffed to the car is in custody and that a knife has been recovered."

Wade said, "Ok. I'm ready to answer questions and tell you what I can remember. One thing though, can you tell me first why that bloke attacked us? It makes no sense."

Munro took over again. "Officers attending the scene released a young girl from the boot of the car you stopped. She was bound and gagged, having been kidnapped several days earlier. It may be that you and Steve Brown saved her life, certainly you saved her from a frightening ordeal and put an end to her parent's nightmare."

"Now I understand why he was so desperate to get away. I'm glad something good came from it all. I suppose somebody else must have seen what happened with us though?"

Once again Munro considered Wade's words carefully before replying, "We have not located any other witnesses so far, and frankly I'm not sure we will. It was a very quiet road."

Wade laid back, looking at the ceiling, requested a drink of water and a minute or two to let things sink in. After a few minutes he told the officers he needed to use the toilet and that he would need the nurse to help him get there if they could call her. Clark pressed the call button.

The same nurse they had seen earlier returned to the room and the officers went outside to wait until he had completed his ablutions. The nurse wanted to get a bedpan, but Wade insisted on using the en-suite toilet. With her help he managed to get there, but not without considerable pain. Once inside he told the nurse he could manage and would call her when he was ready.

The truth was that Wade didn't need the toilet at all, but he did need to think. He now remembered very clearly everything that had happened yesterday, including his own part in events. He was aware that most of his actions were nothing to be proud of and that if he told everything just as it had happened it would not reflect too well on him. In fact, there was not much he did that would look anything other than pathetic. However, he now knew Brown was dead and that there were no other witnesses, nor likely to be any. He reasoned it was therefore possible to be a little economical with the truth and so show his own actions in a better light. After all, he didn't owe anything to Steve Brown, who would still be alive if he'd listened to his inspector. The more he thought about it, the more he decided it was the way to go. It wouldn't harm anyone and may even help his own career, after all he had been seriously injured in the line of duty and a young girl had been saved. If he just concentrated, he could pull this off. Get this right and there would be no holding him, the sky really would be the limit with this on his record. He realised he was nodding at his image in the mirror, and thought, 'Yes, this is definitely the right thing to do'.

Wade was about to call the nurse when he had a sudden thought. What about the arrested man? Would he tell the truth of what had happened? The whole incident only lasted a couple of minutes, he was in a panic, desperate to escape, and probably couldn't remember things exactly, he concluded. Hold on a minute here, he was a seriously injured officer whose actions had led to the safe release of a kidnapped girl. Who would believe a kidnapper, a police killer over a wounded hero? That was how he was actually beginning to see himself; half convinced the version he was going to give was what really did happen.

Richard wasn't a bad man. However, he was a weak man who wanted to be liked, but more than that he wanted to be respected by his colleagues, to be seen as someone who could do the job and be relied on in tight situations. If anything, he was viewed very much as an office man, an administrator. To be truthful he didn't really have much time for most of his colleagues, particularly those junior in rank to him, considering many of them to be stupid.

He reasoned that an edited version of events would help him to achieve his dreams and would not do any real harm. It couldn't damage the already dead Steve Brown and his murderer would not escape justice. It could work, would work, he told himself.

In many ways Wade and Karl Smithson were very similar. They were both angry and frustrated men engaged in occupations that they were probably not ideally suited to. Neither man was particularly good at their chosen profession, nor did they have the yearned for respect of their peers.

He thought, 'I really can do this, it'll all be alright.' He was sure. His final thought being that he'd be a fool not to take such an opportunity when it presented itself, anybody would.

So, having completely justified what he was about to do in his own mind, he summoned the nurse to the toilet. She helped him back to the bed, fussing over him and making sure he was comfortable. She also reminded him that if he got too tired, he should say so and suspend the interview. That was the last thing he wanted to do, he was excited and eager to tell the story that would change his life.

The nurse was very pretty with a warm smile. She looked at him differently to the way most women normally did, and he was beginning to realise that she was eager to please him, responding eagerly to all his requests, as had other hospital staff to be fair. It dawned on him that his status had changed, and he was already getting the respect he craved. He must not do anything to damage his new standing, especially by revealing the truth of yesterday's events.

As it happened, he had a few more minutes to wait, because Munro was on the phone with the incident room and Clark and gone to fetch coffee for them both. He didn't care, it just gave him a little more time to clarify his thoughts, particularly that he should be suitably upset about the death of his fellow officer, when to be honest all he felt was indifference. Wade was glad of the extra few minutes to think things through again and to rehearse his answers. He realised he could overcome a murderer contradicting his account, but if there were any other witnesses he could be in trouble, even though he knew most of them were pretty unreliable.

He had only been a police officer for six years and in that time had risen rapidly to the rank of inspector but had failed to exhibit any real ability as a police officer, particularly when it came to catching criminals. Brown had been the complete opposite. He was a man confident in his own abilities and in his fifteen years as a policeman he had developed into a gifted thief-taker, often achieving outstanding results by following his instincts.

Wade knew his colleagues didn't think much of him or his abilities and, despite his own rapid rise, sometimes he had envied Brown and his achievements as a police officer, as well as with women for that matter.

He knew he could carry this off, and by the time he had finished everyone would learn to give Richard Wade the respect he was sure he deserved. Certainly there were risks in what he was about to do, but if he could pull it off the potential rewards made those risks more than worth taking.

The two detectives came into the room asking Wade if he was ready to begin. He nodded, but then said, "Sir, before we start, I'd like to say something. I'm obviously going to tell you everything I can remember of what happened yesterday, but it strikes me that our conduct, anybody's conduct, can be criticised after an event. To some degree it is to be expected and I understand that. However, I am here to speak up for myself and Steve Brown is not, so when my statement is prepared, I would hope we do not need to say anything that is detrimental to Steve's reputation."

Munro looked a little surprised, wondering what exactly Wade was about to tell him, but replied, "I understand your thinking and it does you great credit. I can assure you that nothing will be done to damage PC Brown's reputation if it can be avoided. That is the best I can say at the moment."

"Thank you, Sir, I just felt it was important that Steve's memory is not tarnished for his family and friends. He was an excellent officer who I had a lot of time for." Wade thought that was enough, hoping he had established his own sense of decency in their eyes, and he didn't want to overdo it.

When asked for a second time if he was ready to begin, Wade nodded in affirmation.

Amy Clark switched on the tape recorder and placed it on the over-bed table in front of Wade, alongside his water glass and tissues. Munro introduced himself for the benefit of the tape, stating the names of those present and the purpose of the recording. He gave the recording an evidential identification number, making sure Wade understood that, whilst a written statement would be prepared, the tape would be retained as his first account of events, possibly being used as evidence at some stage.

Munro began. "Please tell us how your involvement with the suspect began."

Richard Wade collected his thoughts and began. "We were on Trinity Road heading for HQ when we got stopped at the traffic lights."

"What time was this?"

"We set off at 2 p.m., so it must have been around ten past two."

Munro said, "Who was driving?"

"It was Steve, I had to get a lift with him because someone had taken the car I'd booked. I needed to get to HQ in good time because I was giving a presentation to the chief and other senior officers at 3 p.m."

Munro didn't look unduly impressed and said, "Go on."

"Ok. While at the lights the grey car pulled up alongside us and there was something about it that I wasn't happy with."

DI Clark said, "What exactly aroused your suspicions?"

"I don't know really; I suppose you would call it instinct. The first thing was that I knew we were looking for a grey saloon car, even though I didn't know why at the time, but now I suppose it was in relation to the kidnap. Then, and I know it sounds odd, but the driver of the car never looked at us."

Wade laughed inwardly, aware that he was using almost the same words that Steve Brown had used. He realised it was a good tactic and continuing to use it would ensure he got his account spot on.

DI Clark said, "What do you mean when you say the driver never looked at you?"

"Well, you know what it's like, people always want to look in a police car to see what we're up to. He never even glanced at us; in fact, I got the impression he was trying to turn his face away without making it too obvious. The other thing was he looked quite young and a bit scruffy, it just didn't look like he belonged with that car. I don't have to tell you, do I? In this job you get to feel for when things aren't right."

Munro kept his thoughts to himself and said, "So what did you do?"

"Well, the car pulled away and started to turn right onto the dual carriageway. I asked Steve if he'd seen it and told him we should follow it to check the driver out. Steve hadn't seen the car and, I'm sorry to say, was reluctant to follow it. I don't think he wanted to be late off duty, he told me that once he had dropped me off, he was returning to the station to finish his shift. He said something about a date. In the end I had to insist that he follow the car. We followed it from the dual carriageway into Grimston Lane and once Steve put the blue lights on the driver pulled into the lay-by."

As he lapsed into silence, Munro asked Wade if he was ok to continue. Once again he nodded, but asked for a drink of water first, giving him more time to plan his responses. He had gone too far now to backtrack and would need total concentration to make sure he got this right. No mistakes.

Wade continued, "We stopped about five or six metres behind the car and I got out to speak to the driver."

DI Clark then said, "What did PC Brown do when you got out of the car?

"Well, I knew he wasn't very happy with me and for some reason he didn't like it when I asked him to let control know where we were and do a PNC check on the car."

Munro interrupted, "Are you quite sure you asked Brown to inform control of what you were doing?"

"Absolutely. It's standard officer safety procedure and just plain commonsense."

Munro said, "Well I can tell you Brown didn't contact the control room or do a PNC vehicle check. Have you any idea why that might be?"

"Not really, although I got the impression he thought it was waste of time and he just wanted it finished as soon as possible."

"Richard, you were the front-seat passenger. Is there any reason why you didn't call in about the car whilst you were following it?"

Wade realised he had to be careful. "I thought about it, but I hadn't got the registration number at that time so thought we would just call it in when we stopped."

"Alright, carry on please."

Wade thought for a few seconds, trying to make sure he got this right. He only had the one chance. "Well, I got out and started walking towards the car but, just as I got near to the back of it, the driver got out and looked at me in an odd sort of way. He never said anything."

Clark said, "What do you mean odd?"

"I don't know, he looked a bit vacant and thinking back I suppose there was a tension about him, like he was suppressing his anger. I'm sorry I don't think I'm putting this very well."

Munro said, "You're doing fine. Where was PC Brown at this time?"

Wade looked uncomfortable, then replied, "It's a bit awkward for me to say, but I think he was still in the car at this stage."

Munro was thoughtful once more, staring intently at Richard Wade, before he said, "Never mind. Did you get the man's name at all?"

"No, I asked him, but he didn't answer."

DI Clark asked, "Can you describe him to us?"

"He was in his twenties, not very big and quite scruffy. Oh! I remember his hair was quite long."

Munro said, "For your information his name is Karl Smithson. What happened next?"

Wade considered his answer carefully before replying. "This is where it gets difficult, everything seemed to happen really quickly. I heard our car door open, and Steve came up to me saying something about getting a move on or we would be late. It was then I saw Smithson had a knife in his hand, I think it was his right hand. He lunged at Steve, but I saw it coming and managed to push Steve back away from the grey car, so the knife missed him by a whisker. Smithson then seemed to go berserk and slashed at me with the knife but, because I was off balance, I couldn't avoid it. That's how I got this across my chest. I staggered back and then he had another go at Steve. He just seemed frozen, unable to move, and that's when he got stabbed in the stomach. Steve screamed and fell to his knees, there was blood gushing out all over him. I managed to stay on my feet and made a grab for Smithson, but he broke free and lashed out at me with the knife again. I think that's when he got me in the shoulder, and I believe I went down on one knee. He must have thought I was finished because he went after Steve again. Steve was just kneeling there, not moving, like he couldn't or wouldn't move and then Smithson stabbed down into his neck, I think. There was more blood, seemed like gallons of it, and Steve fell over."

He went quiet seemingly upset, but the truth was that he was thinking what he had said and what he needed to say next. Now was not the time to make any silly mistakes.

Misinterpreting his silence, Det. Supt. Munro asked Wade if he was well enough to continue. Once again Wade nodded and went on. "He seemed intent on killing us. He didn't need to carry on, he could have just driven off, couldn't he? I knew I had to stop him before he could finish us both off, so I managed to pull myself up on the car and then jumped on Smithson. I caught him by surprise, I think, and we both ended up on the floor with me on top of him. I'm not that big, but my weight was holding him down, and I think I winded him as well. Thank God he dropped the knife. I got hold of his hair and kept banging his head on the floor until he seemed to lose consciousness. I reached over and got Steve's handcuffs from his pouch and fastened them on one of Smithson's wrists. Then I realised I needed to fasten him to something, so he couldn't escape or finish us off. I don't know how I did it, but I managed to drag him to the car and fastened him to the back. It was lucky he wasn't very heavy or too far to the car, I'd just about had it. He started to come round, lashing out and shouting, that's when I went to our car. I think I sat on the ground, didn't I? That's when the pain hit home, it was unbelievable. I should have gone to help Steve, but I couldn't."

Both Munro and Clark looked at Richard Wade in silence, almost unable to believe the horror they had just listened to. It was every police officer's nightmare facing an armed and determined attacker on a lonely road.

Munro cleared his throat and said, "Just a few more questions if you can manage to carry on. Is that alright?"

"Yes, fine."

Munro said, "Did PC Brown say anything once the fight started?"

"No, he never had chance."

"Smithson has a broken nose. Do you know how that happened?"

"It was in the fight I suppose, I'm not sure how exactly."

"Which hand did you say he was holding the knife in?"

"Right I think, yes right, I'm sure."

Munro continued, "Whilst you were sat on the ground, did you do anything?"

"At first I think I was a little disorientated, maybe I even lost consciousness. I'm not sure. Then I pressed the red panic button on my radio to try and get some help. I knew Steve was in a bad way, but I couldn't get to him to help."

Munro looked to Amy Clark, who looked at her notes before speaking. "Richard, what radio were you using?"

Wade looked at her as if to say, 'what has this got to do with anything?' and replied, "I couldn't find mine so I just got a new one out of its box in the inspector's office. I didn't have time to look for mine. I was in a hurry."

She said, "Because it wasn't assigned to you, or anyone else for that matter, control room staff couldn't identify who was asking for help. For the same reason the GPS wasn't working, so they didn't know where you were initially."

"You mean if I had had the right radio Steve Brown might still be alive?"

Munro responded to that, "We'll never know, but you certainly have nothing to reproach yourself for. You couldn't have done anymore to save Steve, that's obvious."

So nobody knew where they were. Even Wade, after his catalogue of lies and half-truths, felt some pangs of guilt, but soon pushed them to the back of his mind. Of course he would have called it in when Brown asked him to if he had realised how things would turn out, but how could he have possibly known? Anyway, he certainly wasn't going to take instructions from a PC, it was his own fault for following the car in the first place. It certainly wasn't his fault Brown was dead.

Munro said, "Nearly finished. Why weren't you wearing your stab vest?"

Wade looked surprised that they bothered to ask but replied, "Well I was in a bit of a hurry and they get in the way when you get to Headquarters. There's never anywhere to put them, is there? Besides that, I wasn't operational and didn't expect that I would get involved in anything, did I?"

"Is that why you didn't have your PPE either?"

Looking confused Wade replied, "My what?"

"Your PPE, your handcuffs, baton, and CS gas?"

"I know what it is, I just don't really understand why you need to ask about this."

Munro could see Wade was tiring and becoming defensive. "Last question. Is there anything else you would like to tell us?"

"Yes. Whilst I was sat on the ground, I thought I heard banging. I suppose that was the girl in the boot, was it? The only other thing is that I wish I could have done more for Steve. Maybe I could have done more to save him."

Munro decided to wrap things up. "Thanks Richard, we've got enough for now I think." He looked over to DI Amy Clark, who nodded her agreement. He continued, "We should be able to interview Smithson properly now that we've got the full picture. I'll get a statement prepared for you to look at as soon as possible. I'm sure you realise there will be an inquest and a trial sometime in the future, but if I'm honest I don't think I've ever seen a case with so much evidence against one individual. We'll leave you to get some rest." Clark switched the tape recorder off.

As they were going out of the room Amy Clark suddenly remembered something and turned back to speak to Richard Wade. He felt a slight tremor of panic. 'What had she remembered? Had he slipped up somewhere?'

He needn't have worried. She said, "By the way, John Ross would like to come and see you if you are up to it?"

"Who?"

"Sorry, Linda Ross is the name of the kidnapped girl. He's her father."

Wade thought it couldn't do any harm. He told Clark it wouldn't be a problem.

The two detectives left. Wade laid back on his pillows, breathing a sigh of relief. The nurse, who had returned to check on him, thought Wade must be in pain and took his hand whilst she asked if he needed anything. He was very tired but did enjoy holding her hand. He must ask her name. Thinking back on the interview, he decided it had gone to plan. He congratulated himself on the way he had managed things, keeping it simple. His careful planning had allowed him to follow two simple rules, if you tell a lie make it a big one and when lying tell as much of the truth as possible. Thinking it through he realised that he had pretty much told the story exactly as it had happened, simply swapping his and Steve Brown's parts in the events, making sure he was the one who subdued their attacker, and Brown the one who did nothing. His last thought before falling asleep was that he thought he had got away with it. He had done well, bloody well.

As they drove to Headquarters for the 2 p.m. press conference, Munro asked DI Clark what she thought of Wade's story. She considered her words carefully before saying, "I know of Inspector Wade, but don't know him personally. From all I have heard I've got to say I'm very surprised he had it in him. Having said that, he did very well and because of what he did a dangerous man is off the streets."

Munro responded, "I know what you mean. The way he described things Wade certainly showed great bravery and determination to get the better of a nutter like Smithson. I've got to say, though, for all his talk of Steve Brown's reputation, he pretty well managed to trash it, don't you think?"

With that he lapsed into gloomy silence.

CHAPTER 10

On reaching Headquarters, Munro still had a few minutes before the press conference so contacted the incident room, where enquiries were being co-ordinated into the Ross kidnapping and the assault on the two officers. He spoke to Detective Sergeant Bill Devereux who was able to confirm that he had already interviewed Karl Smithson in company with a detective constable, albeit briefly. His intention, in line with standard police practice, was to obtain an initial account of his actions from the suspect. The interview was tape recorded and Smithson was informed of his legal rights, but he refused to speak at all for about half an hour. He refused to even acknowledge the officers' presence, never mind answering their questions, before suddenly demanding to see a solicitor. The interview was immediately terminated.

The duty solicitor, in this case Mike Adamson, had been contacted and was now in private consultation with his client, taking on the biggest and potentially most difficult case of his career.

Munro quickly thought about things, checking the time and doing some mental calculations before he said, "Bill we've got some custody issues to sort out. We are quickly getting to the time when legally we need to either charge or release Smithson, and we're not going to be ready to charge him and there is no way he'll be released. No doubt his solicitor will be onto that pretty soon, making representations to the custody officer."

Devereux replied, "Are you looking for an extension of custody then, Sir?"

"Exactly, Bill. Please see the custody sergeant and ask them to request that the duty superintendent authorise a twelve-hour extension to Smithson's custody. You know all the reasons. Post mortem is taking place now, video interview with Linda Ross is ongoing, property searches and forensic work still being conducted, and finally the need to interview Smithson under caution so that he can give an account of his actions. It needs to be stressed that enquiries are being conducted expeditiously and conscientiously, ok?"

"No problem, Sir, and if you think it's a good idea, I'll have a quick word with Mike Adamson to let him know where we are."

Munro replied, "Yes, that's a good idea, I'm sure he'll understand considering the seriousness of the offences under investigation. Let me know if you get any problems and drag me out of the press conference if you need to."

Devereux laughed, "Sorry Sir, I don't think we'll need to do that."

Munro nodded ruefully, his desire to avoid the press conference so easily detected by his sergeant.

The superintendent just had time to update the chief constable on Wade's account of events and the state of the enquiry before the press conference began. Charles Newman was more than happy with the progress made but stressed the need to get Smithson charged and remanded in custody as soon as possible, so that the Force could return to some normality. Despite everything that had happened, the demands on the police continued and it was his job to ensure that his staff were able to meet those demands.

On the stroke of 2 p.m. Newman and Munro entered the conference room, taking their places at a table in front of the gathered media. If anything, there were even more newspaper reporters and TV cameras than the previous day. Sitting with the two police officers at the table was John Ross.

Ross had decided, after consultations with the police and his legal advisors, that talking to the press now may prevent harassment to his family and ill-informed speculation.

Newman addressed the assembled throng

"Today's press conference is to update you as far as is possible about the events of yesterday which, as you know, resulted in the death of one of my officers and serious injury to another. At least there was some good news in that, as a result of the two officers' actions, a kidnapped ten-year-old girl was released. I can now tell you that the officer who died is Constable Steve Brown and the injured officer is Inspector Richard Wade. Brief biographies of both officers will be available at the end of this press conference. I wish to extend my sincerest condolences to Steve's family and friends. He was a fine officer who will be sadly missed. Richard Wade is still in hospital having had treatment for his injuries, and I understand he needed over a hundred stitches to repair his wounds. We wish him a speedy recovery. A large number of officers are currently engaged in the ongoing investigation and we are satisfied that only one person was involved in the commission of these offences. I can therefore confirm that we are not seeking anyone else. The detained man has been interviewed and will be further interviewed later today. I can tell you that I am extremely proud of both my officers, particularly Richard Wade who fought valiantly against an armed man in an effort to save a colleague's life. It is thanks to his extreme bravery that a man was detained and the girl released. When the full story is revealed, I am sure you will all marvel, as do I, at his courage, determination, and exemplary sense of duty. I'm afraid that is all I can tell you at this time, but I promise we will continue to keep you up to date with all developments. Now I would like to introduce Mr John Ross. I am now able to reveal that it was his daughter, Linda, who was kidnapped, leading to yesterday's terrible events. At least her release is one outcome we can all celebrate."

He sat down, yielding the floor to John Ross, who introduced himself to the reporters and gave brief details of his background and business interests. On behalf of himself and his wife he thanked them for not publicising the kidnapping, going on to thank the police for their unstinting efforts to find his daughter. He reserved his greatest praise and thanks for Richard Wade and Steve Brown, offering his condolences to the latter's family. He finished by explaining that, on legal advice, he would not be able to discuss any details of his daughter's kidnap and subsequent release. However, he was prepared to give interviews to one print and one television reporter, which they would share with their colleagues. It would be up to the reporters to select their representatives, and then he hoped his family could be left alone to recover from their ordeal.

This was agreed and arranged for the following day.

CHAPTER 11

Det. Supt. Munro returned to the incident room, happy to be free of the press and senior officers. He met Bill Devereux who was there to tell him that the extension of custody for Smithson was sorted and that there had been no objection from the solicitor. That give them time to pursue enquiries and plan for the next stages of the investigation.

He was handed a copy of the pathologist's report completed following the post mortem on Steve Brown, and initial forensic reports. More detailed forensic information would take longer following laboratory analysis of evidence and samples, particularly blood and hair. Lastly, he was informed that Linda Ross's video interview was finished and available for him to see. It was all coming together now. That didn't mean that there weren't weeks of work still to be done, finding witnesses, looking into Smithson's background, marshalling forensic evidence, and taking endless statements. Then, along with the Crown Prosecution Service, the evidence and witnesses would need to be prepared and organised to ensure a successful prosecution at the inevitable trial.

Munro asked DI Clark to set up the Ross video for viewing and whilst waiting quickly scanned the pathologist's report. He was not surprised to see that the cause of Steve Brown's death was given as two stab wounds, to the stomach and upper chest, both causing massive internal injuries. Specifically severe damage to his left lung and extensive damage to his small intestine, both accompanied by substantial blood loss. One thing he saw that caused him to read it twice was the description of a graze and bruised area on the centre of

66

Steve Brown's forehead, which was covered with blood, although it appeared not to be from the actual head injury. He wondered how he got that injury and where exactly the blood came from but expected that Brown had wiped it on his head from his other injuries. This was entirely possible as the report had already described the huge amount of blood he had lost and how it had saturated his clothing. It probably wasn't that relevant anyway. Otherwise, the report was pretty much as he had expected.

Glancing at the forensic report his attention was drawn to the graphic photographs taken at the scene. They included close ups of Steve Brown's body which he could clearly see was indeed covered in blood. Munro couldn't help but think that the stab vest hadn't helped Steve much, a clear illustration of how little real defence there was against a determined and, in this case, ferocious attacker. He was able to see the mark and smear of blood on Brown's forehead but couldn't see any real significance. From personal experiences, in his younger days, Munro knew you often picked up lumps and bumps during a fight without knowing exactly how they had happened. He also examined several shots of the grey Ford Mondeo, noting that it appeared to be covered in fingerprint powder, both inside and out.

When it was ready, he sat with Amy Clark to watch the video interview. He noted that the interviewer had been exceptionally skilled at putting Linda Ross and her mother, who was present throughout, at their ease. The girl briefly recounted how she had been stopped by a man on her way to school who told her that her mother was ill, and she should return home. She got into his grey car without hesitation. Once in the car he threatened her with harm to her parents if she didn't do as she was told and took her to the caravan, but she didn't know where it was. She confirmed being chained to the bed but was positive she had not been harmed in any way. She did not know why the man had tied her up and driven off with her in the boot of the car, although police suspected he was getting ready to make his final ransom demand. She knew when the car stopped and did hear some muffled conversation, but as the engine was still running, she couldn't hear very well. The only things she remembered hearing was somebody shouting, 'please don't hurt me' and somebody else shout, 'get my cuffs'. Then she heard the man who kidnapped her screaming and shouting. She got frightened and was very hot in the boot, so she started kicking the lid for someone to let her out.

Linda Ross was unable to give any other useful information, and police did not want to use her at this stage to identify Smithson.

Det. Supt. Munro thought they were ready to interview their suspect. After careful consideration he had decided that he would conduct the interview in company with Amy Clark. Even in this day and age, some men found it unsettling to be questioned by a woman so it could be a useful tactic against Smithson. He called DS Devereux, asking him to arrange for Smithson's solicitor to be at the custody suite at 6 p.m. so that his client could be interviewed.

Munro and Clark went to the canteen for a drink and something to eat before what could be a long night. More importantly they planned their strategy, refreshing their memories on the known facts from the various files they carried.

They were particularly keen to find out why Smithson had taken the risk of driving a stolen car in broad daylight with Linda Ross locked in the boot. Among the items recovered from the car were another note that appeared to contain instructions for delivering the ransom money, and a mobile phone that had the Ross family number entered into it.

The phone was what is often described as a 'burner'. It was a cheap pre-paid mobile phone that the owner generally doesn't intend to keep long term. These phones have traditionally been purchased with cash to avoid any kind of paper trail that would tie the phone's number to any individual. Clearly of great benefit to criminals and easily disposed of.

As further proof that there was no way he could be considered a master criminal, officers searching Smithson's flat had found the mobile phone box. This enabled them to identify the shop where it was purchased and, with the aid of CCTV, to identify Smithson as the purchaser.

Munro and Clark quite reasonably speculated that this was Smithson's endgame. It looked as if he was planning to collect the ransom money that day and possibly to return the girl. However, with his history of violence there was no guarantee that he would have taken the risk of releasing Linda, a witness who may be able to identify him. His proclivity for violence was amply illustrated by his attack on the two police officers.

Armed with all the available evidence they were in the custody suite just after 6 p.m. but had to wait for almost an hour whilst Mike Adamson consulted, in private, with his client. The two officers, the solicitor, and Smithson then went into an interview room, where proceedings would be video recorded throughout. DI Clark turned on the tape recorder, ensured that everyone, including Smithson, introduced themselves and finally cautioned the accused before any questions were asked.

At that moment Mike Adamson interjected, "My client has informed me that he does not wish to answer any questions you may wish to put to him. However, he has prepared a written statement which he has asked me to read out and, if you are ready, I will now do so now."

This was not an unusual tactic and one which was becoming more and more common, allowing detainees to give their account of events without having to answer often difficult questions.

Munro responded, "We, of course, will listen to the statement with interest, but I must point out that we still intend to ask your client a number of questions. It is entirely his right not to answer them, as has already been explained when he was cautioned. Please go ahead when you are ready."

The solicitor began, "It is a brief statement, as follows:

'Yesterday afternoon I was in the car park at B&Q when I saw a grey-coloured Ford Mondeo car parked near to the fence. As I walked past it, I could see that the keys had been left in the ignition. On an impulse I decided to take the car for a ride, because I was bored and had nothing better to do.

I'd only been in it for about 10 minutes when I saw the driver of that police car looking at me as if he knew what I'd done. I turned off but they followed me and put their blue lights on. I was going to make a run for it but didn't because all I'd done was nick a car.

When I stopped in that lay-by, they came behind me and one of them got out. I didn't like the look of him and to be honest I thought I was going to get a good hiding. It wouldn't be the first time and I was very frightened. I carry a knife because I'm fed up of being bashed so when he first came towards me I got it out and waved it at him. The other one got out as well and then they tried to grab hold of me. All they had to do was get off me and go away, but they didn't so I jabbed it towards them, I don't know if I got anybody. I didn't intend to hurt anyone, and I wouldn't have if they had gone away. I was frightened they were going to hurt me, honest. I would have just left if they had let me.

They knocked me down and I think they must have fallen on the knife while I was still holding it, not my fault, was it? I think I got knocked out and when I came to, I was fastened to the car.

Finally, I would like to say that I had no idea there was anyone in the boot of the car and I wouldn't have taken it if I'd known.

I didn't have anything to do with kidnapping that girl and I only acted in self-defence with them coppers.

I don't wish to say anything else and on legal advice will not answer any of your questions.'

That concludes my client's statement."

Both officers were slightly taken aback by the statement, needing a moment to collect their thoughts. They spent the next hour and a half going through the questions they had intended to ask, showing Smithson and his solicitor various photographs and other evidence including the murder weapon. He answered every question with 'no comment', saying nothing else whatsoever, whilst his solicitor made careful notes.

At the conclusion of the interview, following a further brief consultation with his solicitor, Smithson was returned to his cell, still under constant supervision.

Munro and Clark were ready for another cup of tea, both were beginning to feel the effects of their punishing schedule. It was something you never got used to, the non-stop demands at the beginning of a major enquiry, bearing in mind they had already been working on the kidnapping for two days before Smithson's arrest. Both could badly do with some sleep.

The detective superintendent had been a police officer for thirty-five years, with most of them spent as a detective. Even with all his experience, Munro had to admit he had been caught a little by surprise when Smithson's statement was read out. Its audacity was breathtaking, and it was scarcely believable that he thought he might get away with such a laughable fabrication.

"So Amy, what do you think of his statement?"

"To be honest, boss, I could hardly keep a straight face. I've never heard such a load of crap; does he really think that will work with a jury?"

Munro looked thoughtful. "I agree it's total nonsense, but juries are funny things. We need to be spot on with this, making sure we cover every avenue of escape for him. I know it looks cut and dried, but we must be certain we cover all the angles and collect every bit of evidence we can. Get that message across to the team. I don't think they need much motivating though, not after what he did to that girl and killing one of ours."

"What about Wade?"

"What do you mean?"

DI Clark phrased her response carefully, "Do you think he will be ok in court? He's not very experienced and his evidence will be the crucial factor in convicting Smithson."

Munro, if he was honest, had similar concerns. "I think he'll be ok, but we can work with him so that he knows what to expect when the defence barrister starts on him. He'll do alright, I'm sure."

They lapsed into tired silence, returning to the custody suite once they'd finished their tea.

Munro assessed the evidence they had against Smithson. He was detained at the scene by the officers and there would, no doubt, be a mass of forensic evidence to assist in establishing what had happened. They had the murder weapon and had already established that Smithson's fingerprints were on the hilt, having ensured its examination was prioritised. Of course Smithson had already admitted in his prepared statement that the knife was his and that he was holding it when the officers' injuries were caused. Most importantly, they had Richard Wade's compelling account of the incident which clearly fitted the circumstances much more than Smithson's. To hear him, the officers had practically caused their own injuries, and he had played only a minor part. Finally, if needed, he was sure they could use Linda Ross to provide further identification evidence, although he hoped it would not be necessary.

After Munro had discussed the evidence, they had accumulated so far with the Crown Prosecution Service, it was agreed that Smithson should be charged in connection with the offences.

At 11 p.m. that night, in the presence of Mike Adamson, he was charged with murder, attempted murder, kidnapping, burglary, taking the motor vehicle, and possession of an offensive weapon. He was kept in custody to appear at court the following day, where he would later be remanded to prison pending trial.

CHAPTER 12

Whilst Munro and Clark were busy in the custody suite, Richard Wade was being visited by Mr and Mrs Ross. Even though she had been due off duty some hours earlier, Wade's pretty nurse had remained at work to care for him. He had now discovered that her name was Julie and that she had been a nurse for five years. Most people may have been slightly discomfited by Julie's obvious devotion and hero worship, but Wade seemed to accept it as his due. He had enjoyed the succession of visitors, basking in the warmth of their praise and thanks for a job well done.

So far, he'd had visits from the chief constable, his divisional commander David Moss, the Police and Crime Commissioner, along with assorted officers and well-wishers. With every visitor he made light of his injuries, always careful to praise Steve Brown's contribution.

Finally, it was the turn of Linda Ross's parents, John and Mary. They made their gratitude obvious with John Ross so desperate to thank the man he credited with his daughter's safe return that he offered him everything from a job to money. Wade told him that as a serving police officer he was not allowed to accept gifts and anyway, as he modestly explained, he had only been doing his job. In a final effort to reward Wade in some way, Ross offered him the use of his holiday home in Malta to recuperate once out of hospital. The injured officer thanked him and said he would ask senior officers if that was possible, although he thought it unlikely.

However, the idea appealed greatly to Wade and, as he wondered whether Julie might like Malta, he resolved to ask his boss if there was any way he could accept John Ross's offer. Anyone entering the room at that moment may have been surprised at the smile lighting up Richard's face as he fell asleep dreaming of just what his personal nurse might look like in a bikini.

Five days later Richard Wade left hospital, with Julie now officially his girlfriend. He felt genuinely sorry that Steve Brown was dead but, in all honesty, he had to admit that so far it was the best thing that had ever happened to him, and it looked like things were only going to get better. He was, however, very careful to keep his innermost thoughts to himself, revealing them to no one, not even Julie.

He was amazed to think how quickly and dramatically his life had changed for the better in a matter of only a few minutes. He was a selfish man, but not a stupid one and realised that life can change just as quickly in the other direction, particularly for someone hiding behind such a tissue of lies. He needed to be alert, on his guard at all times.

Wade had been told that before he could return to duty, as well as being physically recovered from his injuries, he would need to see a psychiatrist. It was imperative that he be very careful when speaking to them, but in his arrogance did not feel it would present any problems for him. He had received a number of job offers, including the one from John Ross, and he was starting to wonder if there might be better opportunities for him outside the police. He was toying with the idea of writing a book once the trial was over, something he would not be permitted to do as a serving officer. He even had a provisional title, 'Duty Calls', the irony of which was not lost on him.

Exactly a week after the incident in Grimston Lane, the chief constable's personal car and driver collected Wade from his flat to take him to police headquarters for a meeting with Mr Newman. He was seen off by Julie, who had now moved in ostensibly to care for him, but in reality because she worshipped him. She made sure he was wearing his best suit and that he had his left arm in the clean sling he insisted on wearing, even though she wasn't sure he needed it.

On arrival at HQ the driver suggested that, as they were a few minutes early, Wade might like to wait in the canteen. On reaching the canteen door he saw that it was quite full and he belatedly realised that it was nearly lunch time. He was nervous of being around so many police officers, uncertain of the reception he might receive, but he hesitantly went in anyway. Everyone was immediately aware of Wade's presence, falling silent until one man stood up and began to clap, quickly joined by everyone in the room. He was a little embarrassed, but not much, and enjoyed the acclaim he never ever expected to receive from his fellow officers and the police staff who were there. He gave a carefully self-conscious wave and mouthed his thanks to those present.

Before he was able to get a drink, the chief constable came to the canteen, personally escorting him to his office where he was full of concern for Wade's condition, ensuring he was comfortable, and enquiring as to the state of his injuries. The inspector was once again enjoying the attention and was made only slightly uncomfortable when the chief congratulated him on having his own personal nurse, with a slightly inappropriate wink.

Once the formalities were over, Mr Newman said, "I've had a call from John Ross. He tells me that you quite rightly rejected his offers of money and jobs, but he is still keen to thank you in a tangible way. We had quite a talk and he tells me that the least he can do is to lend you his holiday home for some recuperation in the sun."

"Yes Sir, he made that offer to me. I told him that it was unlikely I would be able to accept."

Newman smiled and said, "Quite right. However, I have been in discussion with various people including the Police and Crime Commissioner, the Force solicitor, and the welfare branch. It seems there may be a way. What we have suggested to Ross is that whilst he cannot offer the Malta villa to an individual it is possible to offer it for the use of the whole Force."

Seeing Wade's puzzled expression caused him to smile even more broadly before he continued, "We have suggested he donate the villa for two weeks each year for the use of officers injured on duty or who have other welfare needs. He has accepted and has also included return flights for two people each year. You will be the first beneficiary of his generosity and will fly to Malta on Monday with Julie if you wish."

Newman was very happy, proud of the elegant solution he had achieved.

Wade agreed enthusiastically.

The chief went on, "I have other news. We intend to nominate you for a bravery award and are taking advice on the level of such an award, but I need to be sure you will accept it if nominated."

"I'm grateful, Sir, but to be honest I would feel like a fraud. All the time during the incident I was very much afraid, and I cannot help thinking I should have done more to save Steve."

Charles Newman, who considered himself an excellent judge of men, was completely fooled by Wade's show of humility. "Richard, I understand what you are saying, however, consider this. Yes, you were afraid, as any sensible man would be, nevertheless you overcame your fear, confronted your attacker, and managed to detain him despite your injuries. You did your duty, and I would struggle to find a better example of individual bravery. Before you answer please consider that such an award would bring great credit to the force and your colleagues, whilst honouring the memory of Steve Brown. I'm sure your family and Julie would also be very proud of you, and I don't think I need to tell you that it will not harm your career."

Newman omitted to mention that anything that made his force look good would not do him any harm either.

Wade chewed his lip as he thought about the chief's remarks. Surely, he didn't think Wade ever intended to turn a medal down, it really was too easy to fool people so long as you were careful. He cautioned himself not to overdo it and slowly nodded his head. "Alright Sir, if you think it's for the best."

The chief constable beamed with pleasure and said, "One final thing. When do you think you will be fit to come back to work, Superintendent?"

Even Wade was taken aback by what had just been said, but if he had heard it correctly it was beyond his wildest dreams. All he could say was, "I'm sorry, Sir?"

By now Newman was enjoying himself immensely. "You heard me correctly, Richard. I'm promoting you to temporary superintendent with immediate effect, you deserve it. Of course, we'll have to send you on a few courses to get you up to speed, but I'm sure you will cope admirably."

Wade quickly regained his equilibrium, already sure his promotion was richly deserved. "Thank you, Sir, I'll try not to let you down."

"I'm sure you won't. Now listen, the press have been clamouring for an interview with you, but we're not going to let them speak to you until after Smithson's trial, so please be on your guard. Finally, I would prefer it if the bravery award idea was kept under wraps."

"No problem, Sir."

"Okay Richard, I won't keep you any longer. I'll see you on Friday at Brown's funeral."

After voicing his gratitude again, Wade left the office to be taken home by the chief's driver. He was sure Julie would be overjoyed to hear all his news.

In truth the idea that Wade be given a bravery award had not really been Charles Newman's, but had originated in the Home

Secretary's office. The press had gone to town on the whole story, which bore all the hallmarks of a cheap novel. The kidnap of a self-made millionaire's young daughter, the death of one brave police officer and serious injuries to another as they rescued her from a dangerous criminal.

They had somehow even managed to uncover Wade's previous military service and focussed on his record of service, even publishing photos of him in army uniform. Once again, the facts were not allowed to get in the way of a good story. He had joined the army direct from university where he had managed to just about get a maths degree. His undistinguished military service consisted of a three-year short service commission in a logistics unit where he had shown minimum aptitude for army life. Both the Army and Wade appeared relieved when he left and neither missed the other. However, the police service were very impressed with him, his degree, and military service, welcoming him with open arms. Two things Wade was good at were examinations and interviews, hence his rapid promotion in the police.

In fact, his military experience and training had led directly to him taking that fateful journey with Steve Brown, and to the confrontation with Karl Smithson. Wade, because of his past, was viewed by his senior mangers as being extremely skilled in logistics and planning, although for some reason they had never seen fit to confirm it in any practical sense. In a sign of his favour, he had been tasked with identifying options and recommendations for massive reductions in both police and civilian staff numbers within the Force. The object being to dramatically reduce the budget as, after all, staff are the biggest single expense in any organisation. On that day he had been taking his report to present to senior officers, hence his desperation not to be late. He had been convinced that the report and what he was sure would be a masterful presentation were to be his route to further success.

After a long period of bad publicity for both the Home Office and the police, particularly concerning cuts to police funding, the powers that be wanted to keep a good news story on the front pages for as long as possible. It was a shame someone had died, but it would be foolish in the extreme not to take advantage of it. This resulted in the Home Office advice to Charles Newman suggesting a medal for Wade and their support when it was proposed that he be promoted, both of which would look good to the newspaper-reading masses. It was all about letting the public know that the police were there to protect them and could be relied on whatever the situation. A hero was good for business. Cuts to numbers did not mean a reduction in the quality of individual police officers or the service they provided, did it?

The offices of the Home Secretary and the Prime Minister were in discussion about meeting Richard Wade and deciding who should announce that he was to be nominated for a George Medal, the highest award he could receive. In the event it was reluctantly agreed they should wait until legal proceedings were completed.

Make no mistake, any suggestions emanating from the Home Office were made with the Home Secretary's full support and approval.

A little reflected glory never did a politician any harm. The local MP had already raised the matter in Parliament, singing Richard Wade's praises, and those of the police service in general. He tabled a motion expressing condolences for the death of Steve Brown and congratulations to Richard Wade along with wishes for a speedy recovery. His remarks were met with murmurs of agreement around the house, with both the Prime Minister and Home Secretary adding brief statements of support.

As one seasoned hack in the press gallery remarked, "It's difficult for a politician to see a bandwagon pass by without jumping on it."

CHAPTER 13

Once Wade left his office, Charles Newman realised there was a job he should have done before he spoke to the newly appointed superintendent, so asked his secretary to arrange for Detective Superintendent Munro to come to see him that afternoon.

Munro arrived at the chief's office just before 4 p.m. and was a little concerned as to why he was there. He'd known Mr Newman for several years, but they could not be described as friends and had never actually worked together.

Newman quickly put him at his ease, thanking him for a good job on the Smithson enquiry, but then irritating Munro by telling him the conversation must remain confidential. He was not the sort of man to discuss private conversations with others.

To say Munro was surprised to hear Wade and had been promoted to superintendent, something it had taken him twenty-seven years to achieve, was an understatement. It was not envy, more that he couldn't understand how anyone could be ready for such a senior position with only six years service and so little experience. He was even more surprised to hear that Wade was to be nominated for a bravery award, the George Medal no less. It all seemed a little soon, especially when Steve Brown's funeral had not yet taken place and the trial was months away. Munro was not even close to being the actor Wade was and his discomfort was spotted immediately by Newman.

"John, look I'll be honest with you. This is not just me; our political masters feel that the publicity around Wade is good for the police service and so is obviously good for them as well. He doesn't know yet that both the Prime Minister and Home Secretary want meetings, which will, of course, be highly publicised. What I need to know from you is if there is anything coming out of the enquiry that I should know about?"

Munro had a very good idea what the chief meant, but decided he would make him spell it out. "I'm sorry, Sir, in what way?"

Newman sighed heavily. "Okay, did Brown or Wade do anything that won't look so good when it comes to court? In short, I don't want the promotion, the medal, the publicity, and all the praise to rebound on us. Is everything going to be above board?"

Munro resented being put on the spot like this as a result of everyone else's agendas and chose his words very carefully. "Smithson has not admitted much. He read a prepared statement denying the kidnapping but admitting the confrontation with the officers and to having a knife. He blamed them for their injuries and said if they had left him alone nothing would have happened. It's absolute nonsense of course and I'm sure it will be laughed out of court. I don't think there'll be any problem convicting him, not with all the forensics."

Slightly exasperated Newman said, "Yes, I know that, but what about the way Wade behaved? Can he be criticised for anything?"

"Well Sir, this is delicate, but I think there may be a couple of things."

"Good God man, spit it out will you."

"Firstly, Wade didn't have his own radio, so control didn't know who wanted help and because GPS wasn't connected didn't know where they were. It's possible if medical help had got there quicker, Steve Brown might still be alive, although in fairness his injuries were very serious. Secondly, Wade wasn't wearing his stab vest, which may have prevented his own injuries, and neither was he carrying his PPE.

As you know, Sir, in different circumstances these omissions could have been treated as discipline offences, but not only that they could have made a significant difference in dealing with Smithson. Also, Wade was the passenger in the patrol car, so why didn't he call in what they were doing before they pulled the car over?"

Newman looked angry. "Is that all?"

"Finally, Wade's is the only account we have of the incident, there are no independent witnesses. In effect the man would be getting a George Medal on his own say so. It doesn't seem quite right."

"Okay, I hear what you're saying, but the facts seem to speak for themselves, don't they? Brown is dead, Wade suffered serious injuries, and Smithson ended up under arrest and locked to the car. I don't see how else it could have happened, do you?"

Munro realised it would be unwise to go any further. "Sir, you asked what I thought, and I am merely stating the facts as I know them, not an opinion."

Newman decided he had all he needed. "Okay Mr Munro, I don't think we need to make too much of the radio issue and the lack of PPE, do you? Please let me know if any other information comes to light, particularly in regard to the matters we have been discussing. Thank you."

Dismissed, Munro was relieved to get out. Politics! Why didn't they just let him do his job? He realised that it had been made very clear that no disciplinary action would be taken against Wade and that any further discussion of his failings would not be countenanced. Nothing would be allowed to spoil the good news story.

That Friday Steve Brown's funeral took place at his local parish church, with eulogies from the chief constable, colleagues and friends. Representatives from all the United Kingdom police forces were in attendance and formed a guard of honour along the route taken by the funeral cortege. The murder of a police officer whilst on duty was a big deal, a huge deal for all their colleagues throughout the country. Needless to say, press and TV coverage was extensive.

By the middle of the following week, Richard Wade and Julie were comfortably settled in John Ross's luxurious Maltese Villa. One evening, looking out to sea from the terrace of a restaurant, enjoying pizza and wine with Julie whilst relaxing in the warm Mediterranean breeze, he could only think 'life was pretty good'.

CHAPTER 14

In the run up to Smithson's trial, Superintendent Munro went through the evidence with Amy Clark to ensure they had everything covered and that they had as watertight a case as possible. However, it being their responsibility to prosecute offenders, the Crown Prosecution Service would liaise directly with the Scenes of Crime Branch to ensure all the forensic evidence they required was available for the trial. Therefore, Munro and Clark paid little or no attention to it. There were a large number of statements, the majority of which provided supporting information, so he restricted his reading to those from the main witnesses. Having been there when Richard Wade gave his description of Steve Brown's murder, he had not felt the need to read the written statement until now.

It was a fairly straightforward transcript of the taped account Wade had given from his hospital bed and the content pretty much matched Munro's recollections, until he got to a paragraph near the end. It said:

Though I was not wearing a stab vest and was already wounded, I was determined to do everything I could to help Steve Brown, and to protect him from further attack. That is why I threw myself on our attacker as I described earlier in this statement. The disregard for my own safety was solely the result of my desire to save my friend and colleague. It is to my eternal regret that I failed.

Munro read it twice, before showing it to DI Clark.

"Amy, I presume this paragraph was added at Wade's request?"

"Yes, it was, Sir."

Munro found it hard to hide his distaste and gave voice to his thoughts. "It's a bit strong, don't you think? He's almost writing his own commendation, isn't he? He clearly doesn't suffer from excessive modesty."

Clark thought it best to keep her head down, whilst Munro, slightly embarrassed by his outburst, carried on with his reading. He made sure everything was as ready as it could be.

Karl Smithson's trial began at the Crown Court four months after the death of Steve Brown, presided over by His Honour Sir William Plunkett. The barristers for the prosecution and defence quickly outlined their cases to the jury before the prosecution began to call its first witnesses.

Presenting the case in a chronological order meant the facts of the burglary where the grey Ford Mondeo saloon car was stolen were the first to be put before the jury. Next were the details of Linda Ross's kidnapping which entailed playing the girl's video interview to the packed courtroom. The barristers had agreed between themselves that there was no need for Linda to give direct evidence via a video link. The prosecution did not feel her identification of Smithson was necessary and the defence had no desire to alienate the jury by cross-examining a ten-year-old girl. Her evidence was compelling and caused some of the jury to cast hostile glances in Smithson's direction. He was unmoved, either by the evidence or the looks.

The following day was to be Superintendent Richard Wade's big day in court and the press were in attendance both inside and outside the court. Resplendent in his uniform, now fully recovered from his injuries, he was led through his evidence by the prosecution barrister. The court was hushed as he described, in detail, the death of Steve Brown and the injuries inflicted on him by Smithson. It was a masterly performance, carefully rehearsed, displaying modesty but making it clear the part he had played. That is, the part he claimed to have played and that he had later recorded in his statement.

As part of the prosecution case the barrister introduced the knife into evidence, asking Wade if he could identify it, which he did as the weapon used by Smithson to cause his own injuries and the death of Steve Brown. The barrister informed the court that he would later introduce evidence from the pathologist identifying the knife as the murder weapon, and further evidence from an expert that it bore Karl Smithson's fingerprints.

Tears were shed by several of those in the court, including at least two of the jury.

Obviously having noted the paragraph Wade had added to his statement, the barrister even managed to say, "Tell me, Mr Wade, were you wearing a stab vest?"

"No Sir."

"And yet despite your serious wounds you were still determined to do everything you could to help Steve Brown, and to protect him from further attack."

Wade appeared to collect his thoughts before replying, "My own safety was unimportant. I was trying desperately to save my friend and colleague. It is to my eternal regret that I failed."

The barrister said, "Mr Wade, I can only salute your extreme heroism."

There were several calls of agreement in the courtroom, which Sir William made no effort to stop, as he himself nodded.

For once Wade decided he had said enough.

No one seemed to notice Smithson staring fixedly at Wade as he gave his evidence, frequently shaking his head. He wanted to contradict him but knew that the only way he could do so would be to tell the true version of events, knowing that would only damage his own position further. He decided to keep quiet and to stick to the plan of not giving evidence, relying on the prepared statement read out during his interview. He knew they would play that in evidence.

His barrister asked Wade a few perfunctory questions, suggesting that the stabbings may have been accidental and that in fact he and Brown had attacked Smithson. This earned a sharp rebuke from the judge who told him that he should be wary of attacking the character and integrity of two brave officers, one of whom was not able to defend himself. This time he did silence the gallery when there were several calls of 'hear, hear'.

In truth Smithson had given his barrister very little to work with, and he likened it to making bricks without straw.

Sir William Plunkett thanked Wade for the clarity of his evidence, acknowledging how difficult it must have been, and brought proceedings to an early close at the end of a very emotional day.

The next day PC Paul Thomas gave evidence of the scene he had encountered on his arrival in Grimston Lane. He finished by telling the court how he had heard noises from the car boot which he reported to Inspector Donovan. Having already been mentioned in the barrister's opening address it was no surprise to anyone when he described opening the boot to find Linda Ross bound and gagged inside.

Thomas was followed into the witness box by Inspector Brian Donovan. Under questioning he reiterated what Thomas had already said, going on to explain that he ordered the girl's release to be videotaped as he had no idea what to expect when the boot was opened.

Then, to a once more hushed courtroom, that video was played. Everyone thought they knew what to expect but, judging by a screamed 'no' from Mary Ross and the tears from all five female jury members, they hadn't. Nothing could have adequately prepared them for the sight of a dishevelled, pale-looking ten-year-old girl with tape over her mouth and her hands bound behind her back. More than anything those present would remember forever the look of absolute terror evident in her large dark eyes. Clearly heard was Donovan's anguished cry, "Get her out, for God's sake just get her out."

The video finished with Paul Thomas holding the girl close on the ground, doing his best to comfort her.

John and Mary Ross walked from the room in tears, unable to take any more, but determined to find Paul Thomas and thank him. Meanwhile several of the men on the jury looked at Smithson with undisguised loathing, and it appeared one or two were close to seeking vengeance for his actions.

Once again Smithson's barrister had little he could say, so didn't try. Sir William, accurately judging the mood of his court, decided it would be a good idea to adjourn for the day.

Most of the remaining testimony was a mass of forensic evidence, linking Smithson to the kidnapping with which he was charged. It was not thought necessary to introduce forensic evidence relating to the assaults on the two officers in view of the weight of the rest of the evidence against him. His barrister tried to discredit the evidence with semi-plausible reasons as to why it was incorrect, mingled with his client's assertions that police had planted the evidence.

Finally, Detective Superintendent Munro gave evidence of the interview with the accused man, including details of his prepared statement which, it must be said, was so ludicrous it brought smiles to some in the court. However, it was made very clear to the jury that the prepared statement included admissions by Smithson that the murder weapon was owned by him and that he used it to cause the officers' injuries, even if he claimed it was unintentional.

Then it was the defence's turn, the sum total of the evidence they presented being a re-hash of Smithson's prepared statement. He did not give evidence in his own defence, so could not be cross-examined by the prosecution.

On the fifth day of the trial, both barristers gave their closing statements, followed by Sir William Plunkett's summing up of the evidence and directions to the jury.

The jury returned their verdict after only two hours of deliberations, which included time for a cup of tea. A unanimous verdict of guilty to all charges was returned. By the end of the day, Smithson was on his way back to prison, having been given three life sentences with a recommendation that he serve a minimum of 40 years.

Following the prisoner's removal from the dock, Wade was called back into the court by Sir William who made the following remarks:

"In all my time on the bench I have never heard a tale of such heroism and devotion to a colleague. You suffered horrendous injuries at the hands of a despicable criminal and yet you continued to defend PC Brown, fighting off your attacker even though you were unarmed and did not have the protection of a stab vest. Despite everything you were able to detain him before you collapsed from those injuries. Thanks to your gallant actions a young girl was rescued from a terrible ordeal and returned to her loving parents. No person could have done more. I cannot praise your conduct and sense of duty highly enough; you are a credit to the police service. I wish to formally commend you for your outstanding bravery, dedication to duty, and selfless devotion to a fallen comrade. I will inform your chief constable accordingly so that this richly deserved commendation can be added to your record. Lastly, I would like to say that, in the difficult times we all face, it is a comfort to know that men of your calibre are protecting us from the forces of evil. Thank you on behalf of the law-abiding citizens of this country. I intend to draw your actions in this matter to the attention of the Home Secretary. Once again, thank you, Mr Wade."

The judge's comments received a round of applause from those assembled in the courtroom, as Wade muttered his stunned thanks and left the court to be surrounded by reporters and television cameras. It was all working out better than he could have imagined.

You just have to take your chances when they arise, don't you?

Wade was not the only one stunned by Sir William Plunkett's fulsome praise and extravagant commendation. Det. Supt. Munro, sitting at the back of the court, could scarcely believe what he had heard and was unable to totally accept that it was fully deserved. He was sure Wade had fought Smithson bravely, but was it for Steve Brown's life or his own? As well as that, it seemed Wade was being praised for facing his attacker whilst not wearing a stab vest. Well, whose fault was that? If a PC had gone out without his vest, he would have faced disciplinary proceedings, a fact he had already pointed out to the chief constable. Nevertheless, he had to admit Wade had sustained severe injuries and still managed to detain Smithson, leading directly to the release of Linda Ross. It was just the nagging thought that Wade wasn't quite what he seemed.

Munro decided to let it go, what was the point? The right result had been achieved, a vicious criminal was in prison for a long time, and that was all that counted.

Richard Wade was almost overwhelmed by the sheer number of journalists and their shouted questions, but typically he enjoyed being the centre of attention, particularly with a proud Julie at his side. Once he managed to quiet them by raising both hands palm outwards, he stood ready to read a statement prepared by him with help from the Force Press Office. However, although he had been told to expect a commendation, he had been caught a little on the hop by the extent of the judge's praise so needed to make small changes. He began,

"I am a serving police officer and it is my job is to keep the public safe, not to give press interviews for which I am ill-equipped. For that reason I do not propose to answer questions today and hope the statement I am about to make will provide all the information you need."

He took a deep breath and continued,

"On that horrible day four months ago when myself and Steve Brown stopped the grey Ford Mondeo car on a lonely country road, I had little idea of what was to come. We were attacked by a vicious and determined criminal who inflicted severe injuries on us with a razor-sharp knife. These senseless and heartless acts saw Steve lose his life and, despite my best efforts, I was unable to save him. Not a day goes by when I don't think of Steve and ask myself if we could have done things differently, if I could have done more. Perhaps, if I had, a fine man would still be alive.

Of course, on the plus side, Steve's sacrifice resulted in Linda Ross being saved from God knows what and for that we should be eternally grateful.

I would like to thank the enquiry team headed by Superintendent John Munro and the Crown Prosecution Service for bringing matters to a successful conclusion. I take great comfort from the fact that Smithson is now in a place where he cannot harm anyone else, as I hope do Steve's family.

I would also like to extend my gratitude to friends and colleagues for their support which, I confess, has been sorely needed at times. My girlfriend Julie has been my constant companion, without her love and patience I may not have been able to carry on.

The trial judge, Sir William Plunkett, surprised me greatly with his generous remarks, for which I am very grateful, even if I am far from certain they are fully deserved.

Thank you all."

Despite the continuing question he strode away to a waiting car and drove off.

CHAPTER 15

Superintendent Richard Wade returned to work at the Force Headquarters on the day following the trial. He was hoping his life might settle down a little as even he was finding all the attention a bit too much to cope with at times. He had two major concerns in his life, both of which were putting him under levels of stress that he was having difficulty dealing with.

The first being his relationship with Julie. Whilst she was undeniably pretty and very accommodating, it was sadly true that she was not educated to his level and had little interest in current affairs. In short, she was not all that bright, and they had little to talk about. She still adored him and was very good for his ego, but she did bore him at times and in his arrogance he believed he might do better. He decided to wait before making any decisions about the relationship.

His second, and more pressing, concern was his job where he was struggling to perform the role he had been given, clearly having been promoted too far and too soon. After his return to work, following the attack, he had belatedly made his presentation to the Force Senior Management Team on job cuts and cost savings. It had been an impressive performance which was well received, quickly followed by agreement to implement the programme in full. The new superintendent seemed to be the ideal man to see it through. However, Wade was finding that theory and practice were very different animals, and that every day was a constant battle with disparate groups each intent on preserving their own powerbase. Among these were the Police Federation, support staff unions, and branch managers each fighting to preserve their own empires. He had neither the diplomatic skill or experience to deal with the competing groups and was slowly sinking.

Even though the chief constable was responsible for Wade's rapid promotion, he was far from certain that the new superintendent had the necessary skills and experience to bring the project to fruition. It was essential that the cost-cutting exercise was a success for the future of the Force and, perhaps more importantly, Newman's own ambitions. It was apparent almost from the beginning that Wade was struggling. The chief's solution was to appoint a senior support staff manager as his deputy, which Wade instantly saw as a criticism. Instead of welcoming them and the expertise they brought to the project, he followed his usual policy of ignoring opinions he didn't want to hear and trying to freeze his deputy out of the decision-making process. There was only room for one star in his team.

A few days after the trial's conclusion, Wade received a message telling him that he and the chief constable were summoned to meet the Home Secretary in London on the next Friday. He avoided travelling with the chief by opting to spend the weekend in London, taking Julie with him. As well as allowing him to keep his distance from the chief, he saw it as a good opportunity to impress his lover by admitting her to the exalted circles in which he now moved. Even a man as self-centred as Wade knew that Julie's love and devotion could not be taken for granted forever. Able to acknowledge his own deep-rooted insecurities, he realised that he needed Julie's unconditional love and support the way a flower needs the sun.

At 11 a.m. that Friday they met the Right Honourable Francis Williams in his office where he shook hands with the chief constable and a very nervous Richard Wade, accompanied by his even more nervous girlfriend. He was very warm in his welcome, saying how glad he was to finally meet Wade and to congratulate him in person for his outstanding conduct, making reference to the judge's flowery commendation. Francis Williams was much taken with Julie, turning on all his old-world charm before insisting she accompany the three men to the press conference to be held in a nearby meeting room.

The Home Secretary began by introducing the two men to the larger than usual group of reporters. He then said, "All too often our police officers face dangers we can only imagine when carrying out their day-to-day duty protecting us, the public. One day last August, Constable Steve Brown tragically lost his life doing just that, whilst his colleague Richard Wade received horrific wounds. Mr Wade, despite those wounds, fought tooth and nail with the armed man in a vain attempt to save his colleague. Thanks to the heroic actions of Mr Wade, a dangerous criminal was arrested and a young girl rescued from a terrible ordeal. I cannot praise highly enough the courage and determination he displayed on that day. I am therefore pleased to make the following announcement,

'Her Majesty the Queen is graciously pleased to approve the award of the George Medal to Richard Wade for his outstanding bravery in the face of an armed and violent criminal."

The Home Secretary turned to shake hands with the shocked and delighted officer whilst the cameras flashed. Wade was surprised and overwhelmed, believing the bravery award mentioned by the chief had been quietly forgotten. The delighted photographers managed to get a shot of a smiling Richard Wade being kissed by the highly photogenic Julie, watched by a beaming Home Secretary and Charles Newman.

Whilst it could never be said that Francis Williams had exerted undue pressure on the committee responsible for recommending bravery awards, including the George Medal, he had certainly used his position and considerable influence to telling effect. He had instructed his senior civil servants to prepare a report for the committee strongly advocating the award of the medal to Wade, shining a very positive light on his actions. Whilst acknowledging that there was no independent evidence of Wade's actions, the report suggested that the facts spoke for themselves, and pointed out that Sir William Plunkett, who had heard all the evidence at first hand, had seen fit to praise Wade in the most glowing terms. A copy of the judge's commendation was attached in support. Great emphasis was placed on the officer's injuries, implying they could only have been received by someone displaying extreme bravery and determination. To top it off, the report had been endorsed by the Prime Minister's office, making it difficult to conceive of two more exalted champions of Wade's cause.

No one can ever know if the George Medal would have been awarded to Richard Wade without the political interference, but it certainly helped. Interestingly all the parties involved were most aware of how the Home Secretary's contacts with the committee may look if it became known, so the report and all notes of conversations were given a very high security rating. It really wouldn't do if the public believed the nation's highest bravery awards were given out to recipients for political purposes.

The simple fact was that the government of the day needed a hero to distract everyone from its own failings in managing crime and the police service, so posing for photographs with a George Medal recipient and a beautiful girl could only be good publicity for all concerned.

Twenty minutes later he found himself in the garden at 10 Downing Street, with an increasingly comfortable Julie, shaking hands with the Prime Minister before yet more cameras. Once more a speech was made congratulating Wade, but now managing to link it to the government's fight against violent crime and continued support of the police. They were then entertained to tea by the Prime Minister and his wife, where Julie once again shone when engaging in relaxed conversation with the couple.

Wade found his old confidence returning, he was a superintendent, he had a medal and a stunning girlfriend who, he was beginning to realise, was a considerable asset. To add to that he had the approval of a high court judge, the Home Secretary, and the Prime Minister, not to mention, if the editorials were to be believed, every national newspaper editor in the country. He knew that his new rank was temporary, and he had been concerned that it may not be confirmed but, brimful of his old self-assurance, he was now sure they would have to make his position permanent. How could they not, he was going to see the Queen.

He was even thinking about a change in his domestic circumstances, maybe marriage would be a good thing. The job liked married men, and where would he find anyone better than Julie? Typically, it never occurred to him to consider whether he actually loved her or if she would accept a proposal from him.

CHAPTER 16

As Smithson sat in his miserable cell in the maximum-security prison, he was consumed by an overwhelming feeling that life just wasn't fair. He was in prison for forty years whilst Wade was now a national hero, respected and celebrated by both the police service and the wider country, reaping rich, if undeserved, rewards. From what he'd seen in the papers, Wade even had the companionship of a beautiful girlfriend, something he would have to do without for a long, long time, maybe even forever. On the face of it, Smithson had nothing, but he had in fact gained something he had yearned for over many years, namely the respect of his peers in the criminal world. The prison housed every manner of dangerous criminal including murderers, rapists, armed robbers, and gangland figures. Yet he had done something very few of them had managed and something that most would dearly liked to have done. He had killed a copper, the hated enemy. Although he was not in their league as a criminal, he had earned their grudging respect and was considered a bad man, somebody to be left alone.

If he had been the sort of man to think very deeply about such matters, Smithson would have realised that he and Wade had much more in common than was immediately obvious. Even if he had been aware of it, nothing could have made him admit to any such thing. Whilst they could never be described as similar either physically or intellectually, they did harbour many of the same thoughts and ideas. They saw real or imagined slights everywhere and, believing themselves to be superior, often treated others with contempt. Both men resented and envied their colleagues and associates who prospered through what they firmly believed to have been good luck, or just being in the right place at the right time rather than any great skill. Wade and Smithson both firmly believed that with a little more good fortune they would have achieved much more in their chosen fields of endeavour. Each was a selfish loner who found it hard to establish relationships with others, especially women, and believed only misfortune had held them back. They saw each setback as fate conspiring against them, not for one second accepting that their own failings may be responsible. Wade could not see that, even though a poor policeman, he had achieved a meteoric rise to the rank of inspector of which he could be justifiably proud. Now he was a superintendent, the sky was truly the limit.

Now, following events in that lonely lay-by on a sunny August afternoon, they had both achieved the fame and respect they felt fully entitled to, but not in a manner either could be proud of. Of course Smithson was incapable of such thoughts and would never have accepted that he was in any way similar to a man he so despised.

The true difference between them was that they operated on opposite sides of the law. Even that gap had narrowed because of Wade's willingness to lie, cheat, and finally to commit perjury in order to achieve his ends. Along the way, of course, contributing to a colleague's death before besmirching his good name.

Smithson was almost incandescent with rage as he looked at the papers. All he could see were pictures of Wade's smiling face as he posed with the great and good in the land, accompanied all the time by that gorgeous woman. He found it hard to suppress his anger and frustration, not able to believe they were actually going to give him a medal after all his lies, especially when he remembered him on his knees begging for mercy. It was so unfair Wade had everything and he had nothing. That was the true difference between them now.

He was aware that his defence had been almost non-existent so was fairly relaxed about the outcome of the trial and his sentence, it was only what he'd expected, perhaps even deserved. He was just amazed at the extent of the totally undeserved praise Richard Wade was receiving. Initially he hadn't understood why Wade would lie the way he had, other than to cover up his cowardice, but in the days since his trial finished, he had seen all the newspaper headlines about the hero policeman and all the rewards that were being showered on him. Now he understood and it made him so angry that he felt he had to do something about it, but what?

He wanted revenge and the more Smithson thought about it the angrier he became, but other considerations slowly began to run through his head. If he could establish that Wade was a lying bastard, then that would prove he had committed perjury, surely grounds for a re-trial, and who knows, with their main witness discredited he might have a chance. He liked the sound of that.

His problem was how to go about gaining his revenge on Richard Wade, who he was beginning to believe was the cause of all his problems. Slowly he was coming round to the idea that he was only in prison because of the intervention by the two police officers and not because of his crimes. He reasoned that if Wade and Brown had not interfered, he would have collected the ransom money and released the girl unharmed, the coppers would not have been hurt, and they could all have carried on with their lives. Most importantly he wouldn't be in prison. He was certainly no criminal mastermind, very conveniently overlooking the fact that he had left a trail of evidence that would surely have resulted in his capture even without Wade and Brown's actions. As he continued to dwell on what had happened, Smithson's sense of victimhood increased with a corresponding increase in his desire to strike back at the person he blamed, above all others, for his situation. The more he was able convince himself that his present situation was not of his making and to transfer his guilt to another, the more his own feelings of self-worth were enhanced.

Overwhelmed by a huge sense of injustice he considered his options. Smithson's first thought was to contact his solicitor, but when he thought about that useless bastard he realised that would be a waste of time. His next thought was the press. There were always newspapers ready to have a go at the police, but he was astute enough to realise that in the current climate he wasn't liable to get much sympathy from them. There was no way they would attack a national hero on the word of a man serving forty years for his crimes.

He'd been in prison for several months, thinking constantly about what to do before the solution came to him. He spent the next two days in his cell slowly writing a letter that he hoped would set him on the road to freedom. He conveniently continued to ignore the fact that even if Wade's testimony was excluded from any potential re-trial, there was still plenty of other evidence to make his conviction almost certain.

Somewhat belatedly, after sending his letter, Smithson realised that things were not going to be quite as straight forward as he thought. His only option, if he truly wanted to discredit Richard Wade, was to reveal the full truth about what had happened and exactly what part he had played. That was the only way he could let everyone know the extent of Wade's duplicity, but by doing so he would admit his own guilt.

There must be a way, there always was. The more he thought about it the more he acknowledged that his motives were based entirely on a desire to get back at Richard Wade and if he got out of prison that would be a bonus. After looking at it from every angle he conceded that his chances were not all that good, after all he had admitted to the stabbings already, his only mitigation being to claim that it was in self-defence.

Smithson decided he needed some advice so considered an approach to one of the cell-block lawyers for advice, intending to outline his thoughts, but only in the most general of terms. You couldn't trust anyone in here though, they'd all grass you up if they thought it was beneficial to them. Cell-block lawyers were usually prisoners who had spent time in prison studying the law and subsequently dispensed advice in return for favours. He decided it would be most unwise to approach one of them in the circumstances, finally settling on a disgraced solicitor by the name of Henry Marchant who had been convicted of murdering his adulterous wife.

Both Smithson and Marchant agreed that his chances of getting out ranged somewhere between a dog's chance and no chance, but the former solicitor did give him some practical advice about how he could try to minimise the likelihood of anything he revealed being used against him in future court proceedings.

Whatever, he was so desperate to get Wade that he would do what was necessary and face the possibility that he would never get out. It was only a risk if you had something to lose, and what did he have to lose? He was already doing forty years!

It hadn't registered with Smithson until his new best friend, the solicitor, pointed out that if it was proved Wade had committed perjury, a prison sentence was almost inevitable. Perhaps they could share a cell, he mused.

CHAPTER 17

John Munro had returned to his normal duties with some relief following the high-profile court case against Karl Smithson. His role as a detective superintendent was to manage a number of detectives and police staff, split into teams, who investigated major crimes. Currently they were dealing with two murders and one particularly nasty rape. It seemed odd to feel more relaxed dealing with these offences which, in their own way, were just as horrendous as the crimes committed by Smithson. Perhaps it was because he was in more familiar territory, after all, police murders and kidnappings were just a little unusual, bringing with them huge levels of publicity and pressure.

On this morning he had already met with the officers heading each team, satisfying himself that enquiries were proceeding satisfactorily. The good news was that everything was going as it should with one man already in custody and suspects identified for the other offences. He would be able to update the detective chief superintendent and ACC(Crime) accordingly, thus keeping them off his back and, more importantly, ensure they left his teams alone to do their jobs without interference.

He was feeling quite relaxed, enjoying the day's second cup of coffee, knowing that his day, apart from a couple of staff appraisals, was fairly steady. He took a moment to consider his wife's comments prior to him leaving the house that morning, trying to decide what he felt about them. She had started talking about how nice it was that the mortgage was paid off after all these years and that the kids were all settled in their own homes. Then she mentioned her friend who had just been on a cruise and how nice it must be to have time to do want you wanted when you wanted. He knew she was talking about retirement.

If he was honest, Munro had been thinking about it more and more lately. He was realistic enough to know he had gone as far as he could in his career, especially at his age. For goodness sake his boss was fifteen years younger than him! He was tired and getting fed-up with all the politics and in-fighting which seemed so different to his early days in the job when good bobbying and catching criminals was all that mattered. Perhaps he would speak to Brenda tonight, although he already knew what she would say.

Anyway, that could wait for later, when he got home. He concentrated on his morning mail and was surprised to see an unopened letter which had obviously originated in prison. His surprise was not that inmates wrote to the police, but that one had found its way to his desk and even more that it was addressed to him personally.

Opening the letter, he was shocked to see that it was from Karl Smithson. His initial reaction was to tear it up without reading it, but Munro was intrigued to see what he had to say. He was somewhat disappointed when he did read it to find that Smithson was requesting a visit from Munro where he would be given information of great interest. The usual thing when convicted criminals wrote to the police was that they wanted to confess to other offences they had committed, but this didn't sound quite like that.

Det. Supt. Munro was not that keen to visit Smithson, or any other criminal for that matter, in prison. He hadn't made such a visit for some years as it was usually the job of more junior officers, but despite his misgivings he was intrigued and wondering whether he should go. After all, a man who had kidnapped a young girl and murdered a police officer may possibly have something interesting to say. He was still undecided when, after further consideration, he sent for DI Amy Clark.

When she arrived, he showed her Smithson's letter and asked her opinion. Her response was enthusiastic. "If you're going, Sir, I'd like to go as well please. As you know I'm just completing my criminology degree and my dissertation is on police murderers and their motives. I've already included some of my observations following the enquiry, but I'd love to get the chance to talk to him, to try to find out what his reasons were and especially how he feels now about what he did. Anything I can do to get a better understanding would be a great help and, of course, this is so current. Most of my research so far has been into people like Harry Roberts and Dale Cregan, nobody else will have anything from Smithson."

"Okay Amy, but apart from your degree is there any benefit to us in seeing Smithson?"

"Seriously, I think maybe there is. It's unusual to go from petty crime to kidnap and murder so it's just possible he's got other serious offences he wants to admit."

Munro thought for a moment and said, "Right we'll go, but first check with his solicitor and find out if he knows about it. Please check my diary with Mrs Webb, organise a convenient date for us to see him in prison, and don't forget we'll need the equipment to record what he has to say."

"Yes boss." Clark left the office with a big smile on her face.

CHAPTER 18

On the way to Karl Smithson's new home at the maximum-security prison, Munro wondered aloud why Smithson had sacked his solicitor.

Amy Clark laughed and said, "Well Mike Adamson told me he got the bullet because, and I quote, 'he was a useless bastard' according to his client. I get the feeling Mr Adamson was not too upset about it."

"Has he been replaced?"

Clark replied, "No, it looks as if he is going to speak to us on his own."

A few minutes later they entered the prison for their pre-arranged visit and, after numerous security checks, were shown to an interview room, where Smithson was waiting, accompanied by two prison warders. Once the two officers entered the warders left, but reminded everyone, especially Smithson, that they would be just outside.

On the advice of his 'legal advisor', Smithson had made an effort with his appearance, having been told the police were liable to take him more seriously if he didn't look so much like a thug. Accordingly, he'd had his hair cut and a fresh shave that morning so, along with clean prison uniform and shoes, he looked about as presentable as he could. He had also been advised to be businesslike and professional in his dealings, making sure above all else they he remained calm.

Smithson surprised the two officers by welcoming them and thanking them for coming.

John Munro responded, "Thank you, Karl. I'm sure you remember DI Clark."

"Yes of course, but I'm afraid I really don't want her to stay. Don't get me wrong, it's nothing personal, but what I'm going to tell you is totally confidential and could prove to be dynamite. I don't want what I say recorded or written down either."

Smithson had managed to take Munro completely by surprise and for a moment he was lost for an answer, not a usual occurrence. He eventually managed to say, "That may not be possible. If I remain in this room alone with you, I will be open to, shall we say, allegations from you. Also, it will make it almost impossible to use anything you say in evidence at any future trial."

"My point exactly. I don't want anything I say to be used at a trial, either against me or anyone else. I certainly don't intend to give evidence in court."

Munro was confused. "So what is the purpose of this meeting?"

"I'm going to give you some information that I think you'll want to hear, and once you do it'll be up to you to decide what you do with it."

"That's all well and good, but if I can't take written or recorded evidence from you how exactly do I use what you tell me?"

Smithson was finding it difficult to stay cool and came back sharply, "You're the detective. If I point you in the right direction, you should be able to find other ways to prove what I tell you. Look at it from my point of view, I'm not going to put myself in danger of even more prison time, am I? I don't need to tell you anything at all, do I?" He certainly wasn't going to reveal his true motives.

Munro, despite his doubts, was intrigued. "Give me a clue. What is this about?"

"Look. I can't tell you until we're alone, but you'll definitely be glad you listened. You're here now, surely you can spare an hour to hear what I have to say. It'll be your choice what you do once I've told you."

"What if I decide not to do anything after I've spoken to you?"

"Well, I'm sure the press will be interested if you're not."

Munro responded angrily, "Let's be clear, I won't be blackmailed. If I agree to your terms, I will take what action I see fit, not because of any threats from you. Understand?"

Smithson, slightly taken back, said, "Alright, alright. I'm trying to protect myself, but I think what I know needs to come out somehow."

Munro thought quickly. "I have some conditions of my own. I will need to make notes of the conversation, otherwise there is no guarantee that I will remember accurately what you tell me. I understand you are not prepared to sign them. This room has video surveillance which will be left on to protect both of us from any allegations, but the sound recording will be switched off. Do you agree?"

Now it was Smithson's turn to think quickly. "What guarantee do I have that the sound recording will be turned off?"

"That's easy. We get an assistant governor in here and in his presence you can stipulate, on video with the sound recording, that the sound is to be turned off from that point and state clearly that you are only talking on the strict understanding that the subsequent conversation is not recorded. That way if we tried to use a recording in evidence it would be inadmissible. How does that sound? Bear in mind that these current negotiations are being recorded."

Smithson really wished he could have his cell block advisor with him, but it all sounded alright. He nodded to Munro. "Okay, I'll go with that. As long as I sit with my back to the camera that is, I'm not having you getting lip readers on to it."

Munro had to laugh at Smithson's paranoia. He still had his misgivings, but as the prisoner had pointed out, he was already here. What did he have to lose?

"A couple of final things." He held his hand up as he saw Smithson was about to object. "I only want you to confirm when the assistant governor is present that you are happy to proceed without a solicitor. Lastly, DI Clark would like to interview you separately for a research project, not as part of any enquiries. Okay?"

He certainly didn't think he needed a solicitor and couldn't see a problem talking to the woman, he could soon stop if he didn't like anything. Besides, she was quite attractive and it was going to be a lot of years without pretty women.

Once again, he nodded and said, "Alright."

The two police officers left the room to make the necessary arrangements, leaving Smithson with a packet of cigarettes, having received permission from the warders, who remained with him. Once outside they contacted the governor's office to seek authority for Munro's proposal and, once given, arranged for an assistant governor to attend.

Whilst waiting, DI Clark couldn't help saying, "It's a bit of a bugger that he wants to leave me out, boss."

"Yes, sorry about that, Amy, but I hope I've at least got you a private interview with him. You should still get some good stuff for your thesis."

"I wonder what the hell is so shocking that he'll only talk to you. Maybe he knows the identity of Jack the Ripper," she joked.

Munro looked concerned and in a moment of perceptiveness said, "Amy, my big worry is that I'm not going to like what he tells me and, if that's the case, my next problem will be what to do about it, especially if he's prepared to go to the press."

"Yes, but there's no way the press can get in here to speak to him, is there?"

"You know they can get messages out easily enough, a visitor or a warder can smuggle them out. They can even get access to mobile phones, so if he wants to, he can tell the press. I just wonder what is so important."

He would find out soon enough and maybe he would wish he hadn't.

Three-quarters of an hour later, having completed everything to Smithson's satisfaction, Munro was alone in the room with a man he despised, prepared to talk to him as if he was a normal human being. The things you had to do in the police force.

Munro began, "If everything is to your satisfaction, would you like to make a start?"

Smithson took a deep breath. "Yeah, but I don't think you'll like what I have to say. Your Superintendent Richard Wade is a lying bastard." He smiled triumphantly, pleased to have got it off his chest.

Munro frowned and said, "If that's all you've got to say then I'm clearly wasting my time here."

"No, you don't understand," he said with an edge of desperation, fearing Munro was about to leave. "Wade lied about everything. He never did anything, except beg for his life, it was the other copper, the one who died, he did everything."

Munro couldn't help but think that he really didn't need to hear this, but he'd started now. "Look, PC Brown is dead and Superintendent Wade is the only witness to what happened in Grimston Lane that day. I understand you want to discredit him, but I'm telling you now that if you're thinking about a re-trial, your chances of getting off are pretty slim with all the other evidence stacked against you."

Smithson was surprised that Munro had so easily seen through his plans, but he hadn't had much faith in getting out anyway. He did, however, remain determined to do as much harm to Richard Wade as he could.

"Yes, I know that, but everything Wade said in court was a lie. He claimed all the credit when really he's a snivelling coward."

The detective superintendent had to admit that he found Smithson's desperation to tell him about Wade oddly convincing, especially since he already harboured suspicions about the man's claims. His face gave nothing away as he thought for a moment before saying, "Okay. Tell me what you've got to say, right from the beginning, and I'll listen, but no promises."

Smithson marshalled his thoughts and began. "He lied about everything, right from the beginning. When Wade was giving his evidence in court, he said he saw me in the car and was suspicious, but he never even looked at me. It was the driver, he was the one, I could tell he was suspicious."

Munro interrupted, "Are you sure you're not getting mixed up? He could have seen you as well."

"No chance. I was watching them all the time; don't forget I was in a nicked car, wasn't I? Wade was looking at something on his knee the whole time we waited at the lights. He never looked up at all."

Munro found it hard not to challenge Smithson. "That wasn't the only reason for you to be concerned, was it?"

"Sorry?"

"Have you forgotten about the 10-year-old girl in the boot?"

He grinned. "I didn't know about her, did I?"

Munro smiled ruefully and nodded for the prisoner to continue.

"Look, Mr Munro, it's really hard to remember everything I need to tell you. Can I just say what I have to, so I don't get mixed up?"

"Alright, but don't go too fast so I can make notes."

"I've had a lot of time to think about this and I think the best way to describe what Wade did is to say he claimed the credit for everything the dead copper did, it was like he swapped places with him. It was PC Brown who took me on, it was him that saved Wade and it was him that stopped me. Do you get what I'm saying?"

"I do, but I need more detail than that."

Smithson continued, "I can't remember everything Wade said in court so I'll just tell you what really happened, and you can sort out where he lied."

Munro remained silent.

Karl Smithson cleared his throat and, without a hint of apology or regret, began his account of the day Steve Brown died. "I can only say again that it was the police car driver who was looking at me and him who got out and came towards me. I know now that was Steve Brown. Wade didn't get out of the car straight away and when he did, he was shouting about being in a hurry, that's when I got my knife out and stabbed Brown in the stomach. I knew he was the one who I had to watch. He didn't see it coming because Wade was in the way. When he fell down, I went after Wade, but it was really funny having an inspector on his knees begging me to let him go. He never put up any fight at all and I got him twice. God knows how he managed to do it, but he dodged away from the knife, and I never got him properly. The next thing I know Brown charged me and knocked me down. I don't know how he did it, 'cos I'd stabbed him in stomach and the knife went right in. To be honest I thought he was already dead. He ended up laid on top of me and I stabbed him again near his neck. He was shouting for Wade to help but he never moved. There was blood everywhere and Brown should already have been dead, but somehow he nutted me in the face and broke my nose, the bastard. He must have been a strong bloke because then he got hold of my hair and started banging my head on the floor. I think I lost consciousness because when I came to, I was handcuffed to the car. I'm telling you Wade didn't do anything, he left Brown on his own to die. If it wasn't for Brown, I'd have got away. I'll tell you one thing though, I'd have made sure I finished Wade before I left. Brown definitely saved Wade's life. That's about it I think."

Munro just stared at Smithson, shocked at his callous, matter-of-fact description of the death of another human being, coming as close as he ever had to hitting a man in custody. He was also struggling to think what else he needed to ask and played for time by pretending to study his notes.

He finally managed to say, "Do you know who handcuffed you?"

"No, I've told you I was unconscious."

"Did PC Brown say anything?"

"Only when he was asking Wade to help him."

Munro felt he had to be sure absolutely sure about a couple of things. "Alright, I've got a few points I need to clarify. Mr Wade says that you attacked Steve Brown first but that he managed to push him out of the way, so then you turned on Mr Wade and slashed him across the chest. Isn't that what really happened?"

He shook his head, "No it's not, I've just told you."

"He also says you then went for Steve Brown and stabbed him, without him putting up any sort of fight. What about that?"

Smithson was starting to get angry, "I'm fed up of telling you, Wade's a liar. If it wasn't for Brown and him fighting me off, they'd both be dead, and I'd have gotten away."

Munro said, "Look let's get things straight. You came to me and are busy telling me that a respected senior police officer is a lying coward. I think I'm entitled to ask a few questions, and if I don't make sure I've got a clear picture in my head, how do you expect me to investigate what you're saying?"

He stared angrily and, after taking a deep breath said, "Ask your questions."

"Mr Wade said he grabbed at you to get you way from Steve Brown, and that's when you stabbed him in the shoulder, making him fall to the ground."

Smithson shook his head. "No, he's just turning everything around, twisting the truth."

"Next he says you went back to Steve Brown, stabbing him again whilst he was knelt down and defenceless."

Smithson didn't bother to reply and just shook his head.

Munro went on. "Isn't it true that whilst you were attacking Steve Brown again, Mr Wade got to his feet and jumped on you, knocking you to the ground and causing you to drop your knife? In fact, wasn't it him laid on top of you, banging your head on the floor?"

"No, that's a pack of lies." He was starting to get frustrated when he suddenly remembered something. "Did he tell you how my nose got broken then?"

Munro shook his head. "Not really."

"Well, I've told you how it happened. Why don't you ask him again then?"

Munro had a final read through his copy of Wade's statement and said, "Okay that's about it for now, I think. Of course, this could all be lies and you've just turned it all round to get at Wade. It's only your word against his."

Smithson laughed, "I was told you would say that. I've told you what happened and I think you believe me. Besides, what do I have to gain? No matter what happens I'm not going to get out of here, am I? I just want to see Wade get what he deserves. I said before, it's up to you to prove what I said is true, that's if you want to."

"One final thing. If you believe Wade lied and committed perjury at your trial, why haven't you simply made a complaint against police? The Professional Standards Branch would have looked at it, they are the specialists in investigating wrongdoing by police officers after all."

"You've got to be joking. You can't trust that lot, besides, most of them couldn't investigate their way out of a paper bag."

"What makes you think you can trust me?"

Smithson gave a humourless smile. "For some reason I don't think you like Wade any more than I do, and anyway, you know I've got other options, haven't I?"

"I need to think about this, and it could take some time. I'm sure even you must realise it's not going to be easy. You've certainly managed to put me in a difficult position, I'll say that for you."

"Well time is one thing I've got plenty of, isn't it? But don't take too long, unless you want me to go to the papers."

Inward Munro was angry at the implied threat but managed to maintain an even tone. "Look, this is complicated and a lot of feathers are going to get ruffled if I start re-investigating the case, and, as I've told you, it will take time. I will let you know what happens, but in the meantime, you must keep this to yourself. Do you understand?"

"Okay, okay I was just saying. I'll wait."

With that Munro summoned the warders who took Smithson back to his cell. DI Clark entered the room, bursting to ask questions, but, seeing her boss's grim expression, decided it would be best if she waited.

As they drove away from the prison Munro said, "I'm sorry, Amy, but I don't want to discuss what he said, not yet anyway. He was right, it's dynamite, at least it is if it's true. I need to give it plenty of thought but, I promise, I will tell you as soon as I can."

She had no option but to accept it, she tried to imagine what Smithson could possibly have said to disturb the superintendent this much, a man she always considered to be so unflappable.

CHAPTER 19

Having endured a sleepless night, Detective Superintendent John Munro was no nearer to making a decision about what action he should take, if any. He was fully aware that reopening the enquiry would not be a popular move and that he was unlikely to receive support from either senior officers or the rank and file. As far as they were all concerned, Steve Brown had died an unfortunate death, Wade was a hero, and an evil man was in prison for a long, long time. It was as if there was an unspoken thought that Brown had not acted as well as he could have done, and the less said about that the better.

Did he really want to open this particular Pandora's box, with all the attendant consequences?

Munro considered that he was a very ethical man, acting professionally, impartially, and going where the evidence took him when investigating crimes, whether it was a murder or a petty theft. If he was being totally honest then he had to admit he had always had concerns about Wade, not so much about his account of the incident, more about him as an individual and his conduct in the aftermath of events. He couldn't help but admit that he didn't like the man, which made him all the more determined to be scrupulously fair in his dealings.

Smithson had put him in an extremely difficult position presenting him with a very real moral dilemma, one which he was no nearer to solving. The trouble was that he could see good reasons for taking action and equally good reasons for doing nothing. He was also aware that, should he establish the truth of Smithson's account of events, he would not be the only one to face dilemmas. Senior officers in the Force and politicians who had praised Wade so highly would have their judgement thrown into doubt and could be faced with difficult decisions. As he studied his notes it became clear he needed to discuss the whole issue with someone else, not so much to get advice but more to have a sounding board whilst he verbalised his thoughts. The next problem was who?

Logically if he did decide to investigate Smithson's story, he would require help and that help would need to come from his own team of officers. The fewer people who knew what was happening the better, so once he decided who it was to be they would have to be, by necessity, his sounding board as well.

The next issue he faced was identifying the officers whose help he would enlist, knowing they would need investigative skills and discretion in equal measure. He knew he could pick any of the officers on his team for their skills as detectives, otherwise they wouldn't be there in the first place. The levels of discretion and trust he would need to place in them was another matter, although he did already have a good idea who he wanted to use. He was wise enough to know that any investigation, whichever way it may go, could severely affect an officer's career. For that reason, he would not, could not, order them to assist him.

Munro asked his secretary to arrange for both Detective Inspector Amy Clark and Detective Sergeant Bill Devereux to be in his office at 2 p.m. that afternoon.

Amy Clark was a young and gifted officer with a very bright future who had ably assisted him on several major enquiries already. She had the added advantage of already having been heavily involved in the initial investigation and the subsequent prison visit to see Smithson. The downside was that she had much to lose, and possibly little to gain.

Bill Devereux was a veteran detective sergeant nearing retirement.

He was a methodical and determined man, who had proved many times that he was physically brave, and not in the least bit afraid to upset the police hierarchy if necessary. He was a deep thinker who was, at times, capable of surprising levels of original thought. Devereux had worked for Munro for many years, displaying total loyalty and discretion. In direct contrast to Clark, he had little to gain or lose by being involved in any enquiries.

Both officers arrived on time and were surprised to see coffee and biscuits had been set out on the circular meeting table in Munro's office. They were mystified as to the reason for the summons to the office but, seeing the refreshments, were reassured that they were not in trouble. Munro spent a few minutes putting them at ease, checking on their current workloads and the state of ongoing enquiries. He had thought long and hard before deciding that if they were to investigate this matter the officers would need to work on it full-time, not whilst trying to perform other duties. It seemed that both Clark and Devereux could be detached from their normal duties, if needed, without too many problems.

Munro began, "Amy, I'm sorry, you may be bored for a minute or two as you already know some of this, but I need to recap for Bill's benefit."

Clark immediately knew what her boss was going to talk about and just nodded, whereas Devereux looked even more confused. Munro quickly explained to Devereux that he had been to see Karl Smithson in prison, at his request, and the conditions that had been put on the interview, mainly that no one else should be present and that there be no written or other record of the meeting.

"I don't need to tell you two that it will be almost impossible to use what he told me in any criminal proceedings. Obviously he thought long and hard about what he said and the circumstances. I get the feeling he had some advice from somewhere."

Devereux chipped in, "There's always somebody in prison willing to dispense advice to anybody that will listen. We might be able to find out who he spoke to."

Munro nodded and said, "Hold that thought, Bill. I'm going to tell you what he told me, because I need your help to decide what we should do next, if anything. Once you know what he said you will have to make decisions that may affect your careers and relationships. I must stress that what I tell you is strictly confidential and must, under no circumstances, leave this room. I'm not going to order you to work on this with me and if you want to leave at any time that's alright."

The two junior officers looked at each other, but neither moved.

"Okay then. Not surprisingly he denied anything to do with Linda Ross's kidnap but did admit murdering Steve Brown and attempting to murder Richard Wade. None of which is a big surprise, is it? However, he went on to tell me that Superintendent Wade, far from being a hero is actually a coward and told a pack of lies about the whole incident."

Clark and Devereux both tried to ask questions at once, but he silenced them with a raised hand, continuing to speak. "He claims that it was actually Steve Brown who was the real hero, saving Wade's life and possibly Linda Ross's as well. We'll never know about that, will we? He's given me a detailed account of what he says happened and I've got notes, but there is no way he'll give evidence. He told me it was up to me to prove it."

Munro spent the next hour going through his notes and explaining to his colleagues in detail what Smithson had said during the prison interview. Both sat in stunned silence.

"Amy, Bill, now you know what he said to me, I'd like to hear your ideas about the best way forward. Who wants to go first?"

Devereux looked angry as he spoke first, "Boss if this is true, and I stress 'if', we can't let Wade get away with these lies. Steve Brown is dead; somebody needs to stand up for him. We owe it to Steve to find out for sure, if we can that is. I'm in."

Amy Clark was a little more cautious. "I agree with Bill. Wade shouldn't be allowed to get away with this if Smithson is telling us the truth. I've got to say I wouldn't trust Smithson as far as I could throw him, but if I'm honest I always thought there was something not quite right about Wade. My only concern really is whether anybody is going to want to hear the truth. Still, it'll be interesting to find out, won't it?"

Munro looked at the two officers, knowing he had picked wisely. "Thank you both. Amy, myself and Bill don't have too much to lose, but if this goes wrong it could finish your career. Please be sure."

Clark replied, "Well, the way I look at it is that it could make my career as well, but that's not why I want to do it. If we ignore this, we betray Steve Brown and everything he stood for and everything we should stand for. I'll know for the rest of my life that I looked the other way. We need to find the truth, one way or the other. I'm in."

Munro said, "Thank you both. I've had more time to think about this than you and more time to consider the implications of launching an enquiry and what we may uncover. Firstly, should we bother at all? Smithson is in prison where he belongs, Steve Brown is still dead, and nothing will bring him back. If we prove Wade lied, and don't forget that would mean he committed perjury at the trial, which may give Smithson a re-trial. It's unlikely he would get off, but you never know, do you? The publicity for our chief and the Force will be horrendous, and don't forget all the politicians who have been sucking up to Wade. They won't like looking foolish, will they? Lastly, and probably least, we ran the enquiry and so we are going to look incompetent at the best and dishonest at the worst. Either way it probably won't do too much for our reputations, will it? Our choice is simple, do nothing and we are no worse off, or get into this and the shit could hit the fan big style. Do you still want to go for it?"

Clark said, "What if we do nothing and Smithson does go to the press, what then?"

Munro said, "Yes, I've thought about that, and I don't think anyone will believe him. If they do, what can they prove?"

Devereux looked at Munro and said, "No matter what the outcome, we all know what we have to do. If we don't investigate this properly, we are no better than Wade, are we? Besides which I've been in the shit many times in my career, and it's only the depth that has varied."

The detective superintendent looked thoughtful before saying, "Okay, let's decide how we are going to go about things. Firstly, I'll let your respective supervisors know that you're both working with me on a review of the Smithson case, initially for a week. Of course, that's true, but not quite in the way people may imagine. However, by using that as our cover story it will not look odd when we start asking questions and re-examining evidence. Should anyone want to know more explain to them that it was the biggest case in this force for some time and we need to learn what we can from it. You can let them know that we hope to end up with a report and training package to help improve the way we conduct future major enquiries. If it goes the way we suspect it might, then it will be true anyway. Happy with that?"

Both replied in the affirmative.

Munro continued, "I must confess that the one fear I have is that because Smithson was arrested immediately, and everything was so cut and dry, we may have missed something obvious. So we start at the beginning and question everything, don't assume any of the information is right, treat everything with caution."

Devereux chipped in, "I'll get all the files, but where are we going to work from?"

"We'll use my office, that way we can keep everything secure. I'll get another phone and computer installed by the end of the day. Is that enough?"

Amy Clark said, "What about me, boss, where do I start?"

"This case is a little unusual to say the least. The only witness we have is Wade who is now a suspect if you like, or at least his evidence is suspect so we can't rely on anything from him. For that reason, we don't go anywhere near him yet. What we do have is lots of forensic evidence so that's where I want you to start. We need to go through it with a fine-tooth comb because I truly feel that's where the answer is, but don't ask me where exactly. Bill, as well as going through the files I want you to look closely at Steve Brown, find out what sort of officer he was and we'll need to look at his private life as well. I'm sure I don't need to say that you'll have to be very discreet so nobody finds out what we're really up to, not yet anyway. Any other thoughts?"

Clark said, "At some stage we may need to get the control room tapes of the radio messages, that will make it look like a proper review of the whole incident and, you never know, we may find something useful. I'll set that in motion, but no rush."

"Fine, anything from you, Bill?"

"Yes, it may be worthwhile reviewing Linda Ross's evidence and that from the van driver who called it in."

Munro said, "Good idea, but remember we're not looking at the kidnap enquiry. Wade wasn't involved in that."

Clark and Devereux said nothing so he continued, "Last couple of things, if anybody questions what you're doing, refer them to me, and we don't have a budget so if there are any expenses incurred bring them to me and we'll work something out. That's it then. We start at 8 a.m. tomorrow and we'll have meetings every morning and at 4 p.m. every day. Oh yes, most important, I'll get us a kettle and lay on tea and coffee in here. Unless you've got anything else, go home and we'll start afresh tomorrow."

After the two officers left, he considered the arrangements he had put in place. He realised that his cover story would not stand too much scrutiny, as the reality was that there was no real need to keep such a review secret. It may hold for a while, especially if they kept a low profile. It may also look a little odd to others that he was actually reviewing a case where he had been the senior investigating officer, when such reviews were usually carried out by someone not previously involved. It could look as if they were in effect marking their own homework. So be it. It was the best cover story they could come up with to justify their actions and he knew full well that it wouldn't survive close examination or last very long.

He decided that he could do with an early finish as well, but before he left, he arranged for the two officers to be released from their current duties and tasked his secretary with getting the phone and computer arranged, along with the tea and coffee.

CHAPTER 20

The three officers reconvened at 8 a.m. the next day in Munro's office.

There was nothing new, other than Amy Clark suggesting she would get the custody suite video tapes from when Smithson was first taken in. Again, it was for no other reason than that it might be worth a look and would continue to reinforce their story of a 'case review'.

When the two officers had gone off to begin their enquiries, Munro again considered what he was doing and whether it was worthwhile. Once more he wrestled with the moral implications of his actions, convincing himself he was doing the right thing and truly had no option. If a police officer did not seek the truth, then what was he for? However, two men's reputations were at stake, three if he included his own, and he must proceed with the utmost caution.

He realised he could not carry on in this way, he had made a decision and knew it was the right thing to do, so it was time to stop all the self-doubt and press on. With that he carried on with his normal work whilst trying to work out which budget he would be able to raid if, as he expected, expenses were incurred.

One thing he had done was to tell his wife that he would be working a few late nights, as evenings were realistically the only time he would get to work with Clark and Devereux. She was well used to his hours and took it well but made further oblique references to retirement. Retirement may be much nearer than she imagined if this all went pear shaped, he thought.

Munro had a busy day, including a cordial meeting with the ACC (Crime) who was still full of good humour and basking in the reflected glory resulting from the conviction of Smithson. It was still a major topic of conversation when he attended meetings of the National Police Chiefs' Council and one which he revelled in describing to his colleagues. Of course, it was entirely due to his leadership that there had been a successful outcome, or at least that was the way he now saw things. Whilst Munro never did have any intention of telling the ACC what he was doing, he certainly wasn't going to mention it now, thinking that he was surely storing up trouble for himself at some future date.

He met with Clark and Devereux at 4 p.m. as arranged, but before they could update him on their progress, he had to pass on some information the ACC had given him.

"Superintendent Richard Wade will be presented with his George Medal at Buckingham Palace on Friday morning."

Devereux was the first to react, "I suppose it's too much to hope that we could stop it?"

Munro said, "I'm afraid so. We've only got unsupported allegations from a man doing forty years in prison. If we said anything they'd just laugh us out of the place. We need hard evidence and we won't get it in the time available."

Clark chipped, "I hope it's not the Queen giving him his bloody medal. If Smithson is telling the truth enough people will be embarrassed without getting her involved. God some heads could roll over this."

Munro replied wryly, "Yes, and don't forget they could be ours, so let's be careful and do things right. Bill, what have you got?"

"Right boss, I've got most of the files from storage. I've not had much time to look at it yet, but it does include Linda Ross's video interview and the statement from Frank Hodgson." Seeing Munro's quizzical look, he quickly added, "He's the van driver."

"What about you, Amy?"

"Yeah, I've managed to get the forensic files and the custody suite tapes for us to review. Oh! I've got the pathologist's report as well. I thought me and Bill could start looking through the stuff tonight, if that's okay with you, Bill?"

Devereux nodded. "No problem, Ma'am."

She looked a little surprised and said, "Bill, while we're working this closely together, I think Amy will be ok, don't you?"

He gave a short laugh. "It probably will, Amy."

She laughed as well. "Okay. My first thought was that we try to look at events in a chronological order, but that's going to be really hard to do. So, although Mr Munro and I have already seen it, I propose that we should watch Linda Ross's video and then the video from when Smithson arrived at the police station. That should give us a feel of things."

Both men agreed so she set up the girl's interview tape on Munro's office television. They sorted out tea and coffee before settling down to watch it. It only lasted about half an hour and contained very little information about the events in Grimston Lane, but Bill Devereux suddenly perked up and started making feverish notes.

Once the tape stopped, Devereux could hardly contain himself, blurting out, "Did you see that?"

Both Munro and Clark looked at him in surprise, having failed to spot anything they considered useful.

Devereux had a very satisfied expression as he continued. "The girl said that when the car was stopped, she heard voices above the sound of the engine. She heard somebody say 'please don't hurt me' which fits in with what Smithson said. It was something like, he thought it was really funny having an inspector on his knees begging to be let him go. What the girl says fits with that, don't you think?"

Munro mulled it over, saying, "It's a bit thin, Bill."

"Yes I know, but she also said she heard someone shout 'get my cuffs', didn't she? Well Wade describes Brown as disabled by his injuries and frozen with fear, yet Smithson says it was only Brown putting up a fight. If the girl is right in what she heard, then it must have been Brown who shouted it because Wade didn't have any handcuffs with him, did he? It matches with Smithson's story. Up to now we haven't come up with any real reason why he would lie about it, have we?"

Amy Clark looked at Devereux in a new light, realising there was an observant officer, with a good mind, behind the gruff exterior. "That's good, Bill, very good. It's only ever going to be supporting evidence, it's a hell of a good start though. We need something more concrete, but I think it raises more doubts about Wade in my mind."

Munro came in. "I agree with Amy. Wade could say maybe Brown was begging, but he didn't hear him and that after he grabbed Brown's cuffs he dropped them and was shouting at Brown to get them. I don't believe it for a minute, but we need to be able to knock his every argument. Well spotted, Bill. It just confirms the value of going through this stuff, we're going to find things that were missed the first time round or didn't realise at the time how significant they were."

Deep in thought, all three realised they now had more grounds than ever to doubt Superintendent Richard Wade, but knew they were a long way from proving anything, one way or another.

Munro sent the other two home, telling them that was enough for one night and that they could look at the custody video in the morning.

CHAPTER 21

As luck would have it, Munro was called away the following morning, leaving the other two to look at the custody video without him. Before they did, whilst drinking their morning coffee, they discussed the enquiry and progress so far.

Amy Clark hesitated a little before remarking, "Bill, I don't know about you, but I found last night's meeting a bit unsettling, disturbing even."

"What do you mean?"

"I thought about it a lot when I got home. When we started, we all had doubts about Richard Wade, but I honestly thought we'd find there was nothing in it. I expected to find it was just a difficult and frightening situation, with a tragic outcome, that's been exploited by a ruthless criminal. After what you saw in Linda's video, I'm pretty convinced that Wade lied. So what else has he lied about?"

Devereux answered carefully, "You said yourself that it was not concrete proof."

"Yes, I know that it wouldn't stand up in a court of law, but it was enough to convince me. In a way I'm frightened of what we'll find when we open this can of worms. If Smithson's version is the right one, and we prove it, the repercussions are going to spread far and wide."

"I know what you're saying, Amy. I think we can prove what really happened that day, although I'm not exactly sure how yet, and I too think Wade has got some difficult questions to answer. You're right about one thing though, this will cause embarrassment to a lot of people who will be very unhappy with us."

She said, "I think what I'm trying to say is that I'm now sure, if I wasn't before, that there's something in this and we've got to find out how Steve died and what Wade did or didn't do. I'm determined to get to the truth."

"Absolutely."

Clark nodded. "Okay, we have to go where the evidence takes us and deal with whatever comes our way. Let's get on with it."

They spent the next ten minutes watching the video.

It revealed Smithson to be sullen and uncooperative with the officers dealing with him, but it was his appearance that was most shocking. He had blood in his hair and on his face, which looked as if it had come from his nose, but it was his clothing that took Clark and Devereux's breath away. Almost the whole front of his shirt and trousers were covered in what was obviously blood, and there was clearly far too much to be from his own slight injuries. As the video progressed it could be seen that he also had blood on his hands and arms.

The other thing to emerge from the video was the restraint and sheer professionalism of the officers dealing with the prisoner, particularly Custody Officer Mary Jackson.

Having obtained a copy of Smithson's custody record they then spent some time going through it together. A number of interesting entries were noted. His clothing and shoes had been recovered and placed in evidence bags. Photographs were taken of his injuries, swabs taken from his hands, nail scrapings collected, blood and hair samples obtained.

A later entry, after he had been to hospital, recorded that he had grazing and swelling to the back of his head along with a broken nose.

Clark remarked, "If we actually do come up with a training package from this enquiry, the way he was managed in custody needs to be highlighted as good practice, don't you think?"

"Definitely, they were spot on. Too many officers don't realise you can lose vital evidence if you don't get it right there, and if prisoners are mistreated in any way it can cause massive problems at court, and later."

"Bill, as we already knew, Smithson had grazing to the back of his head and a broken nose. He claimed both injuries were caused by Steve Brown when he butted him and banged his head on the floor. Wade of course said he banged Smithson's head on the floor and didn't know how he came by the broken nose. At this stage we don't know the truth of either account, do we?"

"I suppose if Brown did do it, Wade could have seen him banging his head on the floor and just claimed the credit, but if he saw that why didn't he see the alleged head butt?"

Amy replied, "Well I suppose he may not have seen it in a general scuffle. Anyway, we can't establish the truth of that just yet, so to be fair to Wade we need to keep an open mind. Just because Smithson's story seems a better fit doesn't mean it's right. We need to remember Wade had been stabbed so he would be in a bit of a state."

After a further brief discussion to consider their plan of action for the day, they went their separate ways. Clark was going home so study the forensic files and pathologist's report in peace and quiet, whilst Devereux had an appointment at George Street police station with Inspector Brian Donovan to check into Steve Brown's background. He hoped it would help that he had worked with Donovan in the past. The two detectives confirmed they had each other's mobile number and that they would return for the 4 p.m. meeting with Munro, if he was back.

Devereux found he had time to kill when he arrived at George

Street whilst he waited for Inspector Donovan to finish a briefing. Not one to waste time he found an empty office where he spent twenty minutes having a very interesting telephone conversation with a senior prison officer at the prison where Smithson was incarcerated.

Donovan had been Steve Brown's shift inspector for nearly three years prior to his death and was well equipped to discuss the officer's work performance, also knowing something of his private life. He was, however, somewhat mystified as to what was wanted and especially why. As agreed, Devereux explained that he was engaged in a case review with Det. Supt. Munro to identify any lessons to be learned from how the enquiry had been handled. He told the inspector that they were also trying to identify any training needs emerging as a result of the incident, to include actions by uniform staff, control room staff, and the investigating officers.

Donovan seemed to accept the explanation but was still a little guarded in his responses to questions about Brown. He described the officer's personal life as something of a car crash. He said Brown had been divorced twice, but still liked the ladies, resulting in several liaisons with female officers and staff. Whilst this had caused problems aplenty for Brown, and some for Donovan, it had not affected his work. He was hard working, dedicated, and very professional, so much so that he was used on Donovan's shift to train young officers when they arrived from training school.

When asked how Brown had dealt with violent situations previously, Donovan did not hesitate, saying he was the man you would always want to back you up when there was any trouble and that more than once he had demonstrated his personal courage. Devereux asked what he thought of the description of events in Grimston Lane that had come out at the trial. Donovan was very cautious, clearly realising that contradicting the evidence given by another officer was not the done thing.

"Bill, between us, I think it's a load of bollocks. There is no way

Steve Brown would have hung back, I don't think for one second he would have frozen, it's just not the man I knew. Don't get me wrong, he wasn't perfect, and God knows he caused me enough problems, but he was a hell a good bobby and he never backed off. I think Superintendent Wade must have got mixed up in all the confusion," he said with a slight edge of scorn in his voice.

Devereux then asked if he had any idea why Brown hadn't called in before stopping the car.

"I really can't understand that. As I said, he was a hard worker and was always checking vehicles or people, invariably he called it in first. In fact, it's obvious which officers he trained because they all do exactly the same. It's the safe way to operate, isn't it?"

He added, "You know, I've thought about this a lot. I just can't understand how a man like Steve could be surprised by a thug like Smithson, let alone bested by him in a fight. I know he had a knife, but it was two against one after all. Explain this to me, how does one get a bloody medal and the other gets nothing?"

Devereux wrapped things up, assuring Donovan that he would keep him up to date with progress. He then went for a cup of tea in the canteen, giving him chance to speak informally to some of Steve Brown's colleagues.

Finally, he went off to the control room to meet with Joan Armitage. Once more he used the review and training explanation to Joan and her supervisors, before taking her away from her console to a small office. She was still upset about Steve Brown's death and, to some extent, blamed herself as the radio operator on duty because they had not found him in time. No amount of reassurance seemed to help her.

When questioned, Joan was able to confirm that Brown habitually called in prior to stopping any vehicles, giving his location and the vehicle details. She joked that he did it so often that he was a bit of a pain in the bum. She was unable to stop her tears, even several months after the incident, but when she had composed herself, Devereux was able to elicit further information about Brown. She supported much of what he had been told by Donovan, that Brown was conscientious and always the first to support other officers when they were in trouble. He left her after a few minutes, taking copies of the tapes from the day Brown died, although what use they would be he had no idea.

Devereux arrived a few minutes late for the 4 p.m. meeting to find Munro and Clark waiting for him. Munro apologised for his absence during the day, explaining that he'd had to attend several pre-arranged management meetings. He asked Devereux to update them on his day.

He quickly checked his notes before giving the other two a brief summary of what he had learned. He explained that he had a formal meeting with Brian Donovan, followed by some casual chats with other officers in the canteen. Without exception everyone he spoke to was unhappy with the version of events given by Richard Wade, although none of them could explain why he would be so wrong. They all said that Brown was an outstanding officer and were angry at suggestions that he might freeze when faced by Smithson. He had been given many examples of his bravery when tackling criminals or helping other officers. In fact, they all agreed that, above all else, Brown would never ever fail to help another officer. He was even told that Brown had received three commendations for bravery.

Devereux paused for breath before adding that it was clear Brown was scrupulous about calling in prior to checking vehicles. Many of the officers told him that it was something he drummed into everyone, telling them it was a basic officer safety procedure. Ironically, he apparently used to tell his colleagues that it could save their life one day. The radio operator Joan Armitage confirmed that it was something Brown's did religiously whenever he checked a vehicle or individual.

He looked at Munro before adding, "I've got to tell you that Richard Wade is not a popular bloke in those parts. The general consensus is that somehow he let Brown down and has then ruined his reputation with the evidence he gave. They really resent Wade's medal, while Steve Brown seems to be forgotten like he's an embarrassment."

Munro said, "Thanks for that, Bill. As before it's not direct evidence, but we're continuing to build a picture of Steve Brown and everything we hear suggests there are grounds for concern about Wade's account. Anything else?"

"Yes, one thing. I rang the prison today and I think we've identified Smithson's 'legal advisor'. It's an ex-solicitor doing time for murdering his wife, a bloke by the name of Henry Marchant. According to the P.O.s, they're in the same block and spend a lot of time together. If you agree, it might be worth going to have a chat with him, I thought me and Amy could go."

"Well done, Bill. It might be worth seeing him, you never know what Smithson might have told him. Let's hope he's prepared to talk. Is that okay with you, Amy?"

Clark readily agreed and then said, "Boss I don't think you're going to be as happy when you hear what I've got to say."

"Go on."

"As you know I've been looking at all the forensic records of the samples recovered and there's quite a lot of it, ranging from Linda Ross's clothes through to the knife used to stab the officers. Obviously, I concentrated on the evidence recovered relating to Steve Brown's death and briefly it consists of clothing from Brown, Wade, and Smithson, along with the knife and the blood samples taken at the scene and those taken from Smithson and Wade. I noticed there was also one from Steve Brown which I assume was obtained by the pathologist, but I've not read his report as yet. Swabs were also taken of the blood on Smithson's hands and scrapings from his fingernails. Hair samples were taken from all three men. The problem is that the results of any analysis are almost non-existent, consisting as far as I can tell of blood typing only."

When she paused Munro quietly asked, "What was the result of the blood typing?"

"Well, it didn't help much. It would appear all three men are type O, the most common group which is carried by about 45% of the population."

"What about DNA testing? I requested that."

Clark shook her head and said, "It wasn't done, neither was there any detailed examination of clothing for fibre transfers or hairs. As far as I can see, virtually nothing was done."

Munro thought about things for a moment. "Okay Amy, Bill, clearly the detailed forensic testing that should have been done wasn't, and I intend to find out why. It's possible that I can authorise the testing even now, but I'm sure it will create waves if I do. Before we go there let's try to identify what we hope to achieve by examining the samples and if we think it will help us to establish the truth of what happened that day. In short, do we think it will be worth doing? Amy, you've spent some time looking at this and you've also had a bit of time to think about it. Do you want to go first?"

"When Bill and I looked at the custody video of Smithson, the thing that struck us both was that he was saturated in blood, and it can't have been his because he only had minor injuries. The conclusion therefore must be that it was either Brown or Wade's blood and it can only be as a result of very close contact, not just blood spray when he stabbed them. If you remember, Wade says he ended up laid on top of Smithson whilst he held him down and banged his head on the floor. Smithson describes it exactly the opposite way round, saying it was Brown who was holding him down, even describing how his nose got broken. DNA analysis may well help us to decide who was on top of Smithson, holding him down."

Munro said, "What if it just shows a mixture of blood?"

"Well, it shouldn't, I don't think. The descriptions they both give of the incident are almost identical, the only difference being who ended up on top of Smithson. Neither makes any suggestion that it was a joint action. What do you think, Bill?"

"I think you're spot on and I agree we need to get the DNA done, blood grouping proved nothing."

Munro agreed with them and promised to find out why it hadn't been done already, along with an assurance that he would try to get the testing done now. "Anything else?"

It was Devereux's turn. "I've been looking at the evidence files, including some of the photos. One of them shows the grey Mondeo at the scene covered in fingerprint powder and it looks as if there might be some blood smears as well. Again there are no results so we don't know if any prints were found and who they belong to, or whose blood it was."

Clark said, "Sorry Bill, why is that significant?"

"If I remember right, Wade said he managed to pull himself up by holding onto the car. It may help to prove whether he did or not and, particularly if it proves he's lying, give more credence to Smithson's account."

Once more Munro mentally congratulated himself on picking the right officers to help him. "Okay, I'll get onto all that tomorrow with the head of Scenes of Crime Branch. This stuff could really help us to decide one way or the other."

Devereux said, "One last thing. The van driver Hodgson is on holiday, so I won't get to see him until next week. Not that I'm expecting too much from him, but if I don't ask I won't know. If Amy and I go to see that solicitor Marchant in prison on Monday, I could go to see Hodgson on Tuesday I think."

With that that they finished the meeting, going home for a well-deserved rest.

The following day was Friday, the day Wade was to receive his medal at Buckingham Palace. The three officers were a little subdued at their 8 a.m. meeting, all concerned that the wrong man was being honoured because, they believed, of a monstrous lie.

They had nothing new to discuss and quickly went their separate ways, Clark to study the PM report, Devereux to talk to officers who had attended the scene, and Munro to see Mark Pickering, the head of the Scenes of Crime Branch.

CHAPTER 22

A short time later Munro found himself having a difficult conversation with Mark Pickering, trying to discover why all the blood samples from the Grimston Lane crime scene had not been sent for DNA analysis. Pickering was clearly uncomfortable, going so far as to admit that they should have been examined.

Pickering was a retired senior officer and had been in his current role for about five years. He and Munro knew each other reasonably well and it soon became apparent that he was trying to conceal something. Under pressure from Munro, he eventually conceded that all the samples and exhibits had been packaged ready to be sent to the laboratory when he was ordered not to send them.

Munro was almost speechless, but managed to ask the two questions foremost in his mind, who by and why? The answers were not a surprise. The ACC (Crime) Jack Bryant gave the order on the grounds that it was too expensive, especially when there was enough evidence already for a successful prosecution. At least that was what he had told Pickering, adding that the Crown Prosecution Service were happy with that decision, believing they had more than enough evidence already for a successful prosecution.

Munro couldn't believe it and wanted to know why Pickering hadn't contacted him as the officer in the case. Clearly highly embarrassed, Pickering could only continue to apologise, stressing that he was acting on orders from the ACC. Things became even more awkward when Munro asked him to send the samples off for analysis now, with Pickering demanding to know who would pay for it.

Munro had prepared for that, having already checked that the budget codes for the kidnap/murder enquiry were still open. Briefly all enquiries of this nature were given a code by the Finance Branch, allowing all costs incurred to be allocated to those codes so that they could be correctly accounted for and easily audited. Having established that the costs could be allocated, Pickering's only problem now was authority for the work. He eventually accepted Munro's assertion that new evidence meant that it was now necessary for the samples to be properly examined and should include all blood samples, hair samples, clothing, and fibre transfer evidence. Pickering didn't enquire what exactly the new evidence was, but nervously suggested checking with ACC Bryant before he finally agreed that there was no need as Munro could authorise the costs. Frankly he could do without the grief and, if there was any flak later, he would make sure it all went Munro's way.

Munro left the office, breathing a heavy sigh of relief, not quite believing he had got away with it, but knowing there was sure to be a day of reckoning. He realised that he had gone way out on a limb. Pickering had told him that initial results could be expected by the end of next week as he intended to ask for it to be done as a matter of urgency. It was not that he was being particularly helpful, just that he wanted it all finished with as soon as possible before the roof fell in.

Back in his office Munro tried to get on with his normal work, realising that he needed to catch up with current progress in the cases being handled by his teams. It crossed his mind that he may have been neglecting those cases, but realised he had able officers running the enquiries and that they would be in touch if there was anything he needed to know. He had to admit to some nervousness about Pickering and wondered whether he would check with ACC Bryant before sending all the samples to the laboratory for analysis. However, as the day progressed, he began to relax, knowing that if Pickering had been in touch with the ACC he would certainly have heard something by now.

All he had to do was make sure the invoices from the laboratory were routed through his office, so he could delay their arrival at the Finance Branch for as long as possible. They had to come to him to sign off, so he was fairly sure that Bryant wouldn't find out what he was doing that way. At least for a while.

Munro knew he was taking a big risk, especially if he and his team were wrong. He was even more aware that being right about Wade might be worse because, as far as the senior officers were concerned, the enquiry had been concluded satisfactorily. The last thing they wanted to hear and become public knowledge was that their hero was a fraud, even worse that his behaviour may have contributed to the death of another officer. After all, the tendency to shoot the messenger if they brought unwelcome news was just as strong in the police as anywhere else.

At the 4 p.m. meeting, when Munro outlined what had happened with Pickering, both Clark and Devereux expressed outrage that the prosecution of a police killer had been put at risk for the sake of a few thousand pounds. In truth Munro had been angry about it all day but was not surprised, having become used to the ways of senior officers over the years.

Reminded by a question from Devereux that he had forgotten to ask about the fingerprint examination of the car, Munro promised he would chase it up on Monday, when things had settled down a little. With that the meeting ended and all three went home to recharge their batteries on a welcome and much deserved weekend off.

Munro, realising how tired he was, physically and mentally, wondered if Brenda might be right about retirement. Suddenly the prospect of studying cruise brochures over the weekend didn't seem so bad.

CHAPTER 23

Superintendent Richard Wade couldn't believe how, in the space of ten minutes, his happy Monday morning had turned to absolute shit.

He'd had a brilliant weekend with Julie, realising that she was not only nice to look at but that there was much more to her than he had first imagined. She could be funny and had bags of commonsense, making her a good sounding board when he shared his problems with her. One of her best pieces of advice was to stop fighting the assistant he had been given and to work with the man, using his skills to the benefit of the project. That way, if it all went to plan, Wade would get the praise for a job well done whilst managing a difficult situation and implementing unpopular changes. Of course Wade also realised that, if things did go wrong, he would also have a readymade fall guy, something Julie would never have thought of. He was coming to rely on her more and more as she blossomed, gaining increased confidence from her meetings with the great and good in the land.

The highlight of their weekend in London was meeting the Queen when she presented him with his George Medal. He must admit he had also enjoyed the renewed press attention, seeing his photos, accompanied by a proud Julie, in the weekend papers. A close second was Julie accepting his proposal of marriage. Could life have gotten any better? Then this happened.

It had started with a phone call from one of his few friends at George Street, although a more accurate description might be a hanger-on who was attaching himself to the rising star's coat tails. It was actually a sergeant from Brian Donovan's shift who felt the inspector was not giving him the credit he was sure he deserved, so he was seeking a new sponsor. The information from the sergeant was unsettling, to say the least, letting him know that someone was making enquiries about Steve Brown and that it was somehow related to his murder and the arrest of Karl Smithson. His informant was able tell him that the man making enquiries was Detective Sergeant Bill Devereux, and that he had spent time with Donovan before engaging other officers in casual conversation whilst in the canteen. Wade couldn't understand why anyone would want to make enquiries now, everything was done and dusted, or so he believed.

He thanked his 'friend', telling him that his help wouldn't be forgotten, adding a request to be kept informed of any other developments.

No sooner had he put the phone down when it rang again, this time it was ACC Bryant's office asking what he knew about press enquiries regarding a re-investigation of the Smithson case. Nothing was his brief but truthful reply before promising to make some enquiries and get back within the hour.

His mind was a jumble of thoughts, who was Bill Devereux? What had started this off? What was it all about? How had the press got involved? He started to calm down, realising that finding out who Devereux was would be a good start and may lead to answers for most of his other questions. Because of his current role in rationalising the police establishment, Wade had close links with the Personnel Branch. Contacting them he was quickly able to find out that Devereux was part of Detective Superintendent John Munro's squad and that, at the moment, he was on some form of detached duty. Wade had the presence of mind to ask if anyone else from the squad was on the same detached duty and was given Amy Clark's name. Her involvement in the original enquiry made Wade extremely nervous, particularly as she was so close to Munro. Why were they going over things again? Something serious must have happened, but he was unable to imagine what.

His next call was to the Press Office who were only able to tell him that a freelance journalist had called asking if there was any truth to the story that Superintendent Wade was subject to disciplinary enquiries. Because they had no idea, their response had been to make no comment.

Wade immediately went into panic mode, wondering if he was indeed under investigation and, if so, for what? Once again, when he stopped to think, he realised that it was highly unlikely as normal practice was to inform an officer if he was under investigation and to serve him with notices confirming that fact and the nature of any allegations. The more he thought about it the more he reached the conclusion that something was going on secretly and perhaps without authorisation. After all, the ACC's office were hardly likely to ring him with questions if it was an officially sanctioned enquiry. So what was Munro up to? The question was, did he confront Munro or let the ACC do it?

Munro had completed his morning meeting with Clark and Devereux, who had now set off to see Marchant in prison, when the call from ACC Bryant's secretary came, summoning him to see the ACC in his office at 10 a.m. that day. He was aware of nothing else happening so immediately suspected it was something to do with the Smithson enquiry. He spent the time available marshalling his thoughts and readying his arguments for spending the money on analysing the forensic samples. He didn't think it was going to be a happy meeting, and just wished he had managed to keep things under wraps a little longer.

He had time to reflect on his earlier meeting when all three of them were slightly depressed, having seen lots of coverage of Wade's medal presentation on local TV and in national newspapers. Of course there were non-stop quotes from the chief constable along

144

with the Police and Crime Commissioner among others, all praising Wade to the heavens. It made them realise what a difficult position they were in and how even more problematic it would be to convince anyone that Wade was a liar. They were all realistic and experienced enough to understand that finding out the truth and proving it might not be enough as it was unlikely anyone in authority would want to hear it, let alone do anything about it. If they were right, no one was going to come out of this smelling of roses, but one thing Munro was determined to do was protect Clark and Devereux from any reprisals.

At 10 a.m. exactly, John Munro entered ACC Bryant's office where he was surprised to see Richard Wade already present. He nodded to Wade and sat down when invited to do so by the ACC.

Bryant started and did not beat about the bush. "John, are you running an investigation into the Brown murder?"

Munro decided if he wanted to keep it short, then two could play at that game. "Yes Sir."

Wade was about to say something, but stopped when the ACC shook his head and said angrily, "Why the hell are you doing that, and why don't I know about it?"

Following the maxim that when lying you should include as much of the truth as possible, Munro replied, "A while ago I visited Smithson in prison."

He was interrupted by an almost hysterical Wade; "My God! What did you do that for?"

Munro tried again, "If you'll let me finish, I'll tell you. Smithson contacted us asking me to visit him personally, which is not something I would normally do at this stage of my career. However, because I hoped he wanted to admit other serious crimes I decided to go and took DI Clark with me. In the event he just wanted to yank my chain, making lots of unsubstantiated allegations about Superintendent Wade, claiming he lied about what happened when

145

PC Brown was murdered. Clearly we were not interested, but then he informed us that he intended to go to the press if we didn't take action. I made the decision that we should indeed review the case in order to make us completely bombproof if he did try to get some cheap publicity. This has already been heard in a court of law, so I didn't see any problems at all."

He paused as Bryant nodded and Wade seemed to calm down.

Munro continued, "He told me a couple of things that we were easily able to clarify, so I thought why not get on with it? At the same time, it seemed like a good opportunity to identify any training issues, both from the actual incident and the subsequent enquiry."

A clearly more relaxed Bryant said, "Okay. Don't you think Professional Standards might have been better equipped to deal with this and why didn't you let me know what was happening?"

"To be honest I thought once it was referred to Professional Standards it became an official complaint and may become public. Whilst we obviously have nothing to hide there's no point gaining any more unwelcome publicity than we need. I thought I could deal with it quietly but be ready to respond to any enquiries from the press if necessary. As for not telling you, Sir, that may have been an error but I'm not sure. Firstly, I thought I was capable of deciding whether or not to pursue enquiries and doing so with a minimum of fuss if I went ahead. Secondly, I thought if you didn't know about my enquiries you would have plausible deniability should the press ask you about it."

Wade couldn't contain his anger and blurted out, "Well it hasn't worked, has it? The press are already asking about this cock-up."

Munro responded calmly, "In that case I think as a result of my enquiries we're in a good position to answer whatever questions they ask."

"That may be so, but why are you asking questions at George

Street about Brown?"

Munro answered evenly, "It's part of the identification of any training needs. We are trying to understand why an experienced officer like Steve Brown didn't call in to the control room prior to stopping Smithson's vehicle, as you instructed."

Wade remained quiet, realising this was not a topic he wanted to pursue.

ACC Bryant stepped in. "Is there anything else to add, Mr Munro?"

"Yes Sir. We always knew we couldn't trust Smithson, but he seemed to be getting some legal advice from somewhere, even though he'd sacked his solicitor. Anyway, we discovered he's been spending a lot of time with a prisoner who was a solicitor, before he murdered his wife that is. DI Clark and DS Devereux are on the way to the prison at the moment to see the man and find out what Smithson has told him. We hope to get something to counteract what he says. As for how it got to the press, it seems there are three possibilities, Smithson, the ex-solicitor, or someone at George Street. I can try to find out discreetly if you wish, Sir."

Bryant smiled and said, "Good idea. It looks as if you are well on top of things but keep me posted from now on. I'm not sure keeping me out of things was a wise move, but I understand why you did. Okay, John, thank you."

Munro got up, trying to suppress a smile as he thought, 'He doesn't know about the forensic examinations.'

He nodded again to an unhappy-looking Wade as he left. Munro was pleased with the way things had gone, believing he had given a believable account to Bryant, and he couldn't care less what Wade thought. He'd earned some valuable breathing space.

ACC Bryant was also happy. If things went badly on this it would all be down to Munro and it was about time he retired anyway, they had no need for dinosaurs. He spent a few minutes in conversation with Richard Wade, assuring him that he had nothing to worry about, before he managed to get shut of him. It never crossed his mind that his own involvement in the case might come to light and how it might look. Truth be told he'd completely forgotten about it.

CHAPTER 24

Meanwhile, Clark and Devereux were meeting with Henry Marchant in an interview room where, interestingly, he did not impose any restrictions or conditions before speaking to them. He was more than happy to tell them about his 'client' after the officers had agreed to tell the Governor he had co-operated with them. It was all part of his attempts to be moved to a prison with a more relaxed regime, after all, he wasn't a real criminal, and he certainly didn't belong with scum like Smithson. He knew his chances of getting to an open prison were slim, but you had to start somewhere.

Basically, Marchant supported everything that Smithson had told Munro, confirming that his desire to damage Wade seemed to be all-consuming. He was also able to confirm that Smithson did have an idea that he might get a re-trial out of trashing Wade's reputation. However, he assured them that Smithson swore blind that everything he said was the truth, not a mere fabrication to help his case. Which of course meant that Smithson had admitted to him, as he had to Det. Supt Munro, that he had murdered Steve Brown and attempted to murder Richard Wade.

When DI Clark asked him, Marchant happily agreed to give a written statement outlining everything he told them. It never seemed to cross his mind what Smithson and some of the other inmates might do if they found out about his level of co-operation with the hated police. He was desperate to get out of here.

Superintendent Munro had contacted DI Clark shortly before she and Devereux went in to see the prisoner and explained about the press leak, asking them to find out if it had come from either of the two inmates. Marchant denied any responsibility and thought it highly unlikely that Smithson had done it while he was still pinning his hopes on Munro. When Devereux made enquiries with prison staff, he discovered that neither man had used the phone or sent any letters out in the last week.

Driving away from the prison, with Marchant's statement in her briefcase, Clark couldn't believe how easy it had been. They were now in a position, if Smithson appealed, to produce statements in evidence from Munro and Marchant outlining in detail admissions he had made to them both. Any chance he might have had of a successful appeal had gone straight down the toilet.

The afternoon meeting in Munro's office was an interesting affair. He started by updating them on his meeting with ACC Bryant, specifically what he had told him and Wade who, he confided, looked a little frazzled. He did let them know that so far they seemed okay with regard to the analysis of the forensic samples.

Clark and Devereux produced the statement from Marchant with a small degree of triumph, although they did admit that he had needed little persuading. All agreed that the statement, along with Munro's evidence, should be more than sufficient to scupper any slight chance Smithson may have had of a successful appeal.

More seriously they confirmed that they believed the leak to the press had not come from the prison, unless it was a warder, which seemed unlikely in the circumstances. The inevitable conclusion, no matter how unpalatable, was that someone in the police was talking to the freelance reporter. A brief discussion followed as to how they could get them to hold off on any enquiries for the time being and, more importantly, not to publish anything they might have at the moment. They agreed that finding the informant might prove difficult as journalists, just like the police, did not like to reveal their sources.

It was agreed that Amy Clark would speak to the reporter the following day and offer them a deal they might find hard to refuse in an attempt to diffuse that potential problem. Stopping this journalist was alright but it wouldn't stop the informant speaking to someone else, so she would also try to persuade them to reveal their source.

Shortly after the others had left, Munro received an interesting phone call from Richard Wade.

"John, have you got a moment to speak?"

"Yes, of course, Richard."

"I just wanted to apologise for this morning. I realise I may have been a little rude and I'm sorry. I'm sure you can appreciate how disconcerting it is when you find out that you are being investigated by a colleague and on top of that the press are getting involved as well."

"Certainly, I can understand, but I'm sure you've got nothing to worry about, have you?"

"No, not at all but, as you well know, anything can be made to look bad. I still worry that I could have done more to save Steve Brown, you know. Between us, I'm still getting some counselling for that."

Munro couldn't help wondering where all this was going. "I'm not surprised. It must have been a traumatic and frightening incident, and anyone would take time to put it behind them."

"Thank you for being so understanding. Can I just ask that if you find anything you're not happy with that you run it past me first? It could be that I can clear up any ambiguities for you and your team, saving you some time as well. I think Mr Bryant would like to see this thing finished as soon as possible as well."

Munro saw no harm in playing along and said, "That's no problem. Things are coming together and we should have something soon."

"Anything you can tell me at the moment?"

"Richard, you can rest assured I'll be in touch once I have the full picture."

Then Wade let himself down badly. "I'm sure you realise that the chief and a number of other important people wouldn't be all that happy if this thing got out of hand. Anyone can be criticised in any situation, no matter how well they did, can't they? The trouble is it could affect all of us, even you."

Munro remained calm at the veiled threat, simply saying, "All understood, I will speak to you soon."

After hanging up, Munro couldn't help but wonder at Wade's true purpose in calling him. It obviously wasn't to make friends and he was sure the warning at the end of the conversation was definitely an attempt to intimidate him. Well, if it was, he'd picked the wrong man and had only strengthened Munro's resolve to find the truth, whatever the price he may have to pay. It was proof, if any were needed, that they were getting to Wade, and maybe also that he had something to hide. It was a big tactical mistake.

CHAPTER 25

At the next morning's meeting Munro informed his two colleagues about his telephone conversation with Richard Wade the previous evening. He had made notes immediately after the call in his official notebook, just in case he needed to produce them in evidence at some later stage. Clark and Devereux both expressed amazement at the man's nerve and sheer stupidity.

Clark spoke first, saying, "Well if I had any doubts about Wade's account of what happened they're fast disappearing, and I wonder all the time if Steve Brown would still be alive if Wade had done more."

Devereux spoke quietly, "Well if you've got doubts now, I think you'll have even more when you hear what I have to say."

The other two looked expectantly at the sergeant as he continued; "I spent some time last night checking files for those fingerprints from the car before it eventually dawned on me to look in the Linda Ross kidnap file. Sure enough, there they were with all the other crime scene prints and it's clear from notes in the file that the prints recovered were only deemed to be of value in the kidnap case and not the murder case. In the actual prosecution case at the trial, fingerprint evidence was used, but not that from the outside of the car as it was not believed to be relevant. No one attached any real significance to those prints. Why would they?"

Amy Clark couldn't contain herself any longer. "Come on, Bill, whose prints are they?"

Devereux smiled. "Well Amy I can tell you they're not Richard Wade's. A total of six different fingerprints belonging to Steve Brown were found on the rear offside wing of the grey Ford Mondeo. Two of them were in blood."

Munro said, "Were any prints belonging to Superintendent Wade found on the car at all?"

"None at all, Sir."

Clark jumped in. "Well that's more evidence to doubt what Wade says, isn't it?"

Munro spoke, "Yes, it is. Indeed, it is, but once again it doesn't prove anything on its own. Wade could claim his fingerprints were smudged and not able to be identified. However, they can't have both been next to the side of the car pulling themselves up, can they? This evidence certainly seems to show that Steve Brown did exactly that. We're starting to build a picture. Well done, Bill."

Clark nodded her agreement.

Munro added, "It reminds me of something Smithson said. He described Wade's account of what he did as being almost a complete change of roles, portraying himself as doing what, in fact, Brown did. It fits with that, doesn't it?"

Devereux nodded his agreement.

The meeting finished. Clark and Devereux went off to see Frank Hodgson at this home. They were unable to see the freelance reporter, now identified as Helen Naylor by the Press Office, until the following day so had decided to work together on both meetings. Naylor had agreed not to publish anything until she had spoken to DI Clark.

Frank Hodgson was fairly apprehensive when he met the two officers at his front door, wondering what it was all about. They had told him very little, only referring to a few things from the enquiry that needed clearing up and saying that they hoped he would be able to help. They introduced themselves and were soon seated at Mr Hodgson's dining room table drinking tea with him and his wife.

Amy Clark spent some minutes reassuring Mr Hodgson that he had done nothing wrong and explaining that they were only trying to clarify issues that had arisen since the trial.

Devereux said, "Basically what we would like to do is run through your statement, making sure that nothing was missed by us."

"That's okay by me, but what sort of issues are you talking about?"

Devereux replied using the explanation he and Clark had previously agreed, "Well, to be completely honest, we are pretty sure we missed some things in the original investigation. There is a suggestion that Smithson may make an appeal against his conviction, and we want to make sure he has no chance of ever getting out of prison. I must stress that we have no reason to think there is any problem with your evidence, we're seeing everyone."

Frank Hodgson looked at his wife who nodded before he said, "That's fine by me, ready when you are."

With that they slowly went through his original statement which obviously related to the aftermath of the incident. In simple terms Hodgson described how he had pulled into the lay-by in Grimston Lane to ask for directions, stumbling into the aftermath of the murder. They were unable to identify any significant changes and, whilst disappointed, they had not expected much more.

After they had finished, and being in no particular hurry, the two officers had a second cup of tea with the Hodgsons who were proving to be a very pleasant couple. They chatted about their recent holiday and the general state of the country.

As Clark and Devereux were packing up their papers, prior to leaving, Frank Hodgson said, "Please tell Mr Wade how pleased we were to see him get his medal, he must be very brave."

Amy Clark almost choked on her last mouthful of tea, and it was a minute before she could reply, "Sorry it went down the wrong way. Yes, he must be. I'll certainly pass it on."

Mr Hodgson carried on, "It's so sad to think when I drove by PC Brown was alive and when I came back, he was laid on the ground dying."

Devereux and Clark immediately looked at each other, recognising the significance of what they had just heard. Devereux said, "Do you mind if we sit down for a minute or two longer, I've just thought of a couple of other questions?"

"Of course, anything I can do to help."

Devereux began, "Frank, your statement doesn't mention that you had already driven past the lay-by, does it?"

"No, nobody asked me, and I didn't think it was important. Is it a problem, have I done something wrong?"

"I can assure you that you've done nothing wrong. We should have asked you, we're the police after all. Can you tell me why you drove both ways along Grimston Lane?"

"As you know, I thought I was in Grimston Road but it was actually Grimston Lane. Anyway, I turned in from the dual-carriageway, I was looking for a farm to deliver a parcel. I drove past the lay-by and saw the police car and the grey car parked in front of it, so when I realised that I couldn't find the farm I remembered the police car and headed back to ask for help. That's when I saw what had happened. It was awful."

Clark stepped in. "Yes, it must have been. Do you think another cup of tea might be a good idea, Mrs Hodgson?"

She nodded and, as she left to make it, Clark said, "Frank, please think carefully about this. You said when you drove past the lay-by the first time you saw the two cars, did you see anything else?"

He nodded. "Oh yes! I saw a police officer walking towards the grey car, and I think the man, it must have been Smithson, was getting out of the grey car."

"Do you know which police officer it was?"

"He had very dark hair so it must have been PC Brown, don't you think? I remember Mr Wade had quite fair hair from all the pictures and stuff on TV."

Clark was almost breathless with excitement. "Can you describe him any more than that?"

"Well, he was quite tall, but I can't remember any more. Why is this important, I don't understand?"

Devereux took over, "If you'll bear with us for a moment. Can you remember what he was wearing?"

Frank Hodgson thought for a moment. "Well his uniform obviously, but he didn't have his hat on. I thought you chaps were always supposed to wear your hat. Still, it was a very warm day so that's probably why he didn't have it on. I do remember thinking how hot he must have been though with that black waistcoat thing on you all wear these days."

Devereux just stared before finally saying, "Mr Hodgson, do you mean he was wearing his stab vest?"

"Yes, that's what they're called, aren't they?"

Bill Devereux paused for a moment, shocked by what he had just heard, and then said, "Frank, that's excellent, thank you. Did you see the other officer, that would be Mr Wade?"

"Well I could see someone sat in the police car, but I never got a good look, I was past them in seconds. I suppose that must have been Mr Wade, but I can't be certain."

Devereux looked towards Clark who said, "Frank, can I just summarise what you've told us please?"

He nodded.

"Okay, you were driving down Grimston Lane from the dual

carriageway, having mistaken it for Grimston Road, when you passed a police car and a grey car in a lay-by. You saw a police officer, who you now believe to be Steve Brown, walking towards the grey car and at the same time the driver of that car was getting out. You saw a second person sitting in the police car, who you believe to be Richard Wade although you cannot be sure. You saw nothing of the incident which resulted in Steve Brown dying and Richard Wade receiving his injuries. Is that an accurate account of what happened?"

"Yes, that's it. Does that help?"

Clark replied, "It does, thank you."

Hodgson said, "I'm sorry I never told you this before, but nobody asked me. I didn't realise it was important."

She said, "We should apologise to you and we should have asked you the right questions, I'm sorry. Thank you very much for your help. Are you prepared to give us a fresh statement about this?"

After he had agreed, Devereux took a further statement. In the meantime, Mrs Hodgson made more cups of tea to replace those the two police officers had allowed to grow cold.

It was 2 p.m. before they left and once in the car both officers wanted to speak at once, realising they had just achieved their eureka moment. The inevitable high-five followed. Bubbling with excitement Clark rang Munro, requesting to see him immediately as they had important information. He readily agreed.

By 2.30 p.m. they were in Munro's office. Quickly Amy Clark told him that they had uncovered illuminating new evidence from Frank Hodgson and handed over his new statement which Munro quickly read.

He said, "This is good work, but why didn't we know about it already?"

Clark replied, "I simply don't think we asked the right questions when Frank Hodgson was first interviewed. In all honesty this only came to light with us today while we were chatting with Mr Hodgson, it was a bit of a bombshell I can tell you."

Munro looked at the statement almost sadly. "Well this gives us massive problems, doesn't it? We have an eyewitness whose evidence supports that of a convicted murderer, and directly contradicts the evidence of a George Medal winning hero. To summarise where we are. Firstly, as a result of the fingerprint evidence, it is very doubtful that Wade was ever anywhere near Smithson's car. Secondly, Frank Hodgson provides clear evidence that Richard Wade lied when he claimed to have been the first out of the police car and the one to approach Smithson. It all gives greater credence to Smithson's claim that Wade has just reversed roles with Steve Brown in the account he gives. Lastly, the suggestion that Brown didn't want to call in the check on the car is utterly preposterous in view of what everyone else has told us about the way he operated. What do you think?"

Devereux stepped straight in, "Frank Hodgson is the salt of the earth and I believe everything he says. I think this confirms, along with everything else, that Wade is a lying bastard and that thanks to his actions, or lack of them, Steve Brown died. He cannot be allowed to get away with it."

Clark nodded her agreement but was a little more circumspect in her response. "I agree with Bill, we can't let this stand. It looks like Wade lied and as a result he has gained a great deal and a good man has lost not only his life, but his good name as well. We can't forget that the real villain here is Karl Smithson and whether Steve would have lived if Wade had acted differently is something I suppose we'll never know for sure."

Munro said, "I agree, he cannot be allowed to get away with this. However, we need to think very carefully how to proceed, because revealing what we believe to be the truth will not make us very popular. An awful lot of people are going to be embarrassed when this comes out and don't forget, Wade would appear to have committed a criminal offence when he lied about his actions in court. We need to move with even more caution now and may need to protect ourselves, possibly Frank Hodgson as well."

Devereux said, "So what next, boss?"

Munro thought carefully before replying.

"We do nothing with this for the moment. Amy, you and Bill see this reporter tomorrow, try to get her onside and stop her printing anything yet, if at all. Then, hopefully, when we get the forensic results on Friday, we'll go through everything and decide exactly what we've got and what to do. Okay?"

CHAPTER 26

The next day, Wednesday, with no new information to discuss, the morning meeting was nothing more than a good morning cup of tea with a warning to be careful from Munro.

At 10 a.m. Clark and Devereux met Helen Naylor in the Cosy Corner Tea Rooms, just off the high street. Both parties felt happy meeting there as it was not the sort of establishment frequented by either police officers or reporters, so they were unlikely to be seen or overheard. They introduced themselves and ordered refreshments.

Helen Naylor was a young, thrusting journalist looking for a route into the big time and with a reporter's instinct sensed there may be something in this story for her. It was odd that she had been told there was nothing going on by the police Press Office and now she was meeting with these two officers, at least one of whom she realised had worked on the original Smithson enquiry.

Naylor kicked things off; "Are you DI Clark who worked on the Smithson enquiry?"

"Yes, I am. Before we start, Helen, sorry, is it okay to call you Helen?"

"Please do."

Clark said, "Obviously we are meeting here because we all want our conversation to remain confidential and maybe because we don't want anyone to know we've spoken at all. We don't want this recorded, so can I ask you to put your mobile phone and recorder on the table please?"

Naylor had the good grace to blush as she placed her phone on the table, along with a voice recorder she took from her bag, switching it off as she did so. She then said, "What about you, are you recording this?"

Devereux replied, "No point for us, is there? This is not an interview and I'm sure you appreciate we can't do anything with a recording, whilst you could use one in a story."

"Fair enough. Tell me why you wanted to meet in such a clandestine manner."

Clark took over again. "Alright Helen. What I am about to tell you is not for publication yet, but please remember everything has a price. When you contacted the Press Office, they told you that there was no new investigation into the Smithson case, which is not the whole truth. However, in fairness to them, they didn't, and still don't, know anything."

"So what is the whole truth? Is Wade the subject of a disciplinary enquiry?"

Clark shook her head and told the exact truth. "Mr Wade is not being investigated by the Professional Standards Branch, but we are re-investigating some aspects of the Smithson case."

Naylor looked confused, "I don't understand, what are you not telling me?"

Clark stared at the young reporter for a few seconds before saying, "As I've told you, nothing of this conversation can be printed at the moment and before I tell you anything further, I need something from you."

Sensing she was onto something big, Naylor was ready to agree to anything. "Go on."

This time it was Devereux who spoke, "We need to know how you found out about this. We want you to tell us the name of your source."

Naylor's instinct was to deny that she had a source, but realised that was a complete non-starter, so said, "You know I can't tell you that. You don't reveal your sources, do you?"

He replied, "You know that's not strictly true, sometimes a court will order us to reveal the name of an informant. There are differences between us because our sources can often face serious, even fatal, consequences from other criminals. It is highly unlikely that journalist's sources face the same dangers and certainly not in this case. You've got to decide how badly you want this story."

Naylor looked at them, trying to decide between all her training and personal ethics that said she should never reveal a source and her desire to get the big story that could propel her all the way to Fleet Street.

They knew they had her when, almost admitting it was a police officer, she said, "What will happen to my source if I tell you?"

Clark concealed her joy, simply saying, "I'm making no promises, because I don't know. I will tell you that our main concern is stopping this person from revealing anything else to anyone until the enquiry is completed."

"What do I get? I won't just give them up for nothing."

"What would you like?"

Naylor realised they were quite desperate to get to her source. How big was this story, she thought? She said, "If I tell you, I want an exclusive on the story 24 hours before it's released to the rest of the press. The condition is that if I get a sniff that anyone else is onto this I will go to print immediately and will include this conversation. I also want access to you if necessary."

Clark said, "Well access to me is not a problem although I'm not sure what I will be able to tell you. 24 hours notice may be more difficult. In principle I have no problem with it, but you know what things are like and we may not be able to keep a lid on it. If I get wind it's going to come out, I'll give you a heads up immediately.

How's that?"

Helen Naylor frowned, but the more she thought the more she realised it was one hell of a good deal. She had one more question: "Just how big is this story?"

Devereux looked at Clark who nodded. He said, "We think it's big, potentially very big. The Nationals will be all over it if we're right."

Naylor thought for a moment, justifying her decision to reveal the source by telling herself that they would probably have found out anyway. "It's Nigel Heath."

Devereux looked towards Clark and said, "He's a sergeant on Inspector Donovan's shift at George Street."

Clark said to Helen Naylor, "So how come you managed to connect with Sergeant Heath?"

She coloured slightly before replying, "We had a bit of a fling a few months ago, nothing special but we stayed friendly."

"Alright, who instigated the contact this time?"

"He rang me and said he had something I might be interested in, so we met up in a pub a few days ago."

Devereux said, "It's probably a silly question, but I need to confirm that he knew you were a journalist. Did he?"

"Yes, of course. It's not the first time he's told me bits and pieces, but nothing special."

"You said your relationship is over, is that true?"

"Oh yes, I found out he was married."

"Did he say why he wanted to give you this information?"

"He said it was because you were trying to bring a good man down. At that time, I thought he meant Steve Brown because they worked on the same shift."

Devereux came in once more, "Was he paid for the information?"

She laughed. "No, I don't have access to the funds to pay sources. I think he thought he'd have a better chance of resuming things with me if he helped with information."

He said, "By a bit of a fling, do you mean your relationship was sexual?"

She replied indignantly, "Yes it was, but that had nothing to do with getting information. I liked him."

Clark smiled and said to Naylor, "You're both adults, but we do need the full picture. What would you like to know? Before you ask, please understand that none of this attributable directly to us and no direct quotes. When it breaks, that will change of course."

Helen Naylor returned Clark's smile. "I need to make some notes, is that ok?" When Clark agreed she continued, "You said earlier that you were investigating some aspects of the Smithson case, can you tell me exactly what?"

"As the result of some new information it appears that the original investigation missed some important evidence which we are now following up."

"Does this mean that there may be a re-trial, and could Smithson get off?"

"Yes, to the possibility of a re-trial, but definitely no to Smithson being cleared."

Looking puzzled Naylor said, "I don't understand. If there is a problem with the evidence, how can you be so certain that Smithson will not be cleared?"

Devereux stepped in, "Make no mistake, Smithson is guilty of murder, attempted murder, and kidnapping. Our investigation has done nothing to weaken the case against him, on the contrary it may even have strengthened it."

Getting more confused by the minute Helen said, "So what exactly are you investigating?"

Amy Clark tried to think back to the conversation with Detective Superintendent Munro when they had decided on their tactics for this meeting and exactly how much to reveal to the reporter.

She said, "I can tell you that new evidence has come to light suggesting that the accounts of some of the people concerned may not be completely accurate."

Stunned by what she had just heard, Naylor said, "Jesus, you are investigating Richard Wade, aren't you?"

"I'm not at liberty to say at this stage."

Naylor couldn't believe her ears. Clarke had not denied they were investigating Wade, the George Medal hero who had been promoted and featured in photographs with the Prime Minister and Home Secretary. She was almost breathless with excitement.

"Where did the new evidence come from? Was it Smithson?"

Clark did not reply, just smiled.

Naylor had her answer and asked her next question. "Who is in charge of the investigation?"

Devereux responded, "Detective Superintendent John Munro."

"What is the new evidence that has caused you to re-open this case?"

He replied, "Sorry not now, maybe later."

"When do you expect to complete your enquiries?

Clark said, "Shortly, within the next two weeks we hope. I think that's enough for now, don't you? Before we finish, I'd like to caution you not to make enquiries with anyone else for two reasons. Firstly, because you may jeopardise our investigation and, secondly, because not many people are in the loop."

Naylor got the message loud and clear. The investigation was being done in secret.

"Okay," she said. "But aren't a lot of people going to end up with egg on their faces by the time you finish?"

Clark responded, "That is a possibility of course, but I wouldn't know."

With that they concluded the meeting and went their separate ways, but not before Clark had a brief whispered conversation with Naylor. If Devereux had been looking, he would have seen his colleague pass the reporter a piece of paper containing her home address and phone number. Amy Clark experienced a frisson of excitement as she realised how much she had enjoyed meeting the young reporter, especially as she had responded so positively to the suggestion of a drink one night. She realised her behaviour might be considered reckless, unprofessional even, but hoped Helen's response wasn't just to get the story.

Naylor went for a strong drink to decide which editor she should approach, whilst the two detectives headed back to Munro's office.

When told how the meeting had gone, Munro only had one question. Could they trust Helen Naylor? Both officers believed they could, at least for the time being, certain she was so desperate for the story that she wouldn't rock the boat until she got it, and the glory she was sure would follow. Satisfied, he instructed Devereux to contact Brian Donovan to arrange a meeting in Munro's office as soon as possible.

Once Devereux had gone, Munro contemplated the first casualty of Smithson's revelations. The young reporter, Helen Naylor, had sacrificed her principles by revealing the source of her information in pursuit of a bigger story, career advancement, and journalistic glory. He was sure she was not going to be the last one to fail the moral test they all faced.

CHAPTER 27

At 10 a.m. the next day, Superintendent Richard Wade was having a very uncomfortable meeting in the office of ACC Bryant, who did not beat about the bush. "Richard, but for the intervention of the duty inspector, you would have been arrested last night. Would you like to tell me what happened?"

Wade, displaying all his old arrogance and bravado, said, "I don't think it was that serious. Those two PCs were looking to arrest somebody and were well over the top I can tell you, Sir."

"I'll be the judge of that. Just tell me what happened."

"It was nothing. I had an argument with my girlfriend Julie, and I suppose it did get a bit out of hand."

"My understanding is the shouting was so loud that a neighbour felt compelled to call the police, and when they arrived, they could hear a woman screaming from inside. I'm told that if you had not opened the door at once they would have forced entry. I also understand you were the worse for drink and that Julie was crying as well as having a clearly visible red mark on her cheek. The officers formed the impression she had been assaulted and, in line with the Force domestic violence policy, were going to arrest you."

"I had some wine with dinner, but I certainly wasn't drunk. I definitely never assaulted Julie and if those officers suggest I did I will make an official complaint about their conduct."

Bryant sighed heavily. "Richard, you are a very lucky man that Julie refused to make a complaint, otherwise you would have been in a cell. You made things worse by trying to use your rank to intimidate the officers, which clearly failed as they nearly arrested you to prevent a breach of the peace, so please no more talk of complaints. May I also remind you that your current rank is temporary and the goodwill from previous heroics will only last so long. Do I make myself clear?"

A very chastened Wade replied, "Yes Sir. I'm sorry, I think this stupid investigation by Munro just brought it all back and it got on top of me. It won't happen again."

"Okay. Now go home and make things right with Julie. I know you have been seeing a counsellor and you may want to consider some more sessions."

Wade left the office thinking he had to stop Munro's team somehow and prevent their investigation from getting anywhere. The more he thought about it, the more a sick feeling engulfed him as it dawned on him that he really didn't know how to put a stop to the investigation. His last clumsy attempt with Munro had failed dismally.

Before he went in to see Julie, his final thought was that if things got too bad the job offer from John Ross was still an option. It did not seem to dawn on him that if he was discredited by the new investigation that job offer would soon disappear as well.

Richard Wade was a man under severe pressure. He knew he was in danger of losing everything he had worked for, lied and cheated for. His rank, possibly his job, his reputation, and Julie could all go. It never crossed his mind that his very liberty was at stake.

CHAPTER 28

At the same time that Wade's meeting with Bryant was taking place, Brian Donovan arrived at Superintendent Munro's office wondering what was going on now, suspecting it was still to do with Steve Brown's death.

Munro greeted Inspector Donovan warmly, asking if he had any objection to Clark and Devereux being present. As he had no real idea why he was there, it seemed silly to object to their presence.

Munro began: "Brian, I need to apologise before we go any further. When Bill came to see you the other day, he did not tell you everything that was going on. We are looking at training needs but there may also be some discrepancies in the original investigation. It may surprise you to know that we have spoken to Smithson in prison, at his request I may add, and he tells a very different story to Richard Wade. We are still trying to establish the truth, but it is safe to say we have found enough evidence already to cause grave reservations about Wade's account. I should tell you this is not an official enquiry in that the senior management also believe it is simply an attempt to identify training needs and future best practice. If I could ask you to keep this to yourself please because, if they should find out what we're really doing, I'm sure they'll shut us down in double quick time."

"I thought some of Bill's questions were a bit odd. Nobody will hear about this from me. I can tell you I have never believed Steve Brown would be a coward and be bested by a man like Smithson."

"Right, I can now tell you that details of our enquiry have been

170

leaked to the press and that the same person probably tipped off Richard Wade as well. The leak has been identified as coming from your sergeant, Nigel Heath, who, it transpires, had a sexual relationship with the reporter concerned. As this enquiry is not completely sanctioned, I'd like to discuss with you exactly how we deal with him. By the way it was the reporter, Helen Naylor, who gave us his name and she's now co-operating with us. Thanks to Heath or her enquiries with the Press Office, it seems Richard Wade has been alerted, which has caused him to make some clumsy attempts at interfering with our investigation. We've also had to make a deal with Helen Naylor, which may cause us problems in the future. We'll have to see on that one."

Donovan's expression was thunderous. "The bastard. I could get him posted I suppose, but it might be easier to put him in the custody suite where I can keep an eye on him. I take it you don't want to look at disciplinary action at this stage?"

"I don't think we can as it would shine an unwelcome light on our own dealings. Having said that, we may be able to go public next week, then we'll see."

Donovan considered the plan for a moment before saying, "I take it I can tell him what I know? After all, I expect it's something he wouldn't like his wife to find out about as she surely will if he's disciplined. I'll tell him the reporter will not be taking any calls and should he try to contact her again then things will definitely be in the open."

Munro couldn't help laughing. "Sounds like a plan to me. Maybe we won't have to get Professional Standards involved at all. I'm happy to leave it to you to make his life, how shall we say, uncomfortable. Thank you. As soon as we're ready to go public with our information, I'll make sure you get word first."

Donovan got up. "I think I'm going to enjoy this."

Munro's parting remark was, "Brian, if we're right, an awful lot of people will not want to hear it and may try to suppress our findings, but we intend to do everything we can to stop that happening. You never heard this from me, but that reporter may be a useful asset, so please don't let Heath upset her."

Donovan merely nodded and left the office, intending to enjoy himself putting Nigel Heath firmly back in his box.

Once the inspector had left, Munro suggested to Clark and Devereux that they should spend the rest of the day going through the files looking for any more discrepancies, and that they should begin to prepare a report outlining the new information revealed as a result of their investigation. Obviously they could only go so far whilst they waited for the forensic evidence due the next day. They all agreed that evidence was crucial to finally confirming what they believed really happened.

Munro still found it hard to believe that the submission of the forensic samples to the laboratory had not yet come to the notice of the ACC. He supposed he ought to be grateful and decided he would ring Mark Pickering to confirm the results were still expected the following day.

During the subsequent phone call, he duly thanked Pickering who was able to confirm that, according to the analysts, the results would be there as promised. So, it was a fingers-crossed waiting game.

CHAPTER 29

F riday arrived.

At their 8 a.m. meeting Clark and Devereux confirmed they had found nothing new in their final trawl through the files. All three recognised that everything now depended on the laboratory results despite all their efforts so far. Whilst they had built a good circumstantial case, they knew their only real evidence was the statement from Frank Hodgson which, although good, was probably not enough. Eyewitnesses can always be discredited in some way, but forensic evidence was much more difficult to challenge.

They drank tea and made desultory conversation whilst awaiting the call from Pickering to tell them the results had arrived.

At 10.30 a.m. Pickering rang, telling Munro he had received the results by e-mail and asking where he should forward it to. Minutes later Munro's computer pinged to alert them that a new e-mail had arrived. He immediately opened it and printed three copies off, giving Clark and Devereux a copy each. All three officers studied the reports carefully, amazed how much information there was and how quickly it had been obtained.

It took them some time to go through the reports, each of them reading it twice. Finally, Munro spoke, "Well, there's clearly some interesting stuff here, especially the DNA profiles from the blood. What I propose is that we have a brainstorming session immediately, identifying relevant information and writing it up on the white board as we go. Is that okay with everyone?"

Clark and Devereux readily agreed, both keen to get going.

"You start, Bill. What have you spotted first?"

"As you know the fingerprints on the side of the car were a particular interest of mine. The lab has now confirmed that the only blood found on the rear offside wing of the Ford Mondeo belongs to Steve Brown. There was none of Wade's blood found. I was particularly pleased to see that the blood in which Steve's fingerprints were found was his own. I really don't think Wade pulled himself up on the side of that car, do you? Secondly, there was blood on the road next to the car which was also identified as Brown's and none belonging to Wade."

He wrote both observations on the white board.

Clark had her turn next. "As we know, Smithson was covered in blood right down his front which couldn't have been his because his injuries were so minor. It has been identified as belonging to Brown with no trace of any blood from Wade."

Munro prompted her, "So what's the significance of that, Amy?"

"Well Wade was slashed across his chest and stabbed in the shoulder, both wounds bled profusely as can be seen from his own clothing which was saturated in blood. He claimed to have laid on top of Smithson, holding him down, yet there is not a trace of his blood to be found. Smithson, however, claims it was Steve Brown who laid on top of him and that account is supported by the blood on him. While I remember, there is not a trace of Smithson's blood on Wade, which I suppose is not a surprise as Smithson bled so little. Yet Steve Brown had a smear of Smithson's blood on his forehead which supports very close contact."

She entered her observations on the whiteboard.

Munro said, "Anything else?"

Devereux replied, "Yes, Smithson had blood from both officers on his hands which is not surprising as he admitted stabbing them both. The knife also contained blood from both of them. Incidentally it was not possible to tell who he stabbed first because the blood was so intermingled."

Amy Clark continued, "There's some useful fibre transfer evidence as well. Both Wade and Brown were wearing uniform shirt and trousers and fibres matching them were found on Smithson's clothing, but it was not possible to tell which officer they came from. However, Steve Brown did have fibres transferred from Smithson's clothing on his own, along with some of his hair. Wade had no samples of either clothing or hair transferred to him. As you know, it is inconceivable that he could lay on top of someone else without some sort of fibre transfer taking place. Most damning of all is that fibres matching the stab vest were recovered from Smithson's clothing. Only Steve Brown was wearing a stab vest. Even if someone argues that fibres were transferred from another officer's vest to Smithson while he was being taken to George Street, what is absolutely clear is that Brown had close contact with Smithson and Wade did not. To my mind, it all supports Smithson's account, whilst nothing at all has come to light which supports Wade."

Munro said, "Was any of Wade's hair found on Smithson?"

Clark shook her head.

Munro said, "Anything else?"

Neither Clark nor Devereux responded.

Munro went on, "Well I think there may be one thing you've both missed. Amy, you mentioned that Steve Brown had a smear of blood on his forehead which DNA profiling has identified as belonging to Smithson. If you remember, his only injuries were a graze on the back of his head and a broken nose. The pathologist's report indicates that Steve had a slight bruise on his forehead and if you look at the PM photos you can see the blood and the bruise quite clearly. I think that proves beyond any doubt that Steve Brown butted Smithson in the face, breaking his nose, just as he told us. The nose was the only place Smithson bled from and even then only a very small amount. I don't see any other logical conclusion, do you?"

The other two officers agreed wholeheartedly and entered all their conclusions on the white board.

Amy Clark said, "In a way it's not really what we wanted but it looks to me, without any doubt at all, as if Smithson is telling the truth and Wade is lying. So, what do we do next?"

Munro said, "We all go home and try to have a restful weekend, because when we come back on Monday, we're going to be very busy. We have to collate all our evidence and prepare a coherent case that presents our conclusions in a logical and indisputable form. Then our problems will really begin. When we submit our findings, I'm sure it will cause great alarm in the corridors of power, maybe even extending to some of the politicians involved. Everyone concerned will have to make difficult decisions, including us, and the pressure could be intense. Make no mistake, some people will wish us in hell for what we have done and what we have discovered. In the meantime, everything goes in my safe."

Clark and Devereux left, leaving Munro to make two phone calls. The first was to Brian Donovan who he quietly informed of their conclusion that Steve Brown was the real hero of Grimston Lane and that they would do everything they could to clear his name. The second was to Mark Pickering who he thanked again for his assistance before confirming that the forensic analysis was extremely helpful. He also told him that in the next few days he would be presenting the information to ACC Bryant with the other evidence they had gathered, putting it in its true context. Munro added that he would appreciate it if Bryant did not see the forensic reports before then. Pickering fully understood the warning and assured Munro that no one would hear about it from him.

After locking all the paperwork in his safe, he went home.

Richard Wade spent most of the weekend viewing his life through the bottom of a vodka bottle, whilst Julie wondered if her hero really was the man she wanted to spend the rest of her life with. At least there was no need for any more visits from the police.

CHAPTER 30

Monday morning arrived with a cold, miserable drizzle and three grim-faced police officers facing each other across a paper-strewn conference table. Their conversation bringing home to them the enormity of what they were about to do and the realisation that lives and careers could be damaged, some beyond repair, including possibly their own. They would not have been normal if they did not ask themselves whether it was always desirable for the truth to come out. Would telling the truth really be worth the consequences which were sure to follow? Could not a deal be done, and the damage limited by ensuring only a small circle of people knew what the truth really was?

As their discussion continued, all three officers acknowledged that maintaining the secrets and lies they had uncovered would be much more difficult because of their own actions. Several people already knew part of their discoveries, Bryan Donovan, Mark Pickering and, worst of all, the reporter Helen Naylor. Whether they would be able to put it all together as the enquiry team had was debatable, but who knows? Added to that, there was nothing to stop Smithson and Marchant putting in their ten pennyworths. Even scoundrels may be believed by someone if their story is good enough.

After an hour of to-ing and fro-ing, Munro said, "My opinion is that we have no option but to carry on as we planned, letting events take their course and suffering the consequences. I firmly believe it's the right thing to do. Even though it will not bring Steve Brown back, it may right a great wrong."

Devereux responded, "I agree it's the right thing to do, Wade cannot be allowed to get away with this, and as we have already said, it will probably come out anyway thanks to us."

Clark merely said, "We should carry on. We can't put the Genie back in the bottle, can we?"

There lay the problem for them all. They had started full of moral indignation but were now unsure whether they were going to reveal the truth because it was the right thing to do or because it could no longer be kept secret. That would be something only they would know as individuals when they searched their consciences. Nevertheless, at this moment it was a great comfort to tell themselves that they were doing the right thing for the right reasons. At least they could be confident that nothing they did would help Smithson to get out of prison.

Munro smiled thinly. "Okay let's get this done."

Over the next two days they put together a file including all the evidence they had accumulated from interviews and statements, forensic reports, the pathologist's report, and numerous photographs. A copy of Munro's notes of his prison meeting with Smithson formed a major part of the evidence and was supported by Henry Marchant's statement. A very carefully prepared covering report detailed the discrepancies between Wade and Smithson's accounts of what had happened in Grimston Lane. Frank Hodgson's statement and the forensic evidence was used to dismantle Wade's story piece by piece, proving, they believed, that his whole story was a tissue of lies. This led to the inevitable conclusion that, as he had presented the same evidence in court, he must have committed perjury, and if found guilty of such an offence he could be liable to several years imprisonment.

A second part of the report detailed Steve Brown's history and career, concluding that his actions, as described by Wade, were so far out of character as to be scarcely believable. This section described how neither officer informed control of their intention to stop the car, along with Wade's lack of a stab vest, and PPE.

Wade's failure to wear his stab vest and carry his PPE were highlighted as being of particular importance in what happened in Grimston Lane. Firstly, had he been wearing a stab vest, his own injuries may have been prevented as both his wounds were in areas protested by the vest. Secondly, an aspect which had puzzled Munro's team was why on officer as experienced as Steve Brown had not drawn his baton or used his CS gas, which he would have had time to do if Wade's account was correct. The fact that he had not supported Smithson's account of events because in his version Brown had no chance to use either of them. The final point, again if Smithson was telling the truth, was that if Wade had been in possession of his PPE, he would have had ample time to draw his baton or use CS gas, hopefully disabling Smithson before Steve Brown received the second stab wound.

The inevitable conclusion, as they now believed they had proved Smithson's version to be true, was that Wade's negligence had left him unable to prevent Brown's death and had in all probability directly contributed to it.

Mention was made of the circumstances in which the then inspector came to be using the new radio on the day of the murder. The conclusion of this part of the report, although it could not be proved, was that Brown's life may also have been saved if Wade had been in possession of his own radio. Particular notice was drawn to the fact that no one knew who was using the radio and that the control room staff were unable to trace the caller's whereabouts when the call for assistance was first received. This resulted in a considerable delay in sending assistance and, crucially, medical help.

Once completed they realised, seeing it all put together on paper for the first time, what a compelling case they had and just how damning it was for Richard Wade. However, other less palatable conclusions must also be drawn. The investigation had been far from perfect and clearly chances to challenge Wade had been missed because of an acceptance that he had told the truth and had the injuries to support what he said. If he had been a civilian, would they have delved more deeply into his account of events? Probably. His lies had undoubtedly been more readily believed because he was a police officer and because of Smithson's refusal to answer any questions.

Clearly there had been interference from senior officers, inefficiency and weakness from the Crown Prosecution Service and an all-consuming desire for haste. It seemed inconceivable that there wouldn't be further casualties in the fallout from this investigation. Perhaps that would include Munro as well who, after all, was the senior investigating officer.

Devereux, after reading the file it in its collected form for the first time, could only say, "Wow, this is going to cause some trouble. So, what do we do now?"

Munro said, "I don't think I have any option other than to go direct to the chief constable. Ultimately it will be down to Mr Newman to decide how we progress with this whole matter."

DI Clark couldn't resist adding, "If he does."

Munro continued, "As we've already discussed, I really don't think this can be kept under wraps, do you? Anyway, when I do see the chief, I want you two with me to ensure he gets the full story. Okay?"

They both agreed, but for different reasons. Devereux had always thought Newman to be an office man, not a real bobby, so relished the chance to put him on the spot and witness firsthand how he reacted. Clark realised that it was potentially a defining moment in her short career and a not-to-be-missed chance to enhance her prospects.

Munro finished by saying, "Whatever the outcome, I want to thank you both for your hard work and support. It will not be forgotten. I'll call you as soon as I get something arranged. In the meantime, make sure we have everything we need in the file and then run another copy off for the chief."

Embarrassed, Clark and Devereux left the office.

Once they had left, Munro got straight on the phone to the chief constable's secretary asking for an urgent meeting with Mr Newman. When she enquired what the meeting was to be about, he politely declined to tell her, only saying it was extremely important and that he would need about two hours. After much tut-tutting she put him in for 2 p.m. on Friday afternoon, warning him that once the chief became aware of the meeting, he may demand more information.

When informed of the meeting, Charles Newman did indeed consider demanding to know what his superintendent wanted but decided not to, trusting Munro's assertion that it was a matter of some importance. He knew Munro as a conscientious, hard-working officer who he trusted not to waste his time, although it was unusual for a detective superintendent to come direct to him. He also considered asking ACC Jack Bryant if he knew what was going on, especially as he assumed it to be a crime-related matter. Once again, he decided to wait as, if truth be told, he wasn't overly fond of Bryant nor did he have much respect for his judgement. He'd find out soon enough, he thought.

It was a slow two days. Time spent by Amy Clark and Bill Devereux polishing their file of evidence, making sure they had dotted all the i's and crossed all the t's. John Munro, meanwhile, as well as doing his normal work, spent time considering just how he was going to present his findings to the chief constable in as convincing a way as possible. He knew his boss was not going to like what he heard and felt sure some of the inevitable anger would come his way both for the initial enquiry and the subsequent unauthorised enquiry.

Two o'clock on Friday eventually arrived, with Munro and his two colleagues waiting outside Charles Newman's office. When they were shown inside, the chief constable was clearly surprised to see Clark and Devereux but courteously invited them all to sit down before looking questioningly at Munro.

He introduced the other two officers, going on to say, "Sir, you may remember some time ago you spoke to me about the stabbing of Superintendent Wade and PC Brown, particularly concerned to know if their behaviour could be criticised in any way. At the time I pointed out some issues which you were happy to overlook. You also asked me to let you know if anything else came to light, which I took to mean anything which would reflect badly on them and this Force. I'm sorry to tell you that new information has come to light which, in my opinion, casts serious doubt on the conduct of Superintendent Wade both during and after the incident."

The chief constable found it hard to hide his surprise, particularly at Munro's tone, but said calmly, "Mr Munro, you obviously realise the seriousness of what you just said so you better tell me what it's all about, right from the beginning."

"Yes Sir. I have prepared a copy of our file for you to study later." Clark put it on the chief constable's desk as Munro continued. "Some weeks ago, at his request, I visited Karl Smithson in prison. Basically, he told us that he had decided it was time the truth about what happened when Steve Brown died came out. He went on to tell me that everything Richard Wade told us was completely untrue and that in actual fact Steve Brown was the true hero of the day. At first, I was sceptical but some of his story had the ring of authenticity, and I really couldn't see what he had to gain. I therefore decided to investigate his claims, using Inspector Clark and DS Devereux to assist me, resulting in the final report you now have."

Charles Newman looked thoughtful. "You must have very persuasive evidence to come to me like this. Who else knows about this?"

"Mr Bryant discovered I was carrying out enquiries, but I'm afraid I led him to believe it was to negate Smithson and his threats to approach the press. I also told him I was looking at training needs arising from the incident, which happens to be true."

"Who actually authorised this enquiry?"

"No one, Sir. It was my decision and my responsibility as I felt it was essential my investigation remained confidential."

"Why exactly would that be, Mr Munro?"

Munro couldn't help squirming in his seat. "I think my findings are going to be uncomfortable for a number of people, including myself, and I was concerned attempts may be made to prevent my enquiries."

Newman's expression was growing increasingly dark. "Have a care, Superintendent. I wonder if you have exceeded your authority in this matter. Are you telling me that you don't trust the senior officers in this Force, which, of course, includes me?"

"Sir, I am merely saying that it's possible some people may not have considered it worth the effort, but I did, having been the one to speak to Smithson face to face. He convinced me it should be looked at."

"We'll leave the matter of your conduct for another time. You better tell me what these findings are, please."

Munro was angry with himself. He had managed to antagonise the chief constable and so far he hadn't even told him what the new evidence was and quite how bad things now looked. He had a very grim foreboding that this was only going to get worse, but it was too late to turn back now. He glanced at Clark and Devereux, seeing the anxiety on their faces, which he could do nothing to alleviate at the moment, save for a surreptitious wink in an effort to show them he wasn't bothered.

Newman spoke again before Munro could begin, "On second thoughts, could you all wait outside for a few minutes please?"

Somewhat surprised, they filed out and waited in his secretary's office. Seconds later ACC Bryant bustled by, throwing the trio a surprised look as he went into the chief's office.

After a further five minutes they were called back inside, resuming their previous seats facing the chief constable who was now flanked by Bryant.

Newman spoke first, "I have asked Mr Bryant to join us as this is clearly a crime-related matter, and secondly because he already has some knowledge of what you were doing."

Bryant jumped in first, looking directly at Munro, "Yes, but from what the chief tells me I clearly didn't know everything, did I, Mr Munro?"

It was clear to Munro that Bryant was getting his defence in first and decided silence was the best policy, thinking, 'You'll get yours later, you weak bastard.' The tension in the room was palpable, with Clark and Devereux both doubting the wisdom of being there.

With no hint of a softening in his tone, Charles Newman said, "Alright, Mr Munro, you had better tell us your findings and I hope for your sake they are as persuasive as you seem to think."

Munro, ignoring the implied threat, decided he would not be cowed and tried again to outline his findings. "Leaving aside, for the moment, why I conducted this enquiry at all, I believe my actions have been fully justified by the new evidence my team has uncovered. As you know this investigation began because Karl Smithson told me a totally different story of events to that given by Richard Wade. In fact, he did describe Wade as having swapped roles with Steve Brown, claiming credit for everything he did and transferring his own failings to Brown. He said the truth was that Brown saved Wade's life, not the other way round."

The chief constable said, "Is Smithson using you to establish grounds for a re-trial by discrediting Superintendent Wade?"

"Obviously I considered that and took steps to prevent that happening. He wouldn't give me a statement, but I took notes and can give a statement clearly stating that he admitted the offences to me. We also have another statement from a prison inmate including the same admissions made to him. We should be fine."

Slightly reassured, Newman simply said, "Carry on."

"Sir, if you will allow me, I will just outline the points of difference in their accounts and how we have established what we believe to be the truth of the events of that day. In simple terms, it is the word of a police officer against the word of a convicted murder, and there lies one of our major problems."

Bryant said, "What do you mean by that?"

"We were all too ready to believe what Wade said just because he was a police officer and because he was badly wounded."

Bryant, ever the opportunist, and scenting a scapegoat, said, "So it was your enquiry that was at fault, Superintendent?"

Munro had had enough and retorted, "I didn't promote him and give a bloody medal, did I?"

There was a stunned silence in the room, during which Amy Clark placed a calming hand on Munro's arm. He took a deep breath and nodded his thanks as he calmed down, slightly ashamed he had let them get to him.

Newman tried to regain control. "Let's all remain calm. You had better present your evidence, Superintendent, so we can judge if your actions were justified."

Munro realised gloomily that the chief officers were still focussed on whether he should have mounted the enquiry at all, rather than what it revealed. He hoped he could convince them otherwise.

"I intend to begin with background information and supporting evidence before we get to the concrete facts, using Amy and Bill where they have more in-depth knowledge. We will concentrate mostly on the three main characters in this story."

Charles Newman just nodded.

"The first time I met Richard Wade was when I saw him in hospital with DI Clark to get an initial account of what had happened. At the time, several of the things he said caused me concern, which has only been made worse as more evidence has come to light. He was most anxious to know if Brown had said anything before he died and if there were any other witnesses to events. Once I said no, he knew that his was the only available first-hand account other than that of the defendant. Another thing that surprised me was, despite his protestation to the contrary, he managed to do an excellent job of destroying Steve Brown's reputation."

Bryant sneered, "That's not a lot, is it?"

Munro said calmly, "We'll see. Bill, over to you."

Devereux took up the story. "One of our concerns throughout was that the officers didn't call in prior to stopping Smithson's car, particularly as it was known a grey car was being sought even if they did not know why. Mr Wade claims he asked PC Brown to do it before he got out of the police vehicle, however, as the passenger in the vehicle we would normally expect him to make the call. He claimed he didn't because he hadn't got the registration number."

Once again Bryant chipped in, "Are we actually going anywhere with this?"

Newman was intrigued despite his own misgivings and said, "Let's just let them tell the story for now, shall we?"

Bryant looked put out at the implied rebuke but settled back.

Devereux continued, "I did background checks on Steve Brown

with his supervisors and colleagues, during which I was told repeatedly that he always notified control when he was about to stop a vehicle for a check. So much so that control room staff said jokingly that he was a pain in the bum. He apparently drummed it into colleagues, telling them it was for their safety and that one day it might save their lives."

Devereux left them all to think on that before he continued. "I was told that Brown was known for being the first to respond if there was trouble and would always back colleagues up, no matter what. That directly contradicts what Wade said about his behaviour."

Those present noted the fact that he no longer bothered to give Richard Wade any sort of honorific, clearly showing his disdain for the man.

Munro stepped in, "I will leave you to read the various statement in detail later. Right, Amy, your turn."

DI Clark cleared her throat nervously but when she started speaking her voice was strong and clear. "We reviewed the recorded interview with Linda Ross. Two things stood out. Whilst she was in the boot of the car she heard two snippets of speech, mostly because they were shouted. The first one was someone begging for their life, which fits entirely with Smithson saying that Wade begged him not to hurt him. I suggest it wasn't Steve Brown because Mr Wade's own evidence is that he never spoke. Secondly, the girl heard someone shout 'get my cuffs'. That must have been Steve Brown because Mr Wade didn't have any, suggesting Steve was still fighting, contrary once more to Mr Wade's account."

Bryant couldn't hold back from interjecting once more. "Bloody hell, you can't hang someone on the evidence of a 10-year-old girl locked in a car boot."

Munro responded, "As I said, this is all background and supporting evidence which made us doubt what we had been told, making us determined to establish the truth of what happened. You need to the view the evidence as a whole as we have. Go on, Amy."

"Another thing Mr Wade claims is that he looked into the grey car whilst it was alongside them at the traffic lights and that he became suspicious of the driver. He said it was instinct. He went on to say it was him that got out of the police car to check Smithson out, leaving Steve Brown in the car who, he claims, was not interested. This is contradicted by Smithson who says Mr Wade never looked at him at all and that it was Steve Brown who was looking at him and that it was him who approached the car."

It was Newman's turn to interrupt, "Even I've got to ask if that is relevant, and why should we believe Smithson's unsupported story?"

Amy Clark replied, "I think everything will become clear soon. To continue, Smithson had only two injuries as a result of the fight with the officers, a broken nose and grazing to the back of his head. Everyone is agreed that his head was grazed when it was banged on the floor, although it is in dispute who was responsible. Mr Wade claims to have been the only one fighting Smithson yet he is unable to explain how he sustained the broken nose. Smithson is absolutely clear that Steve Brown head butted him."

As Clark finished, Munro stepped straight in to forestall any further questions. "One thing I found very unsettling was an addition Superintendent Wade made to his original account of events. Simply put, he tried to make a virtue of the fact that he was not wearing a stab vest whilst describing his own bravery and attempts to save Steve Brown. I've got to say it left something of a sour taste in my mouth. You may remember, Sir, I did point out that Richard Wade was receiving a bravery medal pretty much on his own account."

He left that hanging in the air, whilst Newman shifted in his chair with a taught expression on his face.

Munro continued, "Before we go on, I believe it is crucial to remind you that this is the evidence Superintendent Wade gave in court on oath."

Bryant was becoming more and more angry and could contain himself no longer. "Superintendent, you haven't told us anything that establishes, as you claim, that Richard Wade lied. Have you actually got any real proof?"

All Munro could think was that his time was coming, and he was going to enjoy putting Bryant in his place.

Instead, he kept his cool and said, "I believe we do. Bill, go ahead."

Devereux said, "One of the things Wade claimed was that after he had been wounded, he managed to pull himself back to his feet by using the rear offside wing of the grey car as support. Obviously, we would have expected there would have been some of his fingerprints on the car wing. There were none. The only thing we did find were six prints belonging to Steve Brown, two of which were in his own blood. They can't have both been there, suggesting that Wade has told us yet another lie."

Neither of the senior officers had anything to say.

Devereux continued, "As part of any review of an enquiry, it is normal practice to re-interview all the witnesses, but in this case we only had the van driver Frank Hodgson. His evidence concerned the aftermath of the murder when he came across the scene on pulling into the lay-by. Nevertheless, we went to see him. After speaking to him for some time we discovered that he drove into the lay-by to ask for directions from the police officers as he was lost. Under further questioning he revealed that he knew the officers were there because he had driven past them a few minutes earlier, which had not come out when his original statement was taken. We can only assume the officer who took it concentrated on what Mr Hodgson saw when he first arrived back at the scene. Anyway, when he passed the first time, he saw one officer on foot, walking from the police car towards the grey car. He was able to give a reasonable description, saying that he had dark hair and was wearing a stab vest. You may remember Wade has fair hair and was not wearing a stab vest. It was clearly Steve Brown. Mr Hodgson could see another officer still in the police vehicle, which we assume to be Wade. This is evidence from an independent eyewitness and proves Wade did not approach the car first and in my book that makes him a liar."

Newman said, "Interesting, but still only one witness, isn't it?"

Munro said acidly, "Actually it's two if you include Smithson."

Amy Clark took her turn at a nod from Munro. "Sirs, after viewing the custody suite video, we realised that Smithson was absolutely covered in blood, which obviously wasn't his own, so it must have come from one or both of the officers. The main point of dispute in the evidence is exactly who took Smithson on and restrained him, before handcuffing him to the rear of the car. We reasoned that analysis of blood and fibre samples may help, including the blood found at the scene. It came as something of a surprise to find that none of the forensic samples had been sent for analysis at the laboratory. It left us somewhat in the lurch."

Newman asked angrily, "Mr Munro, would you kindly explain exactly why those samples were not analysed? These were offences of the most serious nature, so you better have a good explanation."

Munro smiled grimly, "Sir, I think perhaps Mr Bryant may be able to help us."

Bryant, who had seen exactly where this was going, was totally nonplussed, managing to say, "Perhaps it may be better to discuss this privately, Sir."

Newman would have none of it and said, "This is taking forever, just spit it out."

Looking daggers at Munro and his team, Bryant said quietly, "The number of samples Superintendent Munro wanted to send for analysis would have proved hugely expensive. I discussed the matter with the Crown Prosecution Service who informed me that there was more than enough evidence for a successful prosecution of Smithson, without the need for all the forensic evidence. My decision was that there was no need to waste money on something we didn't need. I've got to say that if a proper investigation had been done in the first place, none of this need have arisen."

Newman refrained from comment, so Munro continued, "Fortunately we managed to retrieve all the samples and send them for analysis and have now got the results."

Bryant never seemed to learn. "Why didn't you speak to me before doing that?"

"Sir, I believe you would have refused permission to have the samples analysed, so I thought it better not to ask. I believed the analysis was essential to the case, and so it has proved. Off you go, Amy."

Clark said, "Very briefly, DNA analysis of blood samples established the following: The blood on the side of the car was Steve Brown's and there was none from Mr Wade. The blood on the ground at the side of the car was all Steve Brown's, none of Mr Wade's. You may remember that Smithson claimed it was Brown who laid on top of him, holding him down, whilst Mr Wade claimed it was him. Whoever did it would have left significant amounts of blood on Smithson as they were both bleeding heavily. All the blood found on Smithson belonged to Steve Brown and there was none of Mr Wade's at all. As you know, it is almost impossible for two people to be in close physical contact, such as laying on top of them, without transferring fibres and hair between them. Fibres transferred from Smithson's clothing and some of his hair was found on Steve Brown's clothing. No similar samples were found on Mr Wade's clothing. Most damning of all is that fibres matching those from a stab vest were recovered from Smithson's clothing. Only Steve Brown was wearing a stab vest.

Nothing was found that had been transferred from Mr Wade to Smithson. The forensic evidence makes it absolutely clear that Brown had close contact with Smithson and Mr Wade did not. To my mind, it all fully supports Smithson's account, whilst nothing at all has come to light which supports Mr Wade."

Bryant looked aghast whilst Newman remained impassive before saying, "Anything else?"

Munro said, "A couple of points, Sir. The post-mortem showed a bruise on Steve Brown's forehead and a slight smear of blood, which puzzled us for a while. DNA analysis showed the blood belonged to Smithson. As Smithson only bled from his nose, the only logical conclusion is that Brown head butted Smithson, causing the broken nose, just as Smithson said. Secondly, Richard Wade contacted me to suggest important people would be unhappy about my enquiries and went so far to make what I took to be a veiled threat. I think it revealed his concern that the truth may come out."

Newman said, "Thank you, Superintendent. So, tell me, what are your conclusions at the end of all this?"

"Sir, I believe Smithson's account to be largely true and that Richard Wade has lied pretty much from beginning to end. He has lied to such an extent that he has managed to portray himself as a hero whilst suggesting a very brave man acted in a cowardly manner. Richard Wade's stupid and unprofessional behaviour may have directly contributed to the death of Steve Brown. By taking a radio that could not be traced, he delayed the arrival of assistance from other officers and medical services. If help had got there sooner, Steve Brown may have had a much better chance of surviving his injuries. If Wade had been wearing a stab vest, his own injuries may have been prevented or at least minimised and carrying his PPE would have meant that he could have been much more effective in dealing with Smithson. Unable to use a baton or CS gas, we believe he did nothing. My final conclusion is that his conduct should be investigated by the Professional Standards Branch and, subject to CPS approval, he should be charged with criminal offences including perjury and possibly malfeasance in public office."

Newman nodded and said, "Once again, thank you, Superintendent, and to you as well, Inspector Clark, Sergeant Devereux. Please leave both copies of the file with me and I will study them fully over the weekend. If you will all return here at 10 a.m. on Monday morning, I will let you know what I propose to do. In the meantime, please do not discuss this with anyone else. Too many people may know about it already."

As they got up to leave, Munro couldn't help thinking that he needed to find a safer place for the third copy of the file he had in his safe.

Once they had left, Newman turned his gaze to ACC Jack Bryant, who just looked away.

"Okay Jack, anything you'd like to say?"

"Sir I was advised by the CPS that we could manage without all the forensic evidence, and we did, didn't we? If Munro and his crew hadn't stuck their noses in there would have been no problem at all."

"Jack, I think we need to get things in perspective. If you hadn't tried to save a few pounds off your budget all the samples would have been examined properly and I'm sure we would have got the true story before we got to court."

"Sir, this is not fair. You put me under pressure to save money and when I do you want to blame me."

"Jack, you're supposed to exercise judgement in these matters. Do you really think saving money on a police officer's murder and the kidnapping of a ten-year-old girl is an acceptable way to save money? If you do, it leads to questions about your fitness for high command."

Bryant, seething with impotence, managed to hold his tongue just for once.

Newman continued, "Having said all that, we have to decide where we go next. This will embarrass a lot of people, including the Police and Crime Commissioner, the Home Secretary, the Prime Minister, a high court judge and, God help us all, Buckingham Palace. That's not to mention the press who have been made to look stupid for the way they praised Wade."

"So, you're convinced by Munro's evidence then, Sir?"

"Jack, please don't be stupid. Have you ever seen a more watertight case?"

"Probably not."

Newman thought for a minute or two and then said, "Okay, we may have to blame your attempt to save money on government cuts. It's a bit thin but I want you to put a case together so we can mount a plausible defence. You'll need to focus on demands from the government and PCC over, say, the last two years, identifying areas where we have made significant cuts. Pay special attention to crimes where we have cut forensic services and the cost benefits to doing so. We need to be able to put up a fight, even if it's a bit weak. I want something ready for Monday morning. Thinking about it, we may be able to drag the CPS into this as a bit of a smokescreen."

Then Bryant did something really stupid: "Sorry Sir, I'm taking my wife away for the weekend."

Newman spoke very quietly, "I think we need to be clear here, very clear. Apart from Wade, someone else's head will roll for this monumental cock-up, and at the moment you are the favourite. So make your mind up which is most important, a dirty weekend or your career."

A very chastened Bryant left hastily whilst the chief constable got ready for some very difficult phone-calls. Before he started though, he summoned Superintendent Richard Wade to his office.

Minutes later, Wade entered the chief constable's office in his usual confident manner, prepared for a pat on the back for the way his department was now operating. He immediately sensed something was not quite right when Mr Newman failed to offer him a seat.

"Mr Wade I understand you have been having some domestic difficulties which I believe are directly related to the trauma you suffered when you were attacked by Karl Smithson. I know you have suffered additional stress as a result of the task I gave you implementing budget cuts and the rationalisation of the work force. I have spoken to the police surgeon and he is happy to authorise you to take the next six months off as sick leave."

Wade stared at the chief constable, totally bemused by what he had just heard, before the penny dropped. "Sir, is this to do with Munro's enquiry? Whatever he has said about me is a lie, I've done nothing wrong. The only thing I did was to risk my life for others."

"Mr Wade, you are correct there is an enquiry ongoing which has cast doubt on some of your actions and the claims you subsequently made. Without making any judgements at this time, it would be wise if you were at home until the matter is finalised."

"Sir, this is not fair. I deserve a chance to answer any allegations."

"I'm sure you will get that opportunity, Mr Wade. However, you either accept the offer of sick leave starting immediately or you will leave me no option but to suspend you. That is all."

Wade was speechless. He left the office in a daze, almost in tears, wondering what he should tell Julie and if he should make that approach to John Ross for a new job. He couldn't help wondering how it had all come to this. What was he going to do? He still didn't realise just how much trouble he could be in.

CHAPTER 31

A nother Monday morning and another 8 a.m. get-together in Munro's office. There was no further information and all three of them were hanging about, waiting for their 10 a.m. meeting with the chief constable.

That's not to say they hadn't been busy over the weekend. John Munro had lodged his copy of the new evidence file with his solicitor, in a sealed envelope, hoping there would be no need to make use of it. Amy Clark had been in contact with the reporter Helen Naylor, mostly to reassure her that she hadn't been forgotten and to confirm that their deal still stood. Bill Devereux had been for a drink with Brian Donovan and had told him as much as he could, without revealing all the evidence, assuring him that they were trying hard to get justice for Steve Brown.

Richard Wade had had a very difficult weekend. Monday morning found him unwashed, unshaven, hung-over, and alone. Julie had gone, with a bruise on her face and sick to death of his self-pity, drinking, and violent outbursts. The only future that he could see was his whole life and everything he had worked so hard for, not to mention lied and cheated for, disappearing down the toilet. Consumed by his own problems, he could only question why John Munro had done this to him, it was so unfair. Unbelievably he really was convinced that he was a genuine hero.

Jack Bryant had spent the weekend in his office working with a number of disgruntled staff to put a case together explaining how government cuts were hampering crime investigation. He remembered his wife's angry words as she left for the weekend without him, shouting that she may stay longer than originally planned.

A serious Charles Newman was tired and depressed, still to make a decision on how to progress matters. He had spoken to the PCC, who if truth be told was the least of his worries, and had been to London for an extremely uncomfortable personal meeting with the Home Secretary Francis Williams. The meeting had surprised Newman as he only expected to deal with Home Office officials. He realised just how difficult things could be as Williams made it abundantly clear that if this went wrong then Newman and his Force would shoulder the blame. The professional politicians, who had been eager to bask in the reflected glory, were now busy distancing themselves from any repercussions. It was made known to him that the Prime Minister was unhappy, but at least he hadn't demanded to see him. The Home Secretary explained to the chief constable that whilst the good publicity generated by Wade's perceived actions had been good for them all, things can soon change. They had managed to show that despite cuts the police were still effective and staffed by heroes, but now they could adopt the high ground, claiming the government believed it was essential to weed out bad apples like Wade. In other words, claim all the glory whilst leaving Charles Newman to manage the best way he could.

At 10 o'clock on the dot Munro and his staff were shown into the chief constable's office to find him once again accompanied by ACC Bryant, but also the Force solicitor Roger Harris. Newman immediately informed them of his consultations with government officials in London and the extreme difficulties the new enquiry had created. He also explained that the matter of Richard Wade was temporarily dealt with in that he was now on sick leave and would remain so for the foreseeable future.

He then said, "Undoubtedly your actions have placed us in what I can only describe as a very difficult position and, to be honest, I have yet to reach a decision on the best way forward. I am shortly meeting with the chief crown prosecutor and Mr Harris to fully understand the legal position. I'm sorry to ask but could you all wait until I send for you, perhaps in the canteen? It shouldn't take long."

In the event, it was almost two hours before they were summoned back to the office to find the chief constable still accompanied by Jack Bryant.

Newman was courtesy itself, offering them seats and refreshments before he began, which only triggered alarm bells in Munro's mind.

The chief constable said, "Once again I have to caution you that everything said in this room is completely confidential and must under no circumstances be disclosed to anyone else. Am I clear?"

By now the alarm bells in Munro's head sounded like klaxons and he was convinced that he wasn't going to like what the chief was about to say. Nevertheless, along with Clark and Devereux, he confirmed that he got the message.

Newman cleared his throat, possibly a little nervously, and said, "As you are already aware, I have consulted widely before making any decisions. I can tell you there is great disquiet in the Home Office at the possible ramifications of your revelations and the adverse publicity that would be generated. The effect on the Force could also be damaging with many of our critics ready to suggest that we are not up to the job. As you know, I have spoken to the chief crown prosecutor who vehemently denies that any of his staff advised us not to have the forensic exhibits analysed. However, he went on to say that, having reviewed all the evidence, his conclusion was that without a shadow of a doubt the right man was in prison. Despite any defects there may be in the original evidence, his advice is that there can be no suggestion of police malpractice as a whole and that there has been no miscarriage of justice. He concluded that Richard Wade may well have committed criminal offences, but that there was little to gain from a prosecution and certainly no public interest benefit in doing so."

Newman paused for a drink of water before continuing. "Mr Harris agrees with this advice, stating that this type of publicity can only damage the Force and individual officers with no tangible benefits. As you know, Richard Wade is on sick leave and will be 'encouraged' to retire on medical grounds. I could not countenance him remaining as an officer in my Force. How does that sound to you?"

Almost speechless, the best Munro could manage was, "And what about Steve Brown?"

"Ah, yes. It may be possible to say that as a direct result of your enquiries we are able to disclose that Steve Brown's performance was much better than at first thought. That may go some way to redressing the wrong done to him."

Munro responded carefully, "So Wade will be allowed to retire on a superintendent's pension with his reputation untarnished whilst Steve Brown, who we have proved died a true hero, still has a cloud hanging over his memory. I've got to say that is no way to treat a man who only showed true courage and devotion to duty, with the added insult that the man who contributed to his death continues to be seen as a hero."

Newman nodded gravely. "John, I can assure you we have considered these matters very carefully, but the bottom line is that PC Brown is dead, and nothing will change that, especially not by inflicting wounds on the Force you rightly say he served so well."

"Sir, if this does come out, you will lose the trust of your own officers."

"Well, we'd better make sure it doesn't come then, hadn't we?"

Munro carried on, "So can I now take it that everyone, including the CPS, agrees the new evidence we have collected does provide the true version of what happened?"

Newman said somewhat coldly, "Yes, you have done an excellent job. It is a pity you weren't as conscientious the first time round."

Munro ignored the barb. "That may well be true, Sir, but it is obvious that others bear some responsibility and may well have a vested interest in this case going away quietly. I have got to say that, in light of this clear and irrefutable evidence, I believe that we will be totally wrong if we do not immediately go public and deal with Wade properly."

Now Newman was becoming angry. "Thank you, Superintendent, but that is enough. A decision has been made in the best interests of this Force and the matter is closed."

Munro would not be silenced, becoming angry as well. "Sir, I feel this to be a hasty and ill-thought-out decision, taken with only short-term objectives in mind and to protect the reputations of all involved. If this should come out the press will have a field day, attacking everyone from Wade through to the Prime Minister. I beg you, Sir, in the best interests of this Force, do not be part of a cover-up."

Newman spoke with icy calm. "Once again, Superintendent, thank you for your comments. Your advice as always is welcome, but on this occasion you clearly do not understand the full ramifications of adopting the course of action you suggest. The decision is made, and I personally resent your suggestion that I am involved in a cover-up."

Munro said, "May I ask what Mr Bryant's opinion is on this?"

Newman nodded to Bryant who, clearly embarrassed, said, "I fully support the chief constable's decision which I believe to be the best one for the Force."

Munro had gone too far now to stop. "No doubt it is best for you as well?"

Newman stepped in. "Mr Munro, you are becoming extremely rude, and your conduct is bordering on insubordination. Please desist immediately."

"Sir, we are all conspiring to conceal the truth and to protect a liar. We are failing in our duty if we carry on with this lie and, by any standards, we are morally deficient if we continue to put self-interest above the truth. It is totally wrong."

Newman did not bother to answer, perhaps because he had no answer. He resorted to shaking his head whilst Bryant merely looked away.

Superintendent Munro made his final attempt, "Sir, I urge you to reconsider this decision before it is too late. Already too many people know something of what is happening, and I am sure it is only a matter of time before the whole story becomes public knowledge. If we release the information officially, we have a much better chance of controlling it. If you truly care about this Force, you will know it is the right thing to do."

Newman finally lost his temper, shouting at Munro, "Superintendent you have gone too far. I don't want to hear any more, my decision is final. Let that be an end to it."

Clark was desperate to help her boss and said, "What if Smithson should appeal?"

Newman visibly took hold of himself, smiled, and said, "Thank you for reminding me, Inspector. I am advised he has few grounds to justify an appeal and if he does it will be fought at the highest level. I don't believe we need to worry about that. Well, if there is nothing else, I want to thank you for your hard work and dedication. That's all."

Having been so peremptorily dismissed, all three left the office in stunned silence.

Once outside, Munro looked at the others and said, "Let's go to the pub."

So the ripples created by the incident in Grimston Lane continued to spread as more people joined Helen Naylor in sacrificing their principles on the altar of career and ambition. The chief constable would doubtless say his actions were for the benefit of his Force, but only he knew his true thoughts. Jack Bryant would probably say the same, but he knew he had made a serious error of judgement which needed to be kept quiet. The Police and Crime Commissioner, the Home Secretary, and the Prime Minister, being professional politicians, it is unlikely that anyone could establish their true thoughts and motives. However, one thing we can all be sure of is that, should the truth come out, none of them would want any of the blame or bad publicity attaching itself to them.

It seemed not to bother any of them that a good man had died doing the job they demanded of him, or that another had been richly rewarded for failing so risibly to do the same job, thereby contributing to the death of a fellow officer.

There is an expression used to describe such people in the police service. They are called Teflon men, because nothing sticks to them.

CHAPTER 32

Munro, Clark, and Devereux stared gloomily into their drinks in a nearby pub, each wrapped in their own dark thoughts. It was left to Devereux to voice his thoughts first.

"Surely that can't be it, can it? All this work for nothing."

Clark answered first. "I don't know what else we can do. The boss couldn't have said anything more than he did."

"Yes, I know, but there must be something. Surely, we can't let them get away with this, boss."

Munro looked at them both before speaking very carefully. "As I see it, we have only the three options now. The first is to do nothing and to let Wade get away with what he has done whilst the higher ups carry on with their cover-up."

He quickly held his hand up as both Clark and Devereux tried to speak at the same time. It was clear from their expressions that that idea did not appeal to them at all.

He carried on quietly, mindful that they were discussing highly sensitive information in a very public place. "I can only see two other ways for us to move forward, and I've got to say that both options could be very dangerous for us all. The simplest and most direct way is for me to go to Richard Wade's house and arrest him for perjury. The second is to use Helen Naylor to get the story out to the wider world. I'm sure you can see that if I arrest Wade, it's likely that I'll be overruled fairly quickly and he'll be released without charge. It's clear the CPS and the senior officers have too much to lose and don't want to know. The drawbacks to getting the press involved are that

204

we could end up facing disciplinary action and possibly serious consequences. Any thoughts?"

Devereux came straight back. "I like the idea of arresting the bastard, it's what I understand and what he deserves, but I think you're right, boss, we'll get nowhere fast. On the other hand, if the press start asking questions, it's difficult to see how the chief and Bryant would be able to avoid the truth coming out. It just goes against the grain to cosy up to a reporter."

Munro said, "So, Amy, what do you think?"

"The first thing that occurs to me is that everyone from the politicians to the CPS and the chief are convinced by the case we've put together. They all know now that Wade is a liar and a coward. However, they are not concerned about seeing justice done, only how it will look for all of them if the truth should come out. I think you're both right that arresting Wade would be nice, but we'll get nowhere with it. I'm pretty sure we can trust Helen Naylor, but our problem is finding a way to involve her that doesn't come back on us."

Munro looked at her carefully. "I agree with you, Amy, the press is our best option. The idea of publicity will frighten them all to death, making sure they all go into full damage limitation mode, wanting to get their version out first. The public spotlight does have a way of making the truth come out eventually. However, we need to be aware that when they start putting out statements blaming each other, we'll come in for some of the criticism. They'll need scapegoats and, as we did the original investigation, it doesn't take a genius to see who the most likely targets will be. Do we all agree that we use the press?"

The other two nodded, Clark immediately and Devereux after a few seconds consideration.

Munro continued, "Okay, I think we are obliged to use Helen Naylor as she already knows something is going on, and I suppose we did promise her. Amy, I've got two questions though before we contact her. Firstly, being freelance, does she have the contacts to get the story out? Secondly, why do you think we can trust her? She dumped Sergeant Heath pretty quickly after all."

Amy Clark blushed as she answered. "I've become quite friendly with Helen, that's why I think I can trust her. To answer your other question, she tells me that she has sounded out a national daily, in the broadest of terms of course, and they are very interested. I understand she only told them it was a case of police corruption and a high-level cover up."

Devereux came in. "I'm sorry, Amy, but just because you've become friendly doesn't mean you can trust her. Hell, she's a reporter, lying comes naturally to them. This is risky for all of us, and we've all got a lot to lose."

"I understand what you're saying, Bill, and your concerns. Look, my private life is my own, but I think I can tell you that our relationship may more truthfully be called close, rather than friendly. I'm sure you get my meaning."

Munro couldn't help laughing as he saw Devereux's initial confusion, followed by the dawning realisation of what exactly Clark was saying and then the resulting embarrassment.

John Munro looked at Clark and said, "Look, Amy, I don't want to labour the point, but there is a lot riding on this for all of us and, if I'm honest, it does go against the grain to talk to a reporter, any reporter. Are you sure you can trust her? As we already know, Heath had a close relationship with her as well."

Clark nodded. "I understand, but don't forget Heath did the dirty on her and she felt she didn't owe him anything. I hope our relationship is a little different. Anyway, to prove how confident I am, I'm offering to be the one who deals with her, leaving you two right out of it."

Munro smiled as he said, "I appreciate the offer, but myself and

Bill are in this up to our necks. I agree that because of your relationship you should be the one to speak to Helen, but we have to develop a plan that involves more than simply telling her the story as we know it. That way we all have a chance to come out of this with our jobs."

To everyone's surprise, Devereux spoke. "Amy, sorry if I asked too many questions, but if this relationship is important to you, then please don't do anything that may jeopardise it."

"Thank you, Bill, I appreciate that. However, if you think about it, telling Helen will not only help to expose the lies and establishment cover up but it has the added bonus of giving a career boost to someone I really care for."

Munro said, "Okay, we need to sort how we're going to do this. Just giving Helen our file will only help her to a point as she can't really disclose the details, but it also runs the risk of us being investigated by Professional Standards. Any suggestions?"

Amy said, "Well clearly there's no way as a reporter that she'll get into the prison for an official interview with Smithson. Could she masquerade as one of his relatives?"

"It's doubtful, and she runs the risk of getting herself into serious trouble if it goes wrong."

Devereux said, "I've got an idea, but it's a bit dodgy." He went on to outline his plan which was far from perfect but was probably the best they could manage. For the next hour they studied his proposal in detail, considering all the pros and cons, before agreeing that whilst it was risky it was the best they had.

They left the pub a short time later, returning to their day jobs with plenty to think about. It was Clark's job to put their plan into operation which she began by calling Helen Naylor to arrange a meeting for later that evening.

When they met at Amy's apartment, the two women exchanged

kisses before settling down with a bottle of wine. Clark told Naylor that their enquiry had been blocked and to all intents and purposes it was over. However, she went on to tell her of the reluctance of the investigating team to let things lie and their decision to let Helen Naylor help them to get things into the public domain. The reporter was also told that it wasn't possible to simply give her the information or to show her their file, instead they had to put a barrier between them as protection in case of a future investigation by the Professional Standards Branch. Nevertheless, they could and would steer her in the right direction. The detective inspector outlined Devereux's plan in detail, covering the proposals one by one, but not being specific about what information Naylor may discover. When she had heard it all, Naylor agreed to her part without hesitation, but did express some concerns as to whether it would work and especially if it would cause Amy any problems. After she had been suitably reassured, Helen settled down with Amy to decide how they would put the plans in motion.

Helen Naylor was beyond excited. She didn't yet know the details of what would be revealed to her if the scheme worked but did know that the findings of the enquiry had been blocked and that the Police Press Office would not speak to her. Richard Wade had refused her requests for an interview, and she had recently learned he was on sick leave. Something was going on, she could smell a big story, perhaps it would be her ticket to Fleet Street.

The next day, as instructed, Helen Naylor submitted an application to obtain a copy of the Smithson trial transcript, whilst Amy Clark made an application to see Smithson in prison. Devereux's plan was in motion.

CHAPTER 33

Two days later Amy Clark faced Smithson across a wooden table in a stark and featureless prison interview room. They were alone.

Clark, who had already made sure that the meeting was not being recorded, immediately got down to business. "We have carried out a new enquiry into what happened the day you murdered PC Steve Brown and wounded Richard Wade. Just as you wanted, we have established what we believe to be the truth which, I have got to say, corroborates almost exactly what you told Superintendent Munro."

Smithson could not contain his emotions. Smiling broadly, he said, "So what happens to that lying dog Wade? I hope he gets his comeuppance."

"Well, not exactly, unless you count probably losing his job."

"That's all? He should be going to prison. There must be more you can do than that."

She looked at Smithson thoughtfully, as if weighing her words carefully, although she already knew what she was about to say. "Maybe there is, but we need more help from you if you are willing to give it."

A clearly frustrated Smithson replied, "What else can I do? I've already told you what happened. Surely that's enough."

It was time to play her ace. "Look, Karl, the simple truth is that we now believe you that Wade lied. We have presented the evidence to those in charge and all they want to do is cover their own backs, they intend to bury this and, as serving police officers, there is nothing we can do. We do think there is something you can do."

"Tell me, whatever it is I'll do it."

In what seemed like a complete change of direction, Inspector Clark said, "Tell me, Karl, are you able to smuggle letters out of here?"

"I'm not telling you about that. If that's all you want to know you can get lost."

Clark laughed as she said, "No, no you misunderstand me, I want you to send a letter out."

She went on to explain why she wanted Smithson to write a letter, what he should put in it and who to send it to, before giving him the recipient's address. However, she made certain he understood that he could not send the letter until he had been visited by Superintendent Munro who would tell him officially that the enquiry had been completed and that no further action would be taken. It would then appear that his letter had been sent as a reaction to that news. He readily agreed, telling her the letter would go out within days of Munro's visit, laughing out loud as he did so.

Clark spent the next hour interviewing Smithson, preparing to use his story as part of her criminology degree dissertation on police murderers, which was the reason she had given the prison authorities as her cover for seeing him. It meant she hadn't lied, plus it was always good to kill two birds with one stone.

Three days after Clark's visit, Munro faced Smithson across the same table in the same prison interview room and passed on the message that the murderer had been expecting. Although he already knew the answer, Smithson asked Munro to explain why no action was to be taken as a result of the new enquiry. Happy to oblige, the officer explained that there was a fear the revelations may generate sufficient concern in legal circles to allow Smithson a re-trial. Secondly, he was forced to admit that the main reason was to prevent criticism of any of the people involved, including members of the government and senior police officers.

Smithson nodded and began shouting at Munro that it was a 'stitch-up' and that they were all 'lying bastards'. He made no physical threat to Munro but made so much noise that the prison officers waiting outside entered the room and removed the apparently hysterical prisoner from the room.

Mission accomplished, thought the detective superintendent as he left the prison. However, he couldn't get rid of the feeling that his contact with Smithson had somehow contaminated him and that he needed a good wash. As a police officer of many years, he was used to dealing with criminals and, on occasion, reaching uncomfortable accommodations with them. However, nothing could ever prepare him for speaking to a police killer in friendly tones and being forced to form an alliance with him. It might be necessary, but it didn't make him feel good about doing it, or about himself. Did the end really justify the means, he wondered?

CHAPTER 34

For the next ten days all those involved in the Devereux plan carried on with their normal jobs, following their usual routines and, most importantly of all, keeping their heads down. They were all acutely aware that in that time Charles Newman had made no announcements about Wade or the restoration of Steve Brown's good name. Had he forgotten or simply hoped it had gone away?

In those long, uneventful days before the next stage of the plan swung into action, Munro had seen both Newman and Bryant more than once and had been greeted cordially. They both looked much more relaxed, clearly believing the danger had passed.

On the tenth day Helen Naylor turned up at Amy Clark's apartment with excitement written all over her face. Amy had hardly closed the door before the reporter, brandishing several pieces of paper, blurted out, "I've got a letter from Smithson."

Clark said, "How was it delivered?"

"By hand to the offices of the Sentinel, marked confidential and for my attention only."

Clark breathed a sigh of relief. The letter had been delivered to the local evening paper where Naylor did freelance work, just as agreed with Smithson. She had to admit she had been beginning to doubt he could do it, despite his confident claims that it would be no problem.

Clark said, "Have you read it yet?"

Helen laughed, seemingly even more excited. "Oh, yes indeed. It's dynamite, as far as I can remember it contradicts everything Richard

Wade said in court, and he makes it clear that if not for Steve Brown he would have got away that day. He describes Wade, and I quote, as 'a yellow-livered coward'. He even says he was begging for mercy, on his knees for God's sake! Smithson says he wants to get his own back on Wade, as if slashing him with a knife wasn't enough. He seems outraged that Wade lied from start to finish and, as he puts it, has been rewarded for doing so."

Amy said, "Have you got the trial transcript yet?"

Helen shook her head. "Not yet, but I've got enough for a cracking story already."

Amy came back immediately, "Helen you're right, I'm sure you could write a good story with the information you've got already, but it will be even better when you get the rest of the information. All you have at the moment is the word of a convicted murderer which won't prove anything, and senior officers will just bat it off. If we stick to the plan, you'll be able to establish Police and Crown Prosecution Service incompetence as a minimum and almost certainly a cover up. You won't get near to hurting the politicians with what you've got so far. Please be patient, I promise it will be worth it."

Looking a little deflated Naylor replied, "Okay, okay I'll wait, it's just so tempting, and I don't want anyone else to beat me to it."

"Helen, you know no one else is looking at this and they wouldn't have your inside track anyway. It will be a bigger story than the one you've got now, believe me."

Naylor nodded her agreement and Clark continued, "Once you get the trial transcript, you'll be able to compare Wade and Smithson's accounts directly. There's evidence from Linda Ross as well to look at and perhaps another civilian witness you might want to visit. Don't forget, if you look closely, you should also spot some omissions in the evidence that need explaining. With a little work you will have a really major story instead of just an interesting one."

The following day Clark was able to inform Munro and Devereux that Smithson had kept his end of the bargain and the plan was fully in motion. For his part Munro was able to tell the other two that it appeared Newman and Bryant were quite relaxed as if they believed all their cares were behind them. Devereux's only comment was that they wouldn't think so soon.

It was to be another full week before Naylor joined Clark in her apartment once more. She explained that she had received the trial transcript two days earlier and had been studying it since. She confided that whilst she now fully understood the discrepancies between Wade and Smithson's accounts, she had not initially noticed any omissions. It was only when she discussed it with a criminal solicitor acquaintance that it was pointed out to her that no forensic evidence was presented during the trial. The solicitor had made her aware just how significant an omission it was in a major criminal case and admitted their own surprise. She quickly reassured Amy that as far as the solicitor was concerned, she was merely gathering background information for an article about the criminal justice system. She was not about to risk her own scoop, was she?

Helen then said, "So why was there no forensic evidence?"

Clark replied carefully, "You remember I'm trying to keep as much distance as I can on this in case Professional Standards come calling, so I won't answer that, at least not at the moment. Do you have any sort of contact in the CPS?"

Helen was a little cagey and said, "I may have, I'm not sure. I might have to use my solicitor friend."

"Well, I think that might be a good place to start, don't you? Let someone there tell you why they appear so incompetent. Now what about witnesses?"

Naylor replied, "Well the only civilian witness to give any evidence about the stabbing was the van driver, Hodgson, I think. He only arrived on the scene when it was all over, didn't he?"

Amy couldn't help grinning as she said, "I think he might be worth a visit and, just a tip, you might want to ask him about his whole day, especially before he found the injured officers."

If truth be told, Clark was finding it difficult not to just tell her friend the full story and the result of their re-investigation of the Smithson case. That may come later but, in the meantime, they needed to establish a sequence of enquiries carried out by the reporter that looked like a thorough examination of the case, providing a plausible explanation as to how she had come by the information that she would later include in her newspaper story.

CHAPTER 35

As she knocked on Frank Hodgson's front door the next morning, Helen Naylor found it hard to believe anything interesting would come from interviewing him, even if Amy seemed to think it was important. Perhaps it showed she wasn't quite the reporter she believed herself to be.

Initially Mrs Hodgson, who answered the door, was reluctant to let the reporter in, or any reporter for that matter. However, by telling the lady that she had already spoken to Detective Inspector Clark, she managed to somehow suggest that her visit was officially sanctioned. When it came to dealing with the press, both the Hodgsons were somewhat naive and in all honesty somewhat overawed. Although Frank Hodgson was fed up with the whole business, he agreed to be interviewed, vowing that it would be the last time.

Settled once more at the dining room table with tea and biscuits, Frank went through the events of that day in Grimston Lane. His memory of the awful events was so vivid it seemed as if it had only happened yesterday. Once again, he concentrated on finding the injured officers in the lay-by, as no one had told him the significance of his other revelations. Naylor lazily jotted a few notes, thinking to herself that this was a waste of time, there was nothing new here. Remembering Clark's tip, she asked Frank what he had been doing in Grimston Lane and why he went to the lay-by. His reply made her sit up straight and start making more detailed notes.

"Like I told those two officers, I was delivering a parcel and got lost, so because I'd seen the police in the lay-by I went to ask for some help."

Helen Naylor said, "So when did you first see the police in the lay-by?"

Hodgson answered a little wearily, "They were there when I first turned into Grimston Lane looking for the farm to deliver my parcel. I thought I was in Grimston Road so there's no wonder I couldn't find the farm, was there?"

"Can you describe what you saw exactly?"

"I thought the officers would have told you that," he said a little suspiciously.

Naylor was used to dealing with reluctant interviewees and responded quickly, "Oh yes, of course you're right, but I always like to hear it first hand from a witness, especially if it's going to be in the paper."

Somewhat mollified, Frank repeated almost exactly what he'd said to Clark and Devereux. "I saw a police officer walking towards the grey car and the driver starting to get out of it. The officer was PC Brown."

"How can you be sure it was PC Brown?"

"When I described him the other two told me that it was PC Brown."

Naylor said, "How did you describe him?"

"The officer had dark hair and was wearing his black vest thing."

Helen Naylor recognised the discrepancy immediately. From reading the trial transcript, she knew that Wade had claimed to be the first to approach the car and also that he was not wearing a stab vest, which is what she believed Frank Hodgson meant when he described the officer wearing a 'black vest'. She had to smile as she remembered reading the description of his bravery in fighting to save his colleague even though not wearing a stab vest as protection. Although she had not met Wade, she had seen enough photos to know that he had fair hair. The officer walking towards the grey car could not have been him, it had to be Brown she concluded.

Naylor had one final question. "During the trial, did the police know about you seeing the officers in the lay-by when you first drove by?"

Hodgson shook his head vigorously. "Oh no, it was only when Miss Clark and Mr Devereux asked me."

"Nobody asked when they took your statement the first time?"

"No, it wasn't mentioned."

So, incompetence rather than cover-up during the first investigation. She had heard enough and quickly wrapped up the interview, thanking Frank Hodgson for his time and confirming that she could return if any further questions arose. As she left, all she could think was that Wade was a liar and that the loathsome Smithson was actually telling the truth about this much at least.

Later the same day Helen Naylor contacted her solicitor friend to ask about any contacts in the CPS who might be prepared to speak to her. He was cagey but did tell her he might know someone and would get back to her. When she had told Amy Clark she might have a contact within the CPS, it was sheer bravado as she'd never spoken to anyone there in her life.

When he did get back to her the solicitor told her an old friend of his was willing to speak to her anonymously on the phone. If she was agreeable her phone number would be passed to the contact who would ring her direct when possible. Naylor readily agreed but was told in no uncertain terms by the solicitor, who had always been attracted to her, that it would cost her.

It was an agonising two days before her 'deep throat' in the CPS rang her mobile phone. The caller reiterated that he would not give his name and that he was not prepared to give information that would harm the service. Having agreed to the conditions, she quickly informed the caller that she was interested in the Smithson trial, using the same story about research into a general feature about the criminal justice system.

Her first question was to ask who the prosecutor was in the Smithson case and was promptly told that it was a matter of public record, easily obtainable. She then pointed out that forensic evidence was used to prosecute Smithson for the offence of kidnap, but none was used to prove the murder charge. Did they know why that was? Her informant merely said that the case was such a 'slam-dunk' that it wasn't needed. When asked who made that decision, she was told that it was the prosecutor handling the case in conjunction with a senior police officer. When asked if they knew who the officer was, the reply was simply a very senior officer.

Growing frustrated, Naylor finally said, "Well can you tell me what where the results of the forensic analysis and what did it show?"

There was only silence at the other end of the phone.

The reporter said, "Hello, hello are you still there?"

"Yes, I'm just thinking. Okay, you must understand I'm only doing this to protect my employers and to make sure any blame is laid at the right door. Do you understand?"

"Yes, I do."

"Alright, the simple truth is that the police never sent all the forensic samples from the scene of the murder for analysis. So that evidence wasn't available to us."

A very surprised Naylor said, "Why ever not?"

"I understand it was purely to save money?"

"Are you sure?"

The CPS employee said, "That's the word around the office."

"That must have been known prior to the trial, so did the CPS just go along with it?"

"Apparently so."

Naylor said, "Is there anything else you think I should know?"

The solicitor was silent before answering. "Not really, only that there is no doubt in anyone's mind that Smithson did it and is in the right place. You won't hear from me again. Goodbye."

Helen Naylor needed a drink and time to think. Ten minutes later, seated in a local pub, she faced rare moments of introspection and, surprisingly, self-doubt. She was honest enough to admit to herself that her main reason for pursuing this story was to further her own career, but did she really believe there were any other benefits to pursuing it? She was aware that by printing what she knew a number of careers would be damaged, if not ended, and reputations ruined forever. Did they deserve that? Did she really believe that the truth must will out?

As she considered the issues, she realised that she honestly believed Richard Wade must not be allowed to get away with his lies and that Steve Brown's reputation must be restored. She reconciled her conflicting thoughts by telling herself that anyone who lost their job had only themselves to blame. They had made their choice.

She knew Smithson was guilty, so it was not the usual crusade to prove someone's guilt or innocence, but to bring the incompetent and dishonest to book. Satisfied that it was the right thing to do, she decided it was her duty to press on, regardless of the consequence for others.

CHAPTER 36

Munro was surprised to be called in to see Chief Constable Charles Newman. When he arrived, he once again found Assistant Chief Constable Jack Bryant and the Force solicitor Roger Harris present. Newman did not beat about the bush, announcing that they had been forced to re-visit their promise to ensure the whole Force was made aware that Steve Brown, contrary to previous beliefs, had performed bravely and in the best traditions of the police service. He said there would be no further official comments on the matter.

When Munro asked why, he was told that, following legal advice, it had been decided that it was not in the best interests of the Force to admit to making such a monumental cock-up. Whilst PC Brown's reputation was important, it was felt that the reputation of the Force was more important still. The chief's announcement had a very distinct whiff of political interference, particularly when he declined to answer if they had changed their mind about what to do with Wade, fuelling Munro's suspicions that they had.

The superintendent protested that it was wrong, warning once again that it would come back to haunt them all, but to little effect. When he continued to argue, he was told that the decision had been made at the highest levels and was not about to be changed, seeming to confirm his earlier suspicions. That was the end of the matter, or so they hoped.

As he left the office, any doubts Munro might have had about implementing Devereux's plan disappeared in that very moment.

Meanwhile, Naylor was once again holding a clandestine meeting with Amy Clark in her apartment where she could clearly see a brown cardboard folder on the lounge table. She didn't need to be told that it was the Smithson re-investigation and stared hungrily at the file as the detective inspector explained what was about to happen.

"Helen, at some time in the future, there are sure to be questions asked about how you came by your information and probably about our relationship. You can prove that you have gathered much of the information yourself, so can quite truthfully tell anyone who asks that you got there on your own. You have the letter from Smithson to prove why you began digging into this case, believing it to be worthwhile because of your previous knowledge that an investigation was already underway. You've read the trial transcript which led you to Frank Hodgson and made you suspicious about the forensic evidence. If necessary, you can establish via your solicitor friend that they told you of its importance and that you spoke to an anonymous contact in the CPS who alerted you to the fact that the samples had not been sent for analysis and why. If you have a problem, it may be in interpreting it all and understanding how important the forensic evidence is to proving that Wade lied. It is vital that I am able to say that I never showed you the file, which by the way doesn't exist, or that I have ever discussed its contents with you. However, once you have read it, I am sure it will join all the dots for you, making anything you don't understand at the moment perfectly clear. You understand, I'm sure, that you can't refer to it in your article, not that I think you'll need to. I'm sure that nobody will believe for one minute that I didn't help you, but I'm equally sure they won't be able to prove I did. Right, I'm off for a shower." She left the room, leaving the file on the table.

Once Clark had gone, Naylor devoured the contents of the file and at last understood the full impact of the forensic evidence and the difference it would have made to the court case. When she had completed her reading, she was amazed at the extent of Wade's duplicity, realising, as had everyone else who knew the full facts, that Wade had claimed all Brown's heroic actions for himself. Even worse, he had allowed Brown to be portrayed wrongly as a coward in the face of extreme danger.

As she thought about it further, Naylor realised that Wade's failure to wear a stab vest was much more important than she had realised, until now believing it was only important in terms of officer identification. She needed to find out more, including the significance of him not carrying his personal protective equipment.

When Clark returned, Helen tried to clarify various points about the forensic evidence and stab vests. Clark's response was to caution Naylor against going into detail about the results of the examination of the blood and clothing samples, pointing out that she was only supposed to know they had not been examined in the first enquiry. She also refused to discuss the impact of not wearing a stab vest or carrying his PPE. Clark told her that any officer could tell her about that without giving away any official information. Doing so would give Naylor the chance to prove that she had gathered her information from many different sources, thus continuing to distance Munro and his team from her story.

Feeling she was nearly ready to write her story, Helen Naylor went to her local police station to seek answers about stab vests. Speaking to a young constable in the foyer, she identified herself and explained that she was researching an article on police safety. Seeing no danger, the officer was happy to answer her questions, telling Naylor that failure to wear a stab vest when on duty in uniform was firstly a disciplinary offence, but also a stupid thing to do. Failure to carry your PPE was likewise a disciplinary offence, but dangerous as well. When pressed, the officer admitted he would hesitate to face an armed attacker if not properly equipped and able to use his CS gas or baton, explaining to her just how valuable the gas could be in incapacitating an attacker. She made a point of obtaining the officer's details, noting the time and date when she spoke to him. She had no intention of quoting him in her article, but as Clark had advised, she would be able to prove she had not got the information from her.

Now she was ready to write the biggest story of her life. This was her big chance, maybe the only one she would ever get, to break a major story exposing high-level incompetence and corruption. She was honest enough to admit, to herself at least, that she was no dyed-in-the-wool campaigner for truth and freedom, but that her main motive was self-advancement and glory. It was an opportunity she could not afford to miss, and she would do everything in her power to ensure that she didn't.

If Clark and the others had been able to see Helen Naylor's innermost thoughts, maybe they would have had more reservations about the help they had given her. However, perhaps they could not have criticised her too much because weren't they all using each other to achieve their own objectives?

The reporter retreated to her own flat, working feverishly on a laptop to put her thoughts and notes into a coherent account stretching from a warm day in August through to the present day. It took her two days before she thought it was ready, having spent some time preparing for the follow ups that would be demanded by any editor worth his salt. She also knew that once this story broke, there would be massive competition from all the other newspapers and TV news channels.

Any follow up stories would largely depend on the police and government response to the exposure of their deficiencies and deceit. Once this broke, they would not be able to ignore it.

Naylor was aware that her big advantage over other journalists was the direct route she had into the follow-up investigation team via Amy Clark. She knew they were using her as much as she was using them, but that was fine, it was the world they all inhabited. She considered ringing Clark to offer her a preview of the article but decided against it, settling instead for sending her a text to let her know it was going to the editor. In the text she promised to let Amy know when the story was due to be published, not for a moment doubting that it would be. Very much as an afterthought, she hastily added two kisses to the text.

On receipt of the message, Clark was absurdly pleased that Helen had thought of her and especially so on seeing the kisses, but she wished it hadn't been sent as, if there was an investigation, mobile phones were easy to examine. She responded with a text of her own, saying, 'Thanx 4 thinking of me. Don't want 2 no anything about it. I can't comment about case. Luvs Amyxx'

Naylor immediately recognised Amy's attempt at putting distance between herself and the article and could sympathise, almost wishing she hadn't sent the first text. Pushing all sentimental thoughts to the back of her mind, she rang her contact at the national newspaper where she hoped her story would be printed, paying her handsomely for the privilege of course. His response was to instruct her to e-mail the article to him and he would get back to her as soon as possible. If truth be told, he didn't sound all that interested. He soon would be, she thought.

For the next three hours Naylor paced the floor of her tiny flat, tried to read a magazine and made an abortive attempt to watch daytime TV. In the end she gave up and just waited, hardly daring to go to the toilet in case her phone rang, which it did twice. The first time was an old friend wanting a chat who had to be cut short with a vague promise that she would ring back. The second was a telemarketer who hung up in disgust at the torrent of abuse she received down the phone.

When eventually the phone did ring, she was shocked to hear the caller identify himself as Tim Reynolds, the editor of the newspaper.

He thanked her for the article, saying that he was very interested in it, but that there were some things that needed to be clarified. He instructed her to get on a train and meet him at the newspaper offices the following morning and to bring with her all the supporting notes and evidence for the article.

CHAPTER 37

Exactly as instructed, a nervous Helen Naylor, holding on tight to her briefcase and laptop, approached the reception desk in the impressive foyer of the newspaper building. On giving her name to the immaculately turned-out receptionist, she was greeted with a warm smile, told that she was expected, and someone would be with her shortly. Within what seemed like seconds a young man approached her, introducing himself as the editor's assistant, before taking her to the nearby lift. Significantly it could only be accessed by means of a key. Realising that it was an executive lift, she was whisked to the senior management floor of the building and escorted to the managing editor's palatial office. A number of people were waiting for her, including Tim Reynolds who introduced her to the features editor, the chief crime reporter, and a woman from the legal department. She was offered coffee, which was served in china cups accompanied by a selection of pastries. If they were trying to impress her, it was working with bells on.

Once everyone was settled around the conference table, Tim Reynolds began. "Helen, this is an excellent story and very well written. You obviously have impeccable sources. Well done."

"Thank you, does that mean you're going to print it?"

Reynolds smiled. "Well, we are thinking about the front page on Sunday, providing there are no major disasters in the meantime."

Helen was almost breathless with excitement; this was beyond her wildest dreams. She found she couldn't speak so just nodded.

The crime reporter laughed out loud at her confusion and said,

"It's very good, we just don't understand how none of us have got a whiff of it before now."

Regaining some of her composure, Helen replied, "That's easy. Only three officers were engaged on the re-investigation, and they were not from the Professional Standards Branch. It has been kept secret from the rest of the Force, including senior management, with those spoken to being led to believe the case was being reviewed to identify training needs. Therefore, there has only been one leak, and that was to me. Although in fairness he didn't know what was happening, he was just giving me some tittle-tattle. Actually, I think he was trying to help Wade, but that's backfired a bit, don't you think?"

Reynolds nodded thoughtfully. "That's as maybe but looking at this I think you may have developed a better source."

Naylor smiled enigmatically but did not reply.

Reynolds nodded. "Fair enough. Right, we need to go through your notes, identifying how you have firmed up the story before we can risk publication. This has the potential to be massive, so we need to be very careful, that's why we have a legal advisor here."

For the next two hours they went through the notes from her first contact with Sergeant Heath, to the letter from Smithson and the trial transcript. She explained how she had noticed the missing forensic evidence which was confirmed by her solicitor friend who put her in touch with an anonymous CPS source. They had confirmed that the police had had no forensic analysis done, purely to save money, although she didn't know who had authorised it. They found her interview with Frank Hodgson particularly compelling as it provided independent evidence to contradict Wade and to support Smithson's account. None of those present could see any motive for Smithson to lie, particularly as he did not deny the offences. They also thought the information that Wade had not been wearing a stab vest or carrying his PPE interesting as it clearly affected his performance during the fight with Smithson. That aspect of the story was highlighted as a good subject for follow-up articles about the dangers police faced in modern Britain and the steps taken to improve officer safety.

Finally, Reynolds said, "It all looks good, but are we sure there has been a cover up?"

Naylor thought very carefully and replied even more carefully, "My source informs me that a new file of evidence has been presented to the chief constable. To date he has taken no action. I cannot say anymore."

The features editor spoke for the first time, "It all looks pretty good to me. I think we can run with it. It's inconceivable that the Home Office have not been made aware of this and the possible repercussions, after all it was them that put Wade forward for the George Medal. They wanted the reflected glory, didn't they?"

When asked for her opinion, the legal advisor could see no problems just so long as nothing leaked prior to publication. She had no doubt that efforts would be made to stop the story if those in authority got wind of it.

Reynolds said, "Have you managed to speak to Wade?"

"No, he's on sick leave and won't speak to me."

The crime reporter chipped in "That's convenient, isn't it? Also interesting because if you've asked to speak to Wade they must know you are sniffing round, yet they've not tried to stop you. They must feel pretty secure."

"They did try at the beginning. Maybe they think they've got me under control."

Reynolds considered things for a moment "Okay, if we're all agreed then we'll run it on Sunday." Following nods of agreement from all around the table, he continued, "Right Helen, I want you to work with Dan here on getting the story sharpened up a little." He indicated the crime reported who nodded to her.

Reynolds continued when he saw her uncertain look. "Don't worry, it's your story and your name will be first under the headline. Okay?" When she nodded he said, "Right one thing we need to do is to give them a chance to answer these accusations. So, we ask the Home Office, Chief Constable Newman, the CPS, and anyone else we can think of for their comments, but we don't do it before early evening on Saturday, that way, even if the story leaks, we keep our exclusive because nobody will have time to do anything with it. It will probably be 'no comment' all the way, but if they do say anything interesting, we will still have time to include it in the story. Once it does break, they'll have plenty to say, you can be sure of that. Anything else?"

Dan said, "Do we know if the forensics have been done now, and if so what did they show?"

Helen replied very carefully again. "I'm not in a position to comment on that, but I understand very compelling evidence has come to light. I think we must all draw our own conclusions as to what that means." She convinced herself that she was not giving away any confidences, although she did come very close to telling them about the contents of the file.

With that the meeting finished. Helen went with Dan to a much smaller office to work on her story and to learn what it really meant to work on a national newspaper.

Later that evening, Helen Naylor rang Amy Clark, intending to update her on events, especially when the story would appear. However, Clark cut her short, saying she didn't want to know, preferring her surprise to be as genuine as possible. However, she did wish her friend 'good luck'.

Most police forces do not have staff on duty in their press office outside of normal working hours, so the task of press liaison is delegated to the Force duty officer, a post manned 24 hours a day. As luck would have it, Sharon Parker was on duty the following Saturday when a call came in just after 6 p.m. from Helen Naylor. She identified herself as a journalist, naming the paper she was working for.

Inspector Parker was expecting the normal mundane request for updates about ongoing incidents but did wonder why a national newspaper journalist was calling. She was somewhat surprised when told that the newspaper intended to publish an article the following day suggesting that Superintendent Richard Wade had given false evidence during the trial of Karl Smithson. Naylor added that she also understood that the Force had conducted a secret enquiry, the results of which had been concealed. Would she like to make a comment?

Parker explained that her role was to deal with current incidents and that she was not able or authorised to make comment on enquiries of that nature. However, she did take a contact number from Naylor, promising that someone from the press office would ring her shortly. She was told that it would need to be quick as they intended to go to print very shortly.

Naylor next tried to contact the Crown Prosecution Service, eventually speaking to an assistant from their press office who was unable to offer any information at all. They did agree that it was their job to decide if an offender should be prosecuted but emphasised that it was the responsibility of the police to gather the evidence. They could not comment specifically on the Karl Smithson case or the forensic evidence and had no knowledge of a second police investigation.

The Home Office offered no official comment on the Smithson case, other than to say that the investigation of crime was the responsibility of individual police forces and that they did not interfere.

Wade simply did not answer his phone.

Shortly prior to the print deadline, Helen Naylor was called by the police press officer who had been contacted and informed of the reporter's request by Inspector Parker. Being aware of how things worked, he had spoken to the head of the Professional Standards Branch, assuming, wrongly as it happened, that if there had been any suggestion of wrongdoing by Richard Wade it would be them who conducted the investigation. He was told in no uncertain terms that Wade was not being investigated and there was no re-examination of the Smithson case. He imparted this information to Naylor, adding somewhat maliciously that she was wasting her time and his as well.

Helen Naylor's final question to the press officer was to ask if it was true that the forensic samples relating to the death of Steve Brown had not been sent to the laboratory for examination. Believing he had the upper hand, the man said he found it highly unlikely that the police would act in such a manner when dealing with an offence of that magnitude. It was a silly thing to do, because if you don't know the answer only two responses are allowed. Either a simple 'no comment' or 'I will find out'.

The ripples continue to spread. Because the press officer failed to recognise how potentially damning Helen Naylor's article was, he failed to contact senior officers to ask them what they knew and secondly just to give them a heads up about the forthcoming revelations. So, his comments put the Force in the position of having denied that there were doubts about Wade's evidence and that the original investigation was being revisited.

However you looked at it, his answers had put the police in what would become a very difficult place, making them appear, at best, simply incompetent or even worse mendacious.

CHAPTER 38

The article appeared the next day, causing widespread dismay to a number of high-ranking officials across the country and ensuring they did not enjoy their breakfasts. Telephones were red hot as they frantically contacted their staff in a bid to find out what was going on and, more importantly, just how it affected them.

Cop Killer Accuses George Medal Hero of Lying in Court, Establishment Cover-up Exposed

By Helen Naylor

Murderer Karl Smithson has contacted this reporter from his cell in a maximum-security prison to make extraordinary accusations against hero police officer Richard Wade.

Smithson was sentenced to life imprisonment earlier this year for a string of offences, including the murder of PC Steve Brown. During the incident, then Inspector Richard Wade claimed to have single-handedly fought the knife - wielding killer, despite his own serious injuries. It has been suggested that the murdered officer played little or no part in the killer's arrest. Smithson, however, claims that Wade continually lied about what happened, taking all the credit for himself when Steve Brown was the true hero.

Readers may remember the officers' actions resulted in the release of kidnapped 10-year-old Linda Ross.

According to Smithson, he has spoken to senior police officers since his imprisonment to tell them his version of events but has grown tired of waiting for them to take any action.

After careful study of the evidence and speaking to witnesses, this reporter has identified areas of concern which need to be addressed by the police and others. Why was no forensic evidence produced in court? Were police aware that an independent witness saw Steve Brown approaching Smithson prior to his murder, in direct contradiction of the evidence given by Wade who claimed he was the first to approach the murderer? One wonders what else he may have lied about.

Police refused to respond when contacted, but a Crown Prosecution Service insider hinted that the police saved costs by not submitting forensic samples for examination. If true, it is scandalous behaviour in such a serious case. Do they routinely seek to save money by doing this in other cases? If true, the CPS need to explain why they went along with it.

Other contacts have confirmed that the police have indeed re-investigated this case, following contact from Smithson. What did they find? Have the forensic samples now been analysed, and what did they reveal? One can only speculate as to why the results of this enquiry have not been made public. We also understand that Superintendent Wade is on sick leave, but no reason why is forthcoming. He has refused all requests for an interview. Just what are they hiding?

Richard Wade was widely praised for his actions by, among others, the Prime Minister and Home Secretary. He was commended by a high court judge and awarded the George Medal as well as being promoted to superintendent, largely on his own say so. Police contacts have informed us that Richard Wade's lack of an issue stab vest, along with his personal protective equipment consisting of a baton, handcuffs, and CS gas, not only breached police regulations but may have meant he was unable to offer his colleague effective help. If Wade had been properly equipped, especially with his CS gas, would he have been able to incapacitate Smithson and so save Steve Brown's life?

When asked to comment prior to publication, the CPS and Home Office have both passed the buck, claiming it is the responsibility of the police to investigate criminal matters and that they cannot comment on the allegations made in this article.

Contrary to the information obtained by this newspaper, a police spokesperson has denied that Richard Wade's conduct is being investigated or that the original *case is being re-examined. The same spokesperson suggested it would be highly unlikely that police would not send the forensic samples for examination. Does this spokesperson actually know what is happening, or are they simply attempting to mislead us?*

What is happening? Can we trust our police and politicians?

What appears to have been an incompetent initial enquiry now seems to have degenerated into an establishment cover-up. We demand answers and will not rest until we have them. The public have a right to know.

At no stage is it suggested that Smithson is innocent of the heinous offences for which he is now rightly in prison, nor does he claim to be innocent. However, just because they achieved the right result, there can be no excuse for such incompetence and complacency from the police and CPS, to be followed by what can only be called a shabby cover-up.

One man has been hailed a true hero for our times, accepting much praise and lavish rewards as his due. Another is dead and unable to defend himself, left with his reputation in tatters. Steve Brown cannot speak for himself, so this newspaper will. The truth must be revealed.

Consider this. What has Smithson to gain by this publicity? He has not denied his guilt, in some ways he seems almost proud of what he has done and the notoriety he has subsequently gained.

Stand by for further updates. Further information appears on pages 5 and 6 with articles on page 7 explaining police regulations in relation to officer safety and the use of personal protective equipment.

The whole front page of the Sunday morning edition was filled with the article, complete with photographs of Smithson and Brown accompanied by one of a happy Wade and Julie at his medal presentation. It was quickly picked up by the radio and TV news, being dissected on all the newspaper review programmes. All the guest reviewers agreed that it was a blockbuster of a story and that the police, along with all those concerned, had many questions to answer. It would appear that no one wanted to act for the defence. A veritable shit storm engulfed all those involved.

Charles Newman's breakfast coffee went cold as he read the article, appalled by the information they seemed to have obtained. His mood wasn't helped following a difficult call from the Home Secretary personally, the basic message being that he was on his own and to get it sorted. He read the article again, and it didn't get any better as he realised his Force had denied there was any investigation of Wade's actions or the Smithson case in general. He wondered how the hell they had discovered about the forensic exhibits and just how much they actually knew. It was clear someone was talking to the press, and he had his suspicions who.

Richard Wade was deeply hungover when he read the article that Sunday morning. In his befuddled state he had not initially realised that the article was about him until he saw the photograph of him and Julie smiling for the camera. His first reading made him angry, but the second caused him to feel an icy chill of fear followed by panic. He didn't know what to do. He ached to speak to someone, but who? He had no friends and he doubted that he would be exactly flavour of the month with his senior officers.

He decided he would feel better after a drink, able to think more clearly, he thought. That's it, just have one drink then decide what to do.

Superintendent John Munro read the article at home, admiring the way it was written, demanding answers to various questions whilst revealing just enough information to give it a ring of authenticity. It was certainly going to cause problems, he thought, then wondered whether he should do some gardening or clean the car whilst he waited for the telephone call.

Both Clark and Devereux read it with some amusement, pleased that things were in the open at long last and that justice now had a chance of being done. Amy was especially pleased that her friend had achieved her dream of writing for a national newspaper, apparently seizing it with both hands. The pair of them were wise enough to the inner workings of the police service to know they would soon be under scrutiny themselves, but if they kept their own counsel there was no real evidence to implicate them in anything.

Even John Munro was surprised by the speed with which the telephone call came, instructing him to assemble his team and get to the chief constable's office immediately.

CHAPTER 39

$\mathbf{M}$unro, Clark, and Devereux waited outside the chief constable's office shortly after lunch, listening to the raised voices coming from behind the closed door. Minutes later a flustered press officer hurried from the office, red in the face and sweating freely, giving every appearance of being glad to get out. The trio were beckoned into the room.

They were met by a grim-faced Charles Newman and a worried-looking Jack Bryant. Also present was the local chief crown prosecutor Philip Webb, sitting slightly apart from the other two in, what was perhaps, a symbolic gesture distancing himself from what was happening.

A clearly angry Newman's first words did not bode well for the remainder of the meeting: "So who leaked this to the press?"

Munro looked him squarely in the face before saying, "Sir, if you are suggesting any of my team are involved then I hope you have some proof."

Somewhat taken back by Munro's tone, the chief said, "Not yet, but rest assured I will."

Munro threw all caution to the winds. "On at least three occasions I have said we should go public to minimise any damage, but because we have not done so it now looks as if we have been engaged in a cover up. Then, just to make matters worse, you want to expend time and energy on finding a possible leak rather dealing with the real issues. As we all know, the basic content of the story is completely accurate and would seem to have originated with Smithson. I'm sure any half-way competent reporter could have filled in the gaps with the minimum of assistance. The real question is what we do now the story is in the public domain rather than wasting time looking for a leak which may not even exist."

Jack Bryant decided to have his say, "You seem to forget that your incompetent investigation in the first place got us into this mess."

Munro, his voice full of scorn, responded angrily, "Why are you still looking to apportion blame? We need to respond to this article before the good name of this Force is dragged any further through the mud." He paused before pointedly adding, "Those responsible for any of this can be dealt with later. Now we just need to limit the damage."

Philip Webb stepped in, "I think Mr Munro is talking sense. It's obvious tomorrow's papers will be full of this. My office has been deluged with requests for comments from all the press and TV. Up to now we have settled for 'no comment' but we won't get away with that for long. I suspect Mr Munro may have some suggestions as to how we may proceed. Am I correct, Superintendent?"

Munro merely nodded.

Newman struggled manfully against the urge to exert his authority, realising that he really had no idea what to do and was desperate for somebody, anybody, to provide a way out. "Okay, Mr Munro, I'm willing to listen to your ideas."

Munro paused, breathed in deeply, and began to speak. Once again, he told them that the newspaper article was correct in all major aspects and that it would be a pointless exercise trying to refute what had been said. He argued that they would be much better confirming that the article was essentially correct but going on to explain their actions and the thought processes behind them. For example, why not confirm that, following contact from Karl Smithson, they had re-examined the initial investigation and had prepared a file of evidence which was to be passed to the CPS for their consideration. They should admit that the forensic exhibits from the murder of Steve

Brown had not been analysed, explaining the reasons why, no matter how weak they were, and putting as good a gloss on it as possible. The CPS should accept they had agreed to the prosecution without the forensic evidence, putting forward a plausible explanation in their defence. Lastly, it must be announced that Richard Wade was to be formally interviewed about his actions that day, giving him the opportunity to answer all the allegations made against him. All this should be announced at a press conference to be held at the police headquarters as soon as possible and attended by representatives of all those involved. It must be stressed that no cover up took place, but that due to the sensitive nature of the new investigation, it was kept secret from the rest of the Force as well as the public, until enquiries had been completed and a decision made. This would also explain why the press officer had denied an enquiry had been carried out because he simply didn't know that it had. Basically, everything that would be said was true or partly true anyway. There would be no need to mention some of the more difficult aspects of the matter. For example, that Mr Newman had decided no further action should be taken and that Wade would be allowed to retire on medical grounds. It was doable, provided they presented a united front.

After hearing Munro's proposal, Charles Newman said, "So you think our best defence is to confirm the substance of their report, but to give our explanations?"

"Yes Sir, after all, we have conducted a further investigation and had the forensic exhibits examined, so we would be telling the truth. In addition, it would give us the opportunity to state that there had been no cover up, just that confidentiality had been maintained, even if that is not completely true."

Newman looked to the crown prosecutor and said, "What do you think?

"I think I can live with that, although I will only say we agreed to proceed without forensic evidence because there was such a strong case, not that we gave advice."

"Jack, what do you think?"

Bryant looked sick as he replied, "I've done the research and can put some arguments forward about us having to cut costs wherever we can because of government cuts. How convincing it is, I don't know." He knew very well who would shoulder much of the blame.

Newman was warming to the idea and said, "Okay, we'll get the press officer in."

Clark nervously said, "If I may, Sir?"

Newman smiled for the first time during the meeting. "You might as well have your say as well, Inspector."

"I think it's very important for us to remember through all this that Superintendent Wade and his actions when Steve Brown met his death are the main focus of the story. No one has any doubt that Karl Smithson is guilty and is exactly where he belongs. We should emphasise that as much as we can, concentrating people's thoughts on the positives. Talking of positives, it's essential that we remind everyone that, no matter what exactly happened at the scene, a 10-year-old girl was released from a frightening ordeal."

Newman responded, "Yes, I agree, Inspector. However, no matter what we do and say, there will still be questions asked about Wade, particularly why he was promoted and presented with a medal. A lot of senior people who praised Wade at the time will be highly embarrassed and have their judgement called into question, including me."

With that, they broke for half an hour whilst they waited for the disgruntled press officer to return.

As they left the room, Assistant Chief Constable Jack Bryant touched Amy Clark's arm to gain her attention before saying, "Inspector, how is your girlfriend, Helen?

With an expressionless face, Amy replied, "Very well I believe, thank you."

Bryant continued with barely disguised menace in his voice, "Just to let you know that if I go down, I'll make sure I don't go alone."

Clark looked around quickly, making sure they couldn't be overheard before turning to face Bryant squarely and, with a sweet smile, said, "With all due respect, Sir, fuck you."

She left the room.

Once more were principles being sacrificed in the name of saving face and careers? They were prepared to deny a cover up even though the chief constable had been happy to overlook the results of Munro's investigation and to let Wade off the hook just to preserve his own reputation. That sounds an awful lot like a cover up. Because danger threatened him personally, not to mention his political masters, he now intended to claim full credit for instigating the second enquiry, attempting to justify why it had been kept secret. He was also ready to publicly sacrifice Richard Wade, despite him having had no chance to answer the allegations against him or to challenge the evidence.

Could Munro and his team be excused? It was their plan, implemented by them, and about to be used to divert criticism from the Force. It should be remembered that Munro was the head of the first enquiry that had manifestly failed to accumulate all the available evidence, and that both Clark and Devereux had been instrumental in that enquiry. Everyone had an interest, even if they didn't want to admit it, least of all to themselves.

When the press officer returned, he was relieved to be greeted by a much calmer chief constable who quickly outlined their proposal to hold a press conference. The press officer readily agreed to set it up for the following day but cautioned them against saying too much, especially in answer to questions which would be designed to trap them into unwise responses. He was experienced enough to know that when confronted with seasoned reporters they would probably drop themselves right in it, but why should he care?

CHAPTER 40

On the Monday morning, Clark and Devereux slipped, unnoticed by the assembled press, into the conference room by a side door. They stood to one side, amazed by the sheer number of reporters present and the mind-numbing cacophony of different sounds, including loud voices, the whirring and clicking of cameras along with the incessant rattle of the feverish bashing on laptop keys as they prepared their articles. The lights were very bright, and it took them a moment to realise that they were for the numerous TV cameras at the back of the room. Obviously, the press conference had drawn considerable attention, both locally and nationally, with one or two well-known faces present among the TV journalists, all of whom appeared to be excited by the forthcoming sport. That was how they saw it, relishing the opportunity to hold authority figures to account, exposing their failings and misdeeds to public scrutiny. It was hard not to compare them with sharks driven to a frenzy by the smell of blood in the water.

Amy scanned the crowd, searching for Helen, who she had not seen for several days, quickly finding her in an obvious position of honour in the centre of the front row. Naylor did not look her way as she was in deep conversation with the man seated next to her.

At precisely 10 o'clock the press secretary entered the room and raised his hands in an attempt to quiet the assembled crowd. Eventually he was able to make himself heard above the hubbub and tried to explain how the conference would operate. Representatives from the police and Crown Prosecution Service would sit behind a table on a small stage facing the reporters and cameras. Chief

Constable Charles Newman would introduce those present before making a short opening statement. The local chief crown prosecutor Philip Webb would not be making an opening statement but was prepared to answer questions from the floor, as would the others on the panel.

Having completed his duty, the press officer nodded to the side of the stage whereupon Charles Newman led a group of men onto the stage, all of them taking a seat behind the table. They were Newman, flanked by ACC Bryant on his right and Munro on his left with Webb further to the left of the superintendent and somehow, once more, appearing to put distance between him and the others.

Once the camera lights had stopped flashing and the noise had settled back down a little, Newman began reading from a prepared statement, at the same time wishing he had asked the press officer to point out Helen Naylor as he belatedly realised that he didn't know who she was.

"Firstly, ladies and gentlemen, let me thank you for coming today. This conference is taking place sooner than we had anticipated and is obviously in response to the article which appeared yesterday. I will make a short statement, but should stress at this point that there has been no cover up, nor will there be whilst I am chief constable of this Force."

The loud hoots of derision and catcalls forced a pause, during which he clearly heard one of the assembled crowd shout, "How much longer will that be then?", generating even more raucous laughter.

Colouring slightly, Newman waited patiently, having been briefed what to expect but finding it was even worse than he had anticipated. Eventually he was able to continue.

"I can confirm that much of the information in Miss Naylor's article is correct, however, some of the conclusions she has drawn are not. For instance, I can confirm that officers from this Force were contacted by Karl Smithson who indicated that he had information to impart. When he was visited in prison, it quickly became clear that he wished to give his account of events in Grimston Lane when Constable Steve Brown was murdered. It transpired that his account differed significantly from the version we understood to be true.

As a result, a second investigation, under the command of Detective Superintendent John Munro, was launched in an effort to establish, once and for all, the truth of what happened that day. I need to make it perfectly clear at this point that neither I, nor anyone else involved in these enquiries, have any doubts whatsoever that Smithson was justly convicted for the murder of Steve Brown and the kidnapping of Linda Ross. Nothing has been discovered to change that opinion and we firmly believe he is where he deserves to be and rightly so, for a very long time.

However, this second enquiry has uncovered certain information that was not available previously and a file has now been prepared for submission to the Crown Prosecution Service for their consideration and advice. Once again, I would like to say that there has been no cover up, only a confidential police enquiry carried out with sensitivity, discretion, and with one aim in mind, to find the truth. We will now take questions from the floor."

Unsurprisingly, Helen Naylor took the lead by asking the first question. "Helen Naylor, Chief Constable. Can you tell me when the second enquiry was completed and when it was submitted to the CPS?"

Newman turned on his highest voltage smile before saying, "A pleasure to meet at last, Miss Naylor. To answer your questions, the file has only recently been completed and will be passed to the CPS this week for their consideration, but it is fair to say that they know of its existence already."

Naylor smiled as well, but because she knew it was her report that had prompted the decision to involve the CPS. Disarmed by her expression, Newman was caught slightly off guard when she said, "Why were the forensic samples not sent for analysis during the first investigation?"

He paused and then stumbled over his reply, managing eventually to say, "Decisions regarding that were taken at a senior level and I have to tell you I was unaware of those decisions, nor was I a party to them. I will ask ACC Jack Bryant to explain more fully." Newman didn't realise that in the harsh TV lights he came across as shifty and evasive, but perhaps, even worse, appeared to be passing the buck and evading responsibility.

Everyone looked toward Bryant who did his best to put on a brave face, answering with fake confidence. "As I am sure you are all aware, the police service as a whole is suffering greatly from the severe financial restrictions imposed by central government and is having to work within stringent financial constraints. This Force is no exception, and we endeavour to make real cost savings whilst trying to maintain a high level of service on a much-reduced budget, sometimes having to make difficult financial decisions. Just such a decision was whether the Force should bear the cost of analysing a large number of forensic samples with minimal evidential gain. By that I mean there was considerable other evidence against Karl Smithson, convincing me that all the other forensic evidence would be surplus to requirements, and it was right to save public money on that occasion. I must stress that each case is considered on its own merits and in this particular instance, the matter was fully discussed with the Crown Prosecution Service before I made my final, and I have to say, difficult decision. On reflection, I acknowledge it may not have been the wisest of decisions."

He could only smile weakly, having achieved the almost impossible feat of shocking a room full of hardened journalists into silence.

The chief crown prosecutor Philip Webb seized his moment. "Ladies and gentlemen, I should point out that the Crown Prosecution Service were not consulted for advice on whether the samples should be analysed. One of my senior prosecutors was asked if he believed there was sufficient evidence to convict Smithson without the full forensic evidence being made available. Considering all the facts, he believed there was a surfeit of evidence, for example Smithson was detained at the scene by the wounded officers with his clothing saturated in blood. His fingerprints were on the murder weapon which he admitted was his and that he had used it to cause the officers' injuries. I believe my colleague was wrong not to ask for the forensic evidence, but his opinion was borne out by Smithson's subsequent conviction for all the offences with which he was charged. In conclusion, I can tell you that the CPS would always want as much evidence as possible at its disposal, especially when prosecuting such serious offences, and would never advise the police that they should not have forensic samples fully analysed. I was not previously aware of this matter but now that I know the full facts in this case, I have taken steps to ensure that nothing of a similar nature happens again. In other words, my instructions are that the Crown Prosecution Service will insist that all forensic evidence is made available in future cases."

Webb sat back, expressionless, whilst Bryant looked daggers at him, wishing he was anywhere else but where he was. Webb's masterful performance had in one fell swoop put all the blame on the police, made it clear that he had not been involved in any of the poor decision making and, finally, now that he did know had taken robust action to ensure it didn't happen again.

Another question came from the floor to Newman. "Two things, Chief Constable, if you please. How much money did you save and have the samples been examined now?"

Newman replied firmly, "Several thousand pounds, and yes they have now been analysed as part of the second investigation."

The same reporter spoke up again, "It appears you didn't save that much and then you ended up spending it anyway. What were the results?"

"I can't go into detail, but I can tell you that the results greatly enhanced the evidence against Smithson, further confirming, in our opinion, his guilt."

The persistent reporter tried once more, "What did they reveal about Richard Wade and Steve Brown?"

A clearly rattled Newman replied, "I cannot say at this stage, but I can tell you that the file of evidence will be examined by the CPS before any further action is taken."

It was Helen Naylor's turn again, "Superintendent Munro, why didn't you and your team know that the van driver, Mr Hodgson, had seen PC Brown approaching the suspect car, in direct contradiction to Wade's account?"

Munro looked straight back at her. "Helen it was a simple error on behalf of an officer taking a statement. There was nothing sinister, I can assure you."

"What else did Wade lie about, Mr Munro?"

"Look all I can tell you is that all the evidence is being considered. Please don't forget Richard Wade received serious injuries during this incident, a life and death struggle. It would not be at all surprising if some events became confused, so I think it is a little too soon to start labelling people as liars until we know all the facts, don't you?"

Naylor would not be denied, "Did you know that the forensic samples had not been sent for analysis to save money?"

Munro maintained his calm and said, "I authorised for the samples to be sent to the laboratory and did not realise, until I began this second enquiry, that they had not."

Bryant looked even more sick this time.

Another reporter took a turn. "Mr Newman, have the Home Office had anything to say to you about this?"

"No this is a local matter and will be dealt with locally."

"So, there has been no pressure on you to deal with Richard Wade?"

"No."

Yet another questioner chipped in. "Why was Richard Wade not wearing a stab vest or carrying his PPE? If he had, would it have led to a different outcome? Specifically, would Steve Brown still be alive?"

The chief constable was becoming flustered, and it showed as he snapped back "Those are matters which have formed part of the current enquiry so I cannot comment. I can say it is impossible to know if Steve Brown would still be alive if circumstances had been different, and stupid to speculate."

The press officer, sensing things were rapidly going downhill, stepped in, saying that it was time to conclude the conference and that everyone would be kept up to date if there were further developments. He foolishly agreed to one further question from Helen Naylor.

She said, "I note the absence of the Police and Crime Commissioner. Do you still retain his full confidence, Mr Newman?"

Newman then compounded the press officer's mistake by not answering the question, simply standing up and leaving the room. The others on the stage, caught unawares, struggled to their feet and left the stage under the gaze of the TV cameras and flashing cameras.

It left the impression of a group of men attempting to defend the indefensible and failing dismally. They had abjectly failed to answer the concerns expressed by the press or to put a halt to the speculation, maybe they had even made it worse, clearly trying to blame each other.

Newman was confused, angry, and not a little afraid as he called Munro into his office. He had been chief constable for five years and this was by far the biggest crisis of his tenure, ironically even more so than the death of Steve Brown. He could admit to himself, if no one else, that he was lost, not really knowing what to do and without any support from the Police and Crime Commissioner or the Home Office. Did he have the stink of failure about him, causing everyone else to keep their distance lest they become too closely associated with his downfall? Make no mistake, he was fighting for his professional life.

He was a proud man who had achieved high office through dedication, hard work, and considerable skill, not to mention an ability to navigate the shark-infested political waters he now inhabited. A major fault was that Newman found it hard to ask for advice, let alone listen to it, but he realised that he needed wise counsel from someone. Hence his call for Munro once more. He saw in the veteran police officer someone nearing the end of his career with nothing to gain or lose by telling him exactly how things were and who would, he hoped, give him sound advice. Munro had the added advantage of being totally involved with all the events surrounding this tidal wave of criticism engulfing both Newman personally and his force.

Whilst he waited for Munro, Newman quickly checked the messages his secretary had left on his desk. In the last few minutes there had been requests for call backs from, in order of priority, the Home Office, the PCC, the National Police Chiefs' Council, and the Police Federation Local Branch Office. He assumed they had all seen and heard some of the press conference and wished to give him the benefit of their opinions and advice. Well, he would get round to them later. The one he least wished to speak to was the Police Federation secretary who had already been very vocal in his criticism of the way Steve Brown had been treated by Newman and the other senior officers. He'd be damned if these people were going to dictate to him how his Force was managed, he wouldn't stand for it. It was too much.

The chief constable was still in high dudgeon about the perceived interference of others when Munro arrived at just the wrong time, becoming the perfect target for his anger. Newman, with a real gift for stating the obvious, said the press conference, advocated by Munro, had been an unmitigated disaster and, with some sarcasm, asked if he had any further advice. It was clear who he blamed, and equally clear that he was not prepared to shoulder any of the blame.

Munro's response was short and sharp. "Firstly, arrest Richard Wade and formally interview him for the possible offences disclosed by my investigation. Secondly, admit all our mistakes and take the criticism, we're getting plenty of that anyway. We need to move on, so does the Force."

None of that was what Newman wanted to hear and all his earlier resolutions to seek and listen to advice disappeared like smoke in the wind. His rage was building and almost out of control.

Full of righteous indignation, Newman almost shouted, "No, we will not do that, instead I'll tell you exactly what I'm going to do. You have served this Force ably for over 35 years and I think it's time you had a rest, don't you? It would make me happy if you were to submit the papers for your retirement today."

"And if I don't?"

Newman smiled thinly. "Well I believe I could find a number of uniform positions for you at a different station, probably meaning a house move or a very long daily commute. I think retirement would be for the best, don't you?"

Munro sighed heavily; this was not the way he envisaged his career ending. He was sure that the press would paint him as another one of those officers leaving the police service before justice could catch up with him. So be it.

He nodded his agreement.

Newman had one further comment. "By the way, I will be instructing the Professional Standards Branch to investigate just who leaked information about this enquiry to the press. They will be paying very special attention to Detective Inspector Clark and her girlfriend."

Munro stared at Newman in disbelief, finally losing patience he said, "Frankly, Sir, you are an absolute disgrace. Instead of dealing with the matter properly, you persist in trying to save your own skin and wasting time in pointless enquiries to discover non-existent leaks. Please take the chance to be honest and admit our shortcomings because if you continue to deny everything, you just make yourself look evasive and unable to own up when we get it wrong. What do you think the press will make of it when they find out you are spending more time and money investigating supposed leaks, rather than our own mistakes?"

When there was no response, he left, his career over.

CHAPTER 41

As expected, the press headlines were brutal. Every daily newspaper led with the Smithson case shambles as its main story complete with lurid headlines calling into doubt the integrity and efficiency of the police service. Newman and Bryant were particularly badly mauled, as there were a number of articles and editorials expressing outrage at the 'pathetic' attempts to save a relatively small amount of money by not having the forensic samples examined. Furthermore, they expressed anger that senior police officers were prepared to risk the successful prosecution of a man who murdered one of their own to save a few pounds.

Unfortunately for the chief constable, many of the news editors took the opportunity in their editorials to have a swipe at the government, criticising swingeing cuts to the police budget in particular and to the public services as a whole. Unsurprisingly this was not well received by senior members of the government or their officials, ensuring that the Home Secretary received a number of unwelcome calls from colleagues and, not unexpectedly, the Prime Minister. The general message being 'to get it sorted'.

Working on the principle that shit invariably rolls downhill, he instructed his senior civil servant Sir George Hammond to ring Charles Newman personally, making it very clear exactly what message he wanted relayed. However, he also gave him other instructions which were to be carried out prior to contacting the beleaguered chief constable.

So later that same morning, Newman received a most unwelcome, though not totally unexpected, call from the Home Office. He had met the civil servant on previous visits to London and was aware of the man's very senior position and his closeness to the Home Secretary. In other words, he knew exactly where the message was coming from.

Sir George was, as usual, the epitome of old-world charm and courtesy, but his message was as subtle as a stiletto between the ribs. Basically, the Home Secretary was not happy with the way recent events had been dealt with by the Force and called into question the general management of the organisation. Therefore, following consultations with the Police and Crime Commissioner, it had been decided to ask Her Majesty's Inspector of Constabulary to carry out an urgent inspection of Newman's Force and the way it was run. He recognised the implied criticism and was left in no doubt just how precarious his own position was.

Newman now understood why he had been unable to contact the PCC who was obviously busily protecting his own position by putting as much distance as he could between himself and the pariah that the chief constable had become. Well so be it, he could play hardball as well as the next man. A sacrifice was needed, and he was damn sure it wouldn't be him. He asked his secretary to request ACC Bryant's presence in his office immediately.

The same afternoon the following press release was issued by the Force press secretary.

'The chief constable announces, with great personal regret, the immediate retirement of ACC Jack Bryant and Detective Superintendent John Munro. They have been able police officers serving this Force with distinction over many years and they will be sorely missed. Both men have been heavily involved in the recent enquiries relating to the death of PC Steve Brown and I'm sure the officers would have hoped their careers could have ended on a more successful note. Because of the recent difficulties experienced by the Force, Mr Newman feels that it is right that Her Majesty's Inspector of Constabulary examines the way we operate, ensuring the public receive the service they deserve and that they can have full confidence in us.'

Following his instructions to the letter, the press officer held separate, off-the-record briefings with selected, trusted journalists during which he made it plain that both the 'retiring officers' had actually been asked to leave by their chief constable. Secondly, it was implied that the skilfully worded press release indicated that it was Newman who had actually requested the HMI to examine his Force and that he expected a clean bill of health. Significantly, on the specific orders of Charles Newman, Helen Naylor was not one of the reporters chosen to be so briefed. Perhaps that piece of spiteful behaviour illustrated how stressful he was finding the whole situation, but once again it showed that his first inclination was to shoot the messenger rather than deal with the message.

By issuing the press release and holding informal briefings, Charles Newman hoped to deflect the criticism coming from all directions squarely onto the shoulders of Bryant and Munro, portraying himself as a victim of their inefficiency. Unfortunately for him, neither the PCC nor the Home Secretary saw his manoeuvring in quite the same way, recognising it for exactly what it was, a crude attempt to save his own neck whilst trying to assume the moral high ground.

They were not happy.

Another man who was not very happy was Richard Wade. Waking with yet another hangover, he really did not need to see his name all over the morning papers, with the story featuring heavily on radio and TV news bulletins as well. He didn't know what to do. Why couldn't everyone just let it go, what difference could any of it make now? The chief constable would not take his phone calls and he had no one else to turn to. Then he remembered that John Ross had said he should contact him at any time if there was ever anything he could do. That's what he would do, go and see the businessman, but he'd better have a shower and shave first.

It was decided at the highest levels of the Home Office that Newman was not to be allowed to seize the initiative and so, to prevent him having everything his own way, they released their own press statement.

We are pleased that Chief Constable Charles Newman has given his backing to the Home Secretary's request for Her Majesty's Inspector of Constabulary to carry out a review of his Force. This action was taken after full consultation with the Police and Crime Commissioner for the area. Should any remedial action prove to be necessary, the public can be assured that swift and decisive measures will be taken."

Thus, quickly and efficiently, one of the small victories Newman believed he had achieved was snatched away as it was made crystal clear that the inspection had been ordered by Francis Williams personally, along with his own PCC. Just to make sure the message got out, they held their own off-the-record briefings to 'trusted' journalists. The problem for Newman was that the Home Office had much better contacts than him and their version was the one accepted as the truth.

It really was quite amazing that when things started to unravel, they did so at an ever-increasing rate, making it difficult for individuals to maintain control, or even to keep up.

As the day progressed it became increasingly clear to Newman that he was running out of allies and for the first time began to realise that he may actually become a casualty of this whole farrago of claim and counter claim. Although he would never admit it to anyone else, he was forced to acknowledge to himself that Munro had been right all along. They should have come clean at the first opportunity, admitting their mistakes, and taking immediate action to put things right, especially with regard to Richard Wade. There would have been one casualty only instead of the many who were now becoming victims of one man's lies. Oddly enough, he did not consider that he had lied, been evasive or economical with the truth, justifying all his actions as being for the benefit of the Force and the good name of the police service. He could not accept that he had tried to manage this, his Watergate Moment, for his own benefit and the preservation of his own career. A career that he recognised was now hanging by a thread and one which he was now seriously considering walking away from, before he was pushed.

As the week wore on, two separate investigations were underway. The first was the Force inspection by the HMIC and the second by the Professional Standards Branch into the possible leaking of information to the reporter Helen Naylor. At least the story was no longer the lead article in the newspapers, but enterprising journalists were still coming up with different angles to ensure it remained of interest to the public. These included lengthy interviews with the Hodgsons and articles full of information from Crown Prosecution Service insiders and forensic science experts. No one had been able to make contact with Karl Smithson whose communication with the outside world and visits had been severely curtailed by the prison service on the direct orders of the Home Office. Any remaining contact was extremely closely monitored.

Interestingly enough, Helen Naylor was no longer involved in the story as her main source of information, Munro's team, had dried up and she was definitely considered to be persona non grata by both the Home Office and police service. Now employed on a permanent basis by the newspaper, Naylor was assigned to other stories.

She had been far too busy lately to contact Amy Clark, not even having had time to return the police officer's messages, which, to her relief, had now stopped. Her only thought being that people move on, don't they?

Richard Wade had managed to make himself presentable for his visit to John Ross's company offices, but for some reason he had decided not to ring for an appointment. Did he think he could just drop in and be welcomed by the businessman, or was he uncertain of the reception he would receive? As he approached the building, Wade could see Ross's car in its usual parking place so, taking a deep breath, he entered the impressive reception area and approached the girl behind the desk. He told her his name before asking to see Mr Ross. He was asked to wait.

Minutes later John Ross, who was not a man to avoid difficult issues, approached Wade with a grim expression on his face. He did not offer to shake hands and enquired tersely why Wade was there.

The police officer's fragile confidence evaporated, and he wished he could have a drink as he stammered a reply, "Well, Mr Ross, you did tell me to contact you if I should ever need anything. I'm considering leaving the police and you did say there would always be a job for me if I wanted it."

Ross found it difficult to conceal his contempt as he answered. "Mr Wade, I am sure you must realise that I have read the newspapers carefully with all the revelations they contain. In addition, I have been fully briefed by Superintendent Munro with regard to the results of his second investigation. It is now clear to me that you did nothing to stop Karl Smithson and in actual fact your cowardice and incompetence contributed to your own injuries and could have cost my daughter greatly. The real hero was Steve Brown and I intend to do everything I can to make sure his heroism is properly recognised. How you could have the nerve to come here is beyond my comprehension. Please do not contact me again. Goodbye."

Stunned into silence, Wade could only stand and stare as Ross turned on his heel and walked away. Already red in the face at his abrupt dismissal, Wade realised that the receptionist and a number of other workers had witnessed his embarrassment, causing him to almost run from the building. Tears were not far off as he desperately wondered what to do next.

Towards the end of the week, Newman was visited by the chief superintendent in charge of the Professional Standards Branch, who did not bring glad tidings. In a nutshell his investigation into the press leaks had proved a total waste of time, bringing no tangible results. He had visited the reporter Helen Naylor who, in the presence of the newspaper's solicitor, had taken great delight in showing him the letter from Karl Smithson which had started off her investigation. She had then explained how she had conducted the remainder of her enquiries through the court transcript, her solicitor friend, the unknown CPS solicitor, and the van driver Frank Hodgson. All perfectly logical and plausible.

She had admitted to a close relationship with Detective Inspector Clark but vehemently denied obtaining any information in relation to Smithson and Wade from her. Clark had been interviewed and likewise denied passing confidential information to the reporter. No evidence had been found to prove a leak.

Newman said, "So Clark is innocent?"

The chief superintendent smiled ruefully and shook his head. "That's not what I said. I don't believe either of them as far as I can throw them. I think Clark fed Naylor with all the information she needed and pointed her in the right direction to find the rest. It is my belief that she must have been acting under the direction of Superintendent Munro, but I can't prove any of it and I don't think I ever will. Sorry Sir."

Once the Head of PSB had left, Newman was left to consider his next moves. There would be no more officers sacrificed to save his career, he must find another way out of his predicament which included deciding what to do with Wade. He was tempted to simply introduce the file containing all the evidence of Wade's deceit and cowardice into the public arena. He could spin it as proof of his own integrity and honesty, a man prepared to follow the evidence wherever it led and whatever the consequences.

The more he thought about it the more he liked that idea. The trouble was that as he considered it further, he realised that it was only a good idea if the outcome didn't make you look stupid and less than honest, as it surely would. As he tried to study the problem from all angles, it slowly dawned on him that he was not the only one with an interest in keeping the contents of the file hidden. Others had praised and rewarded Wade, some would say excessively, using his temporary fame for their own ends. Perhaps he could still walk away from this relatively unscathed after all.

As part of his considerations, Newman took into account the ongoing inspection by the HMIC, which he was sure would find something to criticise him for. If you looked hard enough at any organisation there would always be something that did not meet the standard required or could be interpreted as such. He knew he would not, could not, escape censure. If nothing else, as head of the Force, he was responsible for Bryant's foolish cost-saving exercise and Munro's inept, as he saw it, first investigation into PC Brown's murder.

Self-preservation was paramount in Newman's mind, and he made his mind up to play the only chips he had left in the game. Decision made, he placed a telephone call to Sir George Hammond, requesting a personal meeting at the Home Office, but declined to say why.

CHAPTER 42

Charles Newman considered his strategy as he was driven to the Home Office whilst the others closely involved in the sad train of events went about their lives, with varying degrees of success.

Richard Wade had belatedly realised how much trouble he could be in and the thought of time in a prison cell only served to send him deeper into his downward spiral. The vodka bottle was his best friend, his only friend.

Newly freed of all responsibility, John Munro and his wife were embarking on a hastily arranged Mediterranean cruise.

Amy Clark and Bill Devereux were still part of the Major Crime Unit, obviously with a new superintendent in charge. Both had been surprised at the abruptness of Munro's departure but, following a brief meeting, were reassured that they were safe from similar treatment. Amy sometimes thought wistfully about Helen Naylor, wondering what might have been and if the reporter had ever really cared for her.

Ironically, former Assistant Chief Constable Jack Bryant couldn't be happier, wishing he'd left years ago. He had managed to secure a post as secretary of the golf club where he had been a member for a number of years. He could play as many rounds of golf as he liked, whenever he liked, with the added bonus that he could attend as many of the club social functions as he wished with his wife, who was delighted.

Karl Smithson followed the same routine he followed every day; it was always said it was the sheer monotony that got to you in prison.

He remained frustrated that Wade still hadn't got his just desserts but was really pleased that he'd managed to cause so much trouble. He was smart enough to know that his chance had probably gone, nevertheless it had been good while it lasted. Even though he hadn't got Richard Wade, it would have given him great satisfaction had he known that things were still rumbling along and that there would be further developments. How sad that he would probably never know about them.

Meanwhile, John Ross and his wife returned to their normal, happy, and fulfilling life with their much loved, and better protected, daughter. However, the businessman was still frustrated by his failure to find a suitable way of honouring Steve Brown's memory.

When Newman arrived at the Home Office, he was quickly shown to Sir George's comfortably appointed office, where fine china was used to serve tea and biscuits. The Home Office mandarin was far too polite to enquire into the reason for Newman's visit and contented himself with small talk whilst waiting patiently for him to explain his purpose.

Newman began, "Sir George, I'm sure you would agree this unfortunate matter of my dead officer and his murderer has caused considerable repercussions for us all."

Sir George replied drily, "Not least for PC Brown."

The chief constable, embarrassed by the civil servant's command of the subject, replied, "Very true of course. However, we need to keep cool heads and to manage the situation as best we can, minimising the damage to us all."

Fully aware that Newman was trying to save his own career, Hammond was nevertheless intrigued and said, "Please continue."

"Thank you. At the completion of the second investigation into this matter only two files were prepared, both of which are in my possession. Am I correct that you have not had the opportunity to view the full file?"

"That is correct."

Newman took a deep breath before continuing. "Well I can tell you that the evidence, particularly the forensic evidence, proves beyond any doubt that Richard Wade lied and in actual fact acted in an extremely cowardly manner. I hate to say so, but it was an excellent piece of police work by Munro and his team. I'm only sorry they didn't do so well the first time round."

Hammond looked thoughtful as he asked, "So Brown was the real hero, just as Smithson said?"

"Indeed, he was."

Hammond decided to be blunt, or at least as much as he ever could be. "Interesting as this undoubtedly is, I do wonder why you are telling me this, Chief Constable."

"Well, Sir George, if the contents of this file were to enter the public domain it is likely a number of important people may well be embarrassed, don't you think? Especially so if you include any renewed interest in the cuts imposed on my Force by this government and described so eloquently by my assistant chief constable in defence of his own actions."

"I'm sure that is all true, but none would be more embarrassed than you I should think. However, I am certain you know that already."

Newman said, "It's unlikely that I will come out of it very well. However, I am equally sure that neither the Prime Minister nor the Home Secretary would welcome the adverse publicity which may accompany publication of the file and the continuing focus on public spending cuts. I hardly need remind you that both of them jumped at the chance for photo opportunities with Richard Wade and I believe it was your department which lobbied very hard for the award of the George Medal."

Sir George knew exactly what was going on but wanted Newman to spell it out. "Yes, all true but mostly on your recommendations I believe. Please tell me, Chief Constable, what you are proposing. I assume you do have a proposal for me to take to the Home Secretary?"

"I realise my position is becoming, how shall we say, difficult and perhaps it would be better if someone else took over. That would probably suit all concerned. However, if I had remained as chief constable until the end of my contract I believe the normal reward would have been a knighthood. I do already have the Queen's Police Medal. Maybe some suitable task could be found by your office to keep me occupied until the next honours list is prepared, perhaps overseas."

Sir George's face remained inscrutable. "I see, and what service would you perform to merit such a reward?"

The soon-to-be ex-chief constable smirked as he said, "Sorry, how forgetful of me. Much of the interest in this matter has subsided and I am sure it will soon disappear altogether. It really would be a shame if the file did become public knowledge, perhaps by prosecuting Wade for his wrongdoing. I'm sure I could make certain that didn't happen. After all, renewed interest could make some people look rather foolish and lacking in judgement, not good attributes for politicians to have I would think."

"What will you do with Wade?"

"He doesn't deserve it but before I leave, I will get him out on a medical pension. A superintendent's pension will allow him a reasonable standard of living and I am sure, especially if he is allowed to keep his medal, there will be no chance of him revealing the truth."

Hammond said, "That makes sense, but what about the others?"

"Of course all the police officers are bound by the Official Secrets Act, any breach of which will certainly risk pensions and probably their liberty. That will take care of Bryant and Munro, along with Devereux who is due to retire soon as well. Detective Inspector Clark is overdue for promotion so I think we can make her silence rewarding. If that fails, we can always restart the enquiry into her relationship with that reporter if we need to. Finally, I expect you can make sure we don't hear from Smithson again."

Even Sir George Hammond was a little shocked at Newman's audacity and the naked self-interest he displayed but had to concede that it could work. He reasoned that nothing Newman had asked for was too unreasonable, nor would granting his requests create any great difficulty. Besides which, in time he could make sure Newman was dealt with appropriately.

To shock the senior Home Office civil servant was no mean feat as he had spent a lifetime dealing with Cabinet Ministers and civil servants jockeying for position and personal advantage, using every trick possible, no matter how dirty.

Sir George said, "Alright, I think you have made your position very clear. I will need to put your proposals to the Home Secretary. Is there anything else?"

"Well, it would be nice if the HMIC team were to conclude their inspection very quickly with a favourable report."

Sir George replied smoothly, "I'm sure that can be arranged. Thank you, Chief Constable."

Newman was extremely pleased with the way the conversation had gone and would set things in motion just as soon as he received the Home Secretary's agreement to his proposition. He believed the blackmail, although he did not think of it as such, had worked very well.

CHAPTER 43

Several weeks later Charles Newman received a written request from the Home Office to head an anti-corruption enquiry in a small Caribbean state. As he later explained to his Police and Crime Commissioner, he felt honour bound to agree to the request and so regretfully tendered his resignation as chief constable. The irony of his new role was not lost on either man, but it provided a solution to their problems that they were both happy to accept.

Newman's new appointment and resignation caused barely a ripple, receiving hardly any attention from the press who had long since tired of him and his scandal-ridden force. Similarly, Wade's retirement from the Force on stress-related medical grounds rated only a passing comment, whilst Amy Clark's promotion to chief inspector did not rate any mention at all.

The press had had their fun exposing what they believed to be a scandal, taking the opportunity to implicate the government and its policies wherever possible. However, despite all their pious pontificating, their only real interest was to claim credit for themselves and to sell more newspapers. This they had achieved for a while, but had long since moved on to more, as they saw it, deserving and rewarding stories.

About the same time John Ross received his own letter from the Home Office asking if, at his convenience, he could make an appointment to see Sir George Hammond when he next visited the capital. A week later he found himself, without knowing it, being served tea and biscuits on the same china in the same office as Charles Newman had been previously. He still had no idea why he was there.

Hammond could undoubtedly be very ruthless when the occasion demanded, a fact which many of his enemies could testify to. However, he was an inherently fair man and when he came across an obvious injustice, he would do what he could to make it right. He considered the treatment meted out to Steve Brown and the sullying of his memory to be just such an injustice. Sir George had given the matter considerable thought before coming to the view that there was nothing to be done officially. However, he had arrived at what he believed was a more than acceptable solution and one which he felt sure John Ross would be willing to help achieve.

Polite as ever Hammond said, "Thank you so much for making the time to see me, it is much appreciated. How is your daughter? Has she recovered from her ordeal?"

A still mystified Ross played along, "She seems to be fine and is back at school now, thank you."

"Ah, the resilience of the young. How one envies them."

The civil servant seemed lost in thought and Ross decided to remain silent.

After a few moments Hammond broke free from his reverie. "I assume you are wondering why I asked to see you. Let me explain. I believe you are now fully aware of the results of the second investigation into the arrest of Karl Smithson and all the circumstances surrounding it?"

Having been sworn to secrecy by Munro when he showed him the confidential file, John Ross knew he had to be careful so kept to a one-word answer, "Yes."

"Good. In that case you will know that PC Brown was the true hero of the day and, but for his heroic actions, the outcome for your family could have been very different. One doesn't wish to be too dramatic, but I think it is true to say that the officer gave his life so that your daughter might live. On the other hand, it is now clear that

Richard Wade's performance left something to be desired and his subsequent distortion of the facts led to praise and rewards he definitely did not deserve. Would you agree?"

The businessman did not hesitate when replying, "I would agree wholeheartedly, Sir George, but where are we going with this?"

Sir George was apologetic. "Please forgive me, but it is necessary that we are all on the same page, as our American cousins would say. I assume you were not happy to see that Wade has been allowed to retire from the police service on medical grounds, avoiding any retribution for his dishonesty, and that some of the others involved have also been allowed to escape apparently unscathed?"

"Yes, you could say that, although I do not include Superintendent Munro among those. He came to see me and explained his own shortcomings in the first investigation and how, despite opposition, he had endeavoured to put things right."

"Quite. I do not intend to bore you with the reasons why this has been allowed to happen, but, if it gives you any satisfaction, I can tell you that Wade is a broken man with a decidedly uncertain future. I requested this meeting with you to see if there is anything we can do for PC Brown's memory and to ensure his actions and considerable bravery are never forgotten. However, I am sure you will understand that I cannot be involved in any official capacity. Have you any suggestions, or perhaps it may be helpful if I offered my thoughts?"

Ross was amazed at Sir George's openness. He was wise enough in the ways of the world to know that the lack of action had been entirely due to the possible repercussions for some important people. Though even he did not realise the true level of some of those who had developed severe twitches at the thought of Wade being prosecuted.

"It is something I have discussed with my wife, but so far we have not reached firm conclusions. Any suggestions you could make would be very helpful."

Matters were proceeding exactly as Sir George had hoped. "In that case, if I may. You are no doubt aware that Steve Brown's domestic circumstances were, shall we say, a little chaotic and that he had no children of his own. However, my research suggests he tried to help young people wherever he could, freely giving his time as a supervisor at the Police Boy's Club. It's not for me to suggest how you spend your money, but perhaps a small bequest to the club for new equipment in his name and perhaps a trophy of some kind. I'm sure they could tell you which achievements, sporting or otherwise, would be most suitable. Finally, he was known for encouraging the lads at the club to pursue education and training at every opportunity. Perhaps a Steve Brown Scholarship at the local college linked to an apprenticeship scheme at your company would also be appropriate."

Ross beamed with pleasure. "Both those ideas sound ideal to me."

Hammond allowed a small smile to flit across his face. "Excellent. I have already taken the liberty of speaking to the new chief constable and she has offered her wholehearted support to the schemes and is willing to be an unpaid trustee should it be required. I would also like to put my own name forward should you think I may be able to help."

Totally surprised but realising instantly that Sir George Hammond's patronage would be of immeasurable benefit to any proposed schemes, he gratefully accepted.

Sir George had one final comment, "You may wish to contact the chief constable as I believe she would like to hold a ceremony to officially commend Steve Brown, recognising his extreme bravery and dedication to duty. I believe you and your family would be welcome guests."

John Ross had one final question, "What about the George Medal?"

"That is a little difficult. If the medal is withdrawn it would undoubtedly have the potential to damage senior government ministers and to potentially embarrass Her Majesty. I'm sorry, I know he doesn't deserve to keep the medal, but the risks are too great."

Ross was disappointed, but fully understood the realities of life. After expressing his thanks and shaking hands, he left with promises to be in touch with the civil servant as soon as the scholarship was organised.

Sir George Hammond was quietly pleased with the outcome of the meeting, believing he had done as much as he could to right a grievous wrong. He felt it was unnecessary to mention that the withdrawal of a George Medal would undoubtedly have generated further unwelcome press intrusion, reviving interest in a story best allowed to subside quietly. Or at least that was the message he had received loud and clear from his political masters.

One piece of information that Hammond did not share with John Ross may have given him a greater understanding of his motives and anxiety to right the wrongs done to Steve Brown. Sir George Hammond, despite appearances, did not come from a privileged background, but was in fact the son of a Yorkshire village bobby. That was where he learned about honesty, integrity, and public service. Whilst not a secret, and certainly not something he was ashamed of, it was his own business and others had no need to know about it.

CHAPTER 44

So, the whole tragic saga which began on a sunny August afternoon drew to a less than satisfactory conclusion, with no winners and only two real losers. Steve Brown, of course, and Richard Wade. Steve Brown lost his life because he was an accomplished and dedicated police officer who was as brave as a lion, refusing to give in, no matter what. Richard Wade lost everything because he was a pathetic individual prepared to destroy another man's reputation for his own benefit.

Three men had come together in a lonely roadside lay-by, a career criminal, a weak and ambitious man, along with a hero. They were brought together initially by coincidence, then by Karl Smithson's criminal activities and Steve Brown's instinctive police work, honed by years of experience. The result being that one would die, one would be disgraced, and the other imprisoned for life, whilst their actions would draw a number of other of people into the drama. One can only wonder how differently they might have acted, if at all, had they known in advance the outcome of their fateful meeting.

The coincidence? There were several. The first was Wade's vehicle being taken by someone else, forcing Steve Brown to give him a lift to the Force Headquarters. The second was the route they took and the final coincidence being the two cars stopping side by side at the traffic lights.

Coincidence alone was not the only cause of Brown's death. It could have still been avoided but for a number of avoidable mistakes and wilful omissions by Richard Wade.

A lesser police officer than Brown would have ignored Smithson's behaviour when told to do so by his inspector, but his overriding sense of duty dictated that he do otherwise. Even then his fate was not sealed. If he had been accompanied by a more experienced, capable, and properly equipped officer, with the smallest amount of personal courage, it is possible he would not have received such serious injuries, if any at all.

Contacting control, prior to stopping the murderer's vehicle, would have made sure their location was known and may have meant help, particularly paramedics, could have reached Brown sooner. Finally, what of Frank Hodgson? That poor man made an honest mistake, but if he had been able to give his correct location in the first instance, maybe help would have got to Steve Brown minutes sooner as well, perhaps in time.

It is never one mistake or action that leads to a tragedy, but the culmination of a series of, usually unplanned, events often beyond the control of man. Or, in simple terms, was it just fate that dictated it was Steve Brown's day to die and nothing could prevent the coming together of those three men with the disastrous outcome?

Maybe Steve Brown need not have died but let us remember that despite all Richard Wade's deficiencies, it is Smithson who carried the knife and who used it without hesitation to inflict the officer's horrendous injuries.

Wade can probably be excused for not being a very good police officer, maybe even for being a coward, but in no way can he be forgiven for his subsequent actions. His calculated lies, which embroiled so many others in the tangled web of deceit, were designed for his own glory and to enhance his reputation, portraying him as the man he wished he was. The fact that he succeeded so spectacularly probably led to his own undoing. Indeed, he was a weak man who, despite appearances to the contrary, was a failure at most things in his life.

What of the conduct of everyone else?

Jack Bryant, however misguidedly, was trying to save money as he was expected to do in his position as assistant chief constable. It was a foolish mistake, but was it done with any malicious intent? Probably not, and he certainly paid a high price, perhaps deserving his later happiness.

Munro and his team give every appearance of being stout defenders of the truth, seeking answers with determination and dedication. Perhaps if they had done that in the first place the later problems may have been avoided. Should Munro have known the forensic evidence had not been fully examined and should Frank Hodgson have been properly interviewed the first time round? Both would probably have exposed Wade's lies long before the situation got so out of control, preventing many of the subsequent events. All debatable issues which leave one question remaining. Were they right to collude with a convicted murderer and the press to bring the truth out into the open? Did they abandon the moral high ground by doing so, leaving their own principles in tatters? Surely there were many other options they could have explored, but they didn't try. Instead, they justified their actions on the grounds that the truth needed to be told to protect Steve Brown's reputation and to ensure that Wade wasn't allowed to benefit from his lies.

We have already established that the reporter Helen Naylor was willing to ignore any principles she may have had at the drop of a hat, or perhaps at the drop of some other item of clothing. No more need be said.

Charles Newman and the politicians did not cause Steve Brown's death or Richard Wade to lie, but they were fully prepared to use events for their own cynical ends and political gain. Their day of reckoning would come, especially for the former chief constable, who believed he possessed the only two copies of John Munro's report detailing the findings of his second investigation. He would not have rested so easily had he known of the other copy, now safely back in the possession of a solicitor, even less so if he had known that Sir George Hammond suspected its existence and was hot on the trail.

The only person to emerge from this whole sorry mess with any credit was Steve Brown, whose actions had inadvertently resulted in the rescue of Linda Ross, saving her from whatever fate Smithson had planned for her. Unfortunately, the law of unintended consequences came into play with Brown's actions directly impacting on the behaviour of everyone else. Nevertheless, it was up to each individual to make their own choices.

At the end of a very public period of self-flagellation, which left the police service much diminished in the eyes of the general public, some truths remained. Steve Brown was still dead, and Karl Smithson was still in prison. Nothing was going to change that, so was everything else just a waste of time, a pointless display of breast beating and a vain effort to reveal the truth of one man's perfidy? So did they succeed, and was it worth it?

How many reputations had been tarnished and careers cut short, deservedly or otherwise? Would any more follow?

ABOUT THE AUTHOR

I have spent time as a police officer, along with other jobs. However, this story is way beyond anything I have experienced and is largely the result of my imagination.

I am a firm believer that we all have a book in us, good or bad, and I have determined for some time that I would give it a go.

I am an avid reader of crime fiction, so it was natural for me to try the same genre for my first novel, hoping it is a little different and that other books may follow.

Printed in Great Britain
by Amazon

11057119R00163